AND MARGARET MARON

"Real fun...charming....Margaret Maron bottles the enchantment."
—**Marilyn Stasio,** *New York Times Book Review*

"Plenty of suspense, solid writing...another top tale in Maron's fine series....It gets better with each outing."
—*Cleveland Plain Dealer*

"There's nobody better."
—*Chicago Tribune*

"Maron writes with wit and sophistication."
—*USA Today*

"An entertaining Tilt-a-Whirl of a tale...quickly drawing readers into the colorful carny world."
—*Orlando Sentinel*

"We love her."
—*Winston-Salem Journal*

"Always a writer gifted with the ability to convey an enthralling sense of time and place....Reading Maron is like sipping a Carolina Cooler—solid comfort together with fascinating sensations."
—*Greensboro News & Record* (NC)

Please turn this page for more praise for Margaret Maron and turn to the back of this book for a preview of her upcoming novel, *Last Lessons of Summer*.

"This series is like sweet iced tea on an August day in North Carolina—near impossible to resist."

—*Atlanta Journal-Constitution*

"A multilayered, involving story...fascinating...first-rate."

—*Romantic Times*

"Maron's finely crafted novels about an ever-urbanizing North Carolina are like gathering around one of those legendary storytellers of the South as they spin story after story....In Maron's case, she lets her heroine, Judge Deborah Knott, weave tales about her expansive family in novels that are as personal as they are engrossing."

—*Ft. Lauderdale Sun-Sentinel*

"SLOW DOLLAR works on many levels....Serves up justice with a Southern flavor."

—*Mansfield News Journal* (OH)

"Maron beautifully depicts life in the South."

—*Easy Rider*

"A well-written novel...as much a family saga as it is a clever regional mystery."

—*Midwest Book Review*

"A fascinating, fast-paced look at carny life."

—*Raleigh News & Observer* (NC)

SLOW
DOLLAR

By Margaret Maron

Deborah Knott novels:

Slow Dollar
Uncommon Clay
Home Fires
Killer Market
Up Jumps the Devil
Shooting at Loons
Southern Discomfort
Bootlegger's Daughter

Sigrid Harald novels:

Fugitive Colors
Past Imperfect
Corpus Christmas
Baby Doll Games
The Right Jack
Bloody Kin
Death in Blue Folders
Death of a Butterfly
One Coffee With

Non-Series:

Bloody Kin
Shoveling Smoke

MARGARET MARON

SLOW DOLLAR

WARNER BOOKS

An AOL Time Warner Company

WARNER BOOKS EDITION

Copyright © 2002 by Margaret Maron
All rights reserved. No part of this book may be reproduced in any form or by any electronic or mechanical means, including information storage and retrieval systems, without permission in writing from the publisher, except by a reviewer who may quote brief passages in a review.

Cover art and design by Diane Luger

Warner Books, Inc.
1271 Avenue of the Americas
New York, NY 10020

Visit our Web site at www.twbookmark.com

 An AOL Time Warner Company

Printed in the United States of America

Originally published in hardcover by The Mysterious Press
First Paperback Printing: August 2003

10 9 8 7 6 5 4 3 2 1

For Julia Elizabeth Maron, born in a comet year—

"... for out o' question you were born in a merry hour."

"No, sure, my lord, my mother cried; but then there was a star danc'd, and under that was I born."

Much Ado About Nothing

you went to you today. Put down that book with all the
questions now, and go to sleep. You want to find out
what I said, why did the crier shout and the orchestra
plays the questions are in the back.

FOREWORD

I was introduced to the carnival world by my cousin
Brandy, with it and for it for twenty-five years, and I am
forever grateful. The books she lent, the inside stories
she told, and all the jackpots she cut up with me were
invaluable. If I learned more from my independent research than she intended, if my totally fictional Ames
Amusement Corporation doesn't exactly conform to her
own "Sunday schooler" standards, I hope she'll forgive
me and understand the needs of the story I wanted to
tell.

As always, Judge Deborah Knott's courtroom behavior owes much to the advice of District Court Judges
John W. Smith, Shelly S. Holt, and Rebecca W. Black-
more of the 5th Judicial District Court (New Hanover
and Pender Counties, North Carolina). Unfortunately,
they have no influence at all on her *out*-of-courtroom
behavior.

For the uninitiated, I have included a glossary of carny
terms at the back of this book.

Carnivals are pure Americana: the glitz and flash of
colored lights, the fried-food-on-a-stick, the cotton
candy, the "step-right-up-win-a-prize" pitches. If it's
summer, there's probably one playing somewhere near

you even as you read. Put down this book, turn off the television, load up any available kids, and go find one *now*. Build a memory for the children or for yourself before the carnival disappears into our past.

SLOW
DOLLAR

Deborah Knott's Family Tree

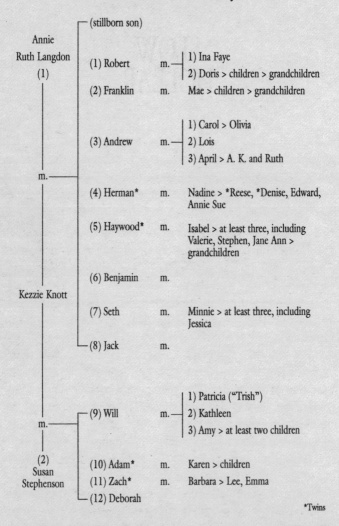

Annie
Ruth Langdon
(1)

— (stillborn son)

(1) Robert   m. — 1) Ina Faye
                     2) Doris > children > grandchildren

(2) Franklin   m.   Mae > children > grandchildren

(3) Andrew   m. — 1) Carol > Olivia
                     2) Lois
                     3) April > A. K. and Ruth

m. —

(4) Herman*   m.   Nadine > *Reese, *Denise, Edward,
                     Annie Sue

(5) Haywood*   m.   Isabel > at least three, including
                     Valerie, Stephen, Jane Ann >
                     grandchildren

Kezzie Knott

(6) Benjamin   m.

(7) Seth   m.   Minnie > at least three, including
                     Jessica

— (8) Jack   m.

— (9) Will   m. — 1) Patricia ("Trish")
                     2) Kathleen
                     3) Amy > at least two children

m. —

(2)
Susan
Stephenson

(10) Adam*   m.   Karen > children

(11) Zach*   m.   Barbara > Lee, Emma

— (12) Deborah

*Twins

PROLOGUE

EARLY MAY
BRAZOS HARTLEY

The back door of the eighteen-wheeler had been pushed up about eight inches from the bottom and one of the side doors was open wide in an attempt at cross ventilation. An oscillating fan moved air around the cavernous interior, but the south Georgia night was so hot and muggy that the fan was having almost no effect.

Beyond odd pieces of furniture stacked on one side, Brazos Hartley hunched over a laptop computer screen at the rear of the trailer. The young man had stripped to the waist but sweat dripped down his back and arms. It turned the snake tattooed the length of his right arm into something glistening and alive as he tapped the keys.

Bare, low-wattage lightbulbs hung by both open doors to decoy night-flying insects. At the computer, a rusty gooseneck lamp illuminated the keyboard and spotlighted the green marbleized fountain pen that lay across the top row of his function keys. As he typed, a stray moth fluttered up into the lamp, showering gray dust on the keys. He caught it and mashed it between his fingers, then wiped his fingers on his pant leg before picking up the pen by its slender barrel to examine it closely again. He scraped away a fleck of old, dried ink from the shining point, screwed the cap back on, and returned to the eBay listing he was composing:

> *. . . circa 1940. Pump filler. Solid 18K nib and trim. Beautiful condition. Original owner was killed in WWII. Reserve price—*

Braz hesitated while greed warred with reality, then confidently typed *$350.*

The fountain pen had been in the pocket of an old Navy jacket, part of a defaulted self-storage locker his stepfather Arn had bought last week down near Jacksonville. The locker had held a bent bicycle frame, a fairly new love seat with matching chairs upholstered in black leatherette, and a pair of tarnished and dented pole lamps. His eyes on the resale value of the furniture, Arn had been high bidder at one twenty-five. Only after he'd paid over the money could they enter the locker and check out what else was there. Usually it wasn't much. This time, over behind the love seat, where no flashlight could reach, they'd found a boxy WWII vintage suitcase.

The old suitcase was locked, and they'd had to wait till they got back to their current base to open it with Arn's set of picklocks. Vintage luggage in good condition brought decent money these days, and Arn was careful not to bust the catch.

Inside was pay dirt. A carefully folded American flag and a small gold-fringed banner with a gold star pinned to the middle lay atop the dark blue wool uniform of a Navy noncom.

American flags were always good sellers at Southern flea markets, and authentic uniforms moved briskly, too, around the military bases that dotted the South.

"Know what we got here?" Arn had said. "This must've been a kid got killed in the war and his folks just packed everything up when they sent his things home."

Beneath the uniforms were yellowed letters with certain parts carefully razored out by a wartime censor. No envelopes, to Braz's disappointment. Old envelopes were what collectors wanted.

But while Arn leafed through the letters, Braz shook out the clothes and surreptitiously felt the pockets. When his fingers discovered the pen, he'd palmed it slicker than an add-up agent working a razzle-dazzle.

Unless it was extremely old or immediately recognizable as valuable, his stepfather never had much patience with anything paper. He preferred hard goods that he could turn over quickly at a decent profit. "A quick dime's better than a slow dollar," Arn always said, and he'd tossed the packet of letters Braz's way, along with a couple of Zane Grey books and a New Testament that had been in the bottom of the suitcase.

A half-dozen tiny black-and-white snapshots slid out of the Bible. Uniformed boys younger then than he was now stood on the deck of a ship, and in the background was another ship with big white numbers on its bow. It would take some detective work, but if he could figure out what ship it was, he could write an ad to put on the Internet auction site that would bring in a few bucks for the pictures. World War Two memorabilia always sold.

Let Arn go for the quick dime. He'd take the slow dollar any day.

Like this fountain pen. Arn would've put it out to auction with no reserve price, happy to take the high bid of whoever happened to be online that day. Ten dollars or a hundred, Arn wouldn't care, Braz thought scornfully. He was like any other carny. All he cared about was the quick profit. And yeah, Ames Amusement Corporation was growing, but it was never going to be big-time. And even if it grew big as Strates, wasn't like his mother and Arn would ever cut him a major piece of it. Not while baby brother Val was around.

He completed the ad, using an e-identity that neither Arn nor Val knew about, then exited from the program and turned off the laptop. As the screen went dark, he closed the lid, neatened the makeshift desktop, switched off his lamp, and stood up to stretch his cramped muscles. It was a little past two A.M. and time to hit the hay, hay being a mattress on the floor by the rear door. He'd quit sleeping in the family's two-bedroom trailer four years ago, preferring to stake out his own private space here in the back of the eighteen-wheeler's van rather than share a pop-out with his younger half brother when they were on the road.

Most of the trailers around him were dark and silent. Somewhere, though, a radio was playing soft jazz, and when he stepped out into the airless night, he heard a burst of laughter that sounded like his mother. She and Polly and some of the others were probably over there sipping ice-cold beers and cutting up jackpots. Arn and Val would already be asleep inside the trailer. Neither of them were the night owls he and Mom were.

He thought about going over and scoring a cold one himself, but on second thought, after what happened last night, maybe not, he decided.

A shower would feel good, but hot as it was, might as well wait and take one when he woke up. Be fresh for if that little blond townie came by tomorrow like she said she would when she was flirting with him at the Dozer tonight.

What couldn't wait was the need to empty his bladder. Portable donnikers were down near the Tilt-A-Whirl, convenient to the midway. Quicker and easier was to go around back to the bushes that grew at the edge of the field where they were parked.

It was dark back there and he'd just finished his business and was zipping up when someone came around the corner.

Male.

Big.

Moving with purpose.

Out of the corner of his eye, he thought he saw a second figure by the truck's front fender.

Before he could speak, an iron fist to his midriff bent him double with pain. Another to his chest spun him around so hard that the third punch landed bruisingly on his right shoulder blade as he crumpled to the ground.

"This is from Polly," the man grunted as he gave a bone-jarring kick to Braz's left buttock and another to his ribs. Not enough to break one, just enough to hurt like hell.

Instinctively, Braz drew up his legs and covered his head with his arms in a fetal position as the punishing blows and kicks continued. Pain blossomed through his body, and he cried out.

At that, someone called in a low voice, "That's enough, Sam! Let him alone!"

The attacker gave Braz another halfhearted kick. "Try to mess over Polly again, you little shithead, and you won't get off this easy. And you better not go running to Arnie or Tal, either. You and Skee keep your mouths shut. They hear about this, I'll beat the crap out of both of you. You got that?"

"He's got it," said the newcomer, a small elderly man. "Now get the hell away before somebody comes."

Despite the venomous words, both men kept their voices down.

The one called Sam stomped off and Skee Matusik bent over Braz, who still writhed in agony on the ground.

"Come on, kid," he said. "Let ol' Skee help you back inside."

He pulled the younger man to his feet and guided him around to the back of the trailer, where he pushed up the retractable rear door and pulled down the folding steps. Braz climbed them shakily and collapsed onto the mattress, half crying in his pain and anger. "The bastard!"

"You got any aspirin?" Skee asked practically.

Braz pointed toward the black zippered bag that held his toothbrush, razor, and other toiletries.

The older man found the bottle, shook out three in his hand. There was a water bottle next to the pillow, and he handed both to Braz.

"Thanks," he muttered, and lay back on the makeshift bed, drained and exhausted and hurting all over.

"Anything broken?"

Braz shook his head wearily.

"Didn't think so. And he stayed away from your face, too," said Skee. In this light, his missing teeth left dark holes in his tight smile. "Smart. Your shirt'll cover all the bruises you're going to have tomorrow, but Tally would've noticed a black eye or cuts on your chin."

"How come you didn't pull him off me quicker?" Braz asked resentfully, wincing as he pushed the pillow into a more comfortable position.

"Like Sam wouldn't make two of me? You're just lucky I could stop him when I did. What'd you do to piss him off like that?"

"None of your business. But I'll tell you one thing: This is my last time out. Come October, I'm finished with the carnival for good and all."

"Yeah, yeah," said Skee, who'd heard it before. He went over and pulled the side door nearly shut and turned the fan full on Braz. "Want me to turn out these lights?"

"I mean it," Braz said drowsily. "Who needs this fuckin' life?"

"Some of us, kid," sighed the old carny. "Some of us."

CHAPTER
1

I was holding court over in Widdington and it was our fifth drunk-and-disorderly of this hot September morning.

Actually our fifth, sixth, and seventh since there were three men involved in the same incident.

"Call Victor Lincoln, Daniel Lincoln, James Partin," said Chester Nance, the ADA who was prosecuting today's calendar.

If James Partin had ever stood before me, I didn't remember, but the Lincoln brothers, Vic and Danny, were husky young white men whom I'd found guilty of larceny more than two years ago. Itinerant carpenters, they had been stealing appliances from the newly finished houses in Tinker's Landing before their owners could move in.

I gazed from one set of bloodshot eyes to the other. "Time sure does fly. I didn't realize you guys were out already."

"Time off for good behavior," Vic said, trying to look

upright and respectable. He and his cohorts had already waived their rights to an attorney.

"Too bad your good behavior didn't last," said Chester Nance. "Class-one misdemeanor, Your Honor. Injury to personal property. Misdemeanor assault. Intoxicated and disruptive."

It was the usual story except that this time, the personal property destroyed was the Pot O'Gold Rainbow.

"The what?" I asked.

"An inflatable carnival ride, Your Honor."

"How do you plead?" I asked the accused.

"Not guilty," Vic Lincoln said confidently. "We might've had a couple of beers, but we won't drunk. Just having a good time. We didn't really hurt nothing."

"Just put a three-hundred-dollar cut in my ride," the woman seated at Chester Nance's table observed.

"Mr. Nance," I warned.

The ADA stood hastily. "Call Mrs. Tallahassee Ames."

The woman rose from the table and moved easily across to the witness stand, where she placed her hand on the Bible.

She looked to be pushing forty—at least three years older than me—and her slender body had an air of muscular hardness to it. Her shoulder-length dark hair framed a square face that was attractive, if a little weather-roughened like farm women who'd sized up too many crops under too many hot suns, which, come to think of it, probably isn't too much different from sizing up crowds in strange towns. The big gold hoops that swung from her ears made me wonder if she ever moonlighted as the carnival's gypsy fortune-teller. Instead of flowing skirts and veils, though, she wore well-cut jeans, high-heeled boots of red snakeskin, and a red silk shirt with the top buttons left open. Several gold necklaces encircled her throat and a diamond-crusted cross on one of them dipped down between her breasts. Danny Lincoln was staring at its resting place and breathing with his mouth open.

The tangle of small gold charms on her bracelet clinked and jingled against the Bible as Mrs. Ames placed her left hand on it and swore that she would tell the truth, the whole truth, and nothing but the truth.

"You may be seated," said my clerk.

"State your name and address," said Chester Nance.

"Tallahassee Ames, currently of Gibtown—sorry, I mean Gibsonton, Florida."

Puzzled, Nance looked at his notes again. "Didn't you give the police officers a local address that night?"

"I might've told him I owned property in this county, but my legal residence is Florida."

"I see." Again he shuffled papers. "Please tell the court your occupation."

"My husband and me, we own and operate Ames Amusement Corporation." The witness chair was one step lower than mine, and when she looked up at me, her eyes were an unexpected deep clear blue. "Three rides, five games, two grab wagons."

"Grab wagons?" I asked.

"Corn dogs, popcorn, cotton candy, soft drinks, okay? Grab-and-go food."

"On July seventh of this year, where were you and your amusements?" asked Nance, virtuously staying on topic.

"Us and another outfit were set up over in the abandoned Kmart parking lot at the edge of town here for the Fourth of July."

I hadn't been to Widdington's Fourth of July celebration since I was a teenager, but I knew they went all out—parade, fireworks, and a ten-day carnival to raise money for their rescue squad.

Under Nance's questioning, Mrs. Ames described the events leading to last month's incident. Her voice had the husky timbre of a heavy smoker.

According to her testimony, it was around eleven o'clock on a Thursday night. Average closing time for a weeknight. Widdington isn't New York. It isn't even Raleigh. The owner of the other rides had already shut down his Ferris wheel and Tilt-A-Whirl, and she herself was in the process of securing her guessing game when she realized there was trouble over at the Pot O'Gold, a contraption that sounded like a large, colorful sliding board.

"It's basically a big plastic balloon shaped like half a rainbow, okay?" She gestured with her hands, and her charm bracelet tinkled like little gypsy bells. "One side looks like a big treetop with clouds over it. Inside, there's a set of spiral steps that go up thirty feet to the top. When you come out of a door in the cloud, you're on top of the rainbow. We've got an air compressor that keeps it inflated. The way it works is that you sit on a slide sack and try to land in the pot of gold at the bottom."

She saw my raised eyebrow and smiled. "Well, actually, the pot's padded and filled with gold-colored sponges that look like gold bars. If you land in the pot, though, you either get a prize or you get to slide again."

"Sounds as if you probably hand out a lot of freebies," I said.

"It's a little harder than you might think," she drawled. "But maybe you'd like to try it yourself in a few weeks. We're booked to play the harvest festival over in Dobbs."

"As to the night of July seventh?" said Chester Nance.

"My husband had gone on up to Virginia to check out a new elephant-ear trailer, okay? So it was just me and my two sons to look out for things."

(At least I didn't have to ask what an elephant ear was. Not with my weakness for fried dough. Hot and crispy, sprinkled with cinnamon and powdered sugar, it's my biggest indulgence when the state fair comes to Raleigh every October.)

"I'd just snapped the locks when I heard Val yelling."

"Val being your younger son?" asked Nance.

"Yeah. He's only sixteen. Hasn't got his full growth yet or he'd've busted them three's butts."

Hastily, Nance pushed on. "When you looked over to where he was, what did you see?"

"I saw them knock him over and start climbing up my rainbow on the outside, but the compressor was still going, so it was twisting enough that they couldn't get a good hold. The plastic's tough, but I was worried they might stomp a hole. Braz and me—"

"Braz is—?"

She gave an impatient toss of her head at having her narrative interrupted yet again. "Braz is my oldest boy, Val's the youngest, Binga's our Bozo, and Hervé was the one working that ride, okay? The others had gone to the bunkhouse."

Nance nodded and let her keep going.

"Braz and me, we ran over. I hollered for Binga to come help, too, but by the time we got there, that one"—she pointed to Vic Lincoln—"had his knife out and before we could get to him, he cut a slit ten feet long and let all the air out. Whole thing collapsed, okay? It was a miracle somebody didn't break an arm or a leg."

A Widdington town police officer who'd been there that night with his wife gave corroborating evidence as to the defendants' presence, general belligerency, intoxication, and possession of knives. He hadn't witnessed the incident, but since the Lincoln brothers and their friend Partin weren't actually denying it, that point was moot.

When the prosecution rested, Vic Lincoln took the stand and the oath and asked if he could tell his story in his own words.

"See, Your Honor, we went there to get back the stuff her old man stole from us, but—"

"Stole from you?" I asked.

"Yes, ma'am. See, when you put us in jail last time, we rented us a storage locker for our tools and stuff. But Danny's sorry girlfriend that was supposed to be keeping up the payments on it? She went off to Myrtle Beach with another guy, and when we got out, the people at the locker place said they'd sold our stuff off for back rent. Her dude's the one that bought it and we were there to find him. I mean, how can we make a honest living if we don't have our tools?"

"And when you didn't find Mr. Ames at the carnival, you decided to take it out in trade?" asked Nance.

"Well, naw, that just sorta happened," said Lincoln.

"Let me get this straight," I said. "You put your tools in storage, nobody pays the rent on it, the company auctions it off, yet you blame the Ameses for your loss? Seems to me, you should be going after your brother's old girlfriend."

Lincoln looked at me as if I were dumber than dirt.

"She ain't the one got our tools," he said.

I let him have his full say, then found the men guilty as charged. Because they each had less than five priors, I could only give them forty-five days max for the injury to personal property, same for the simple assault. It was tempting to send them all back to jail for thirty days, but most victims prefer cash restitution over the satisfaction of seeing their assailants do time, so I suspended the active sentence and put them on supervised probation for two years with the usual conditions. This included a fine, restitution for property damage and any medical bills, an injunction to stay away from this carnival, plus an alcohol assessment at the local mental-health clinic.

Despite the unusual property that had been damaged, it was, as I said, a routine case and I didn't give it another thought for the next few weeks.

And then the carnival came to Dobbs.

CHAPTER
2

🦆 "If she says, 'Oh, Dwight, honey' in that little girl voice one more time," Portland Brewer muttered in my ear, "I'm going to dump orange slush down the back of her shirt."

"Be nice, Por," her husband Avery pleaded from the other side. "Dwight'll hear you."

"Over all this noise?"

Opening night at Dobbs's Annual Harvest Festival carnival and the mild moonlit evening seemed to have brought out half of Colleton County to ride the Tilt-A-Whirl, swings, and Ferris wheel, to throw quarters onto a red dot, sling rope rings around Coke bottles, or toss Ping-Pong balls into bowls of live goldfish against a cacophony of music, clacking machines, and hucksterism.

The air was sweetly redolent of hot grease, fried dough, grilled meats, and spun sugar and one whiff was all it took to send me straight back to childhood, holding my mother's hand, riding on the shoulders of one of my many older brothers, or clinging to my daddy's pant leg, a little farm girl so dazzled by the bright lights that I thought I'd stumbled into Oz.

The lines between our small towns and the surrounding countryside have always been blurred, and now that creeping urbanization is turning tobacco fields into high-density developments, the differences are even fewer. Nevertheless, there are still enough farmers in the area to give meaning to the harvest side of this festival. And even though many now toil in the Research Triangle's high-tech fields, most of the local people crowding the midway had roots that go deep in our sandy loam. These days, the huge gardens that once fed families through the winter might be reduced to little patches of tomatoes, peppers, and cucumbers in the backyards of pretentiously named subdivisions, but even little patches can produce a few jars of piccalilli or spaghetti sauce for pantry shelves and bragging purposes.

In the meeting hall at the front of the makeshift midway, golden bundles of hand-tied tobacco, field corn, pumpkins, and other produce awaited tomorrow's judging; as did rows of spiced peaches, bread-and-butter pickles, and strawberry jam. There would be cakes and pies for sale, and even now, black iron cookers were getting set up for the barbecue contest. With their appetites whetted by the smell of grilled pork basted with spiced-up vinegar, hungry spectators would be able to sample the winners for a charitable donation to the local rescue services.

This wasn't the State Fair in Raleigh, with its huge array of gravity-defying rides and every inch of ground taken up with catch-me-eye game or food stands, and amusements that went nonstop from ten A.M. till midnight. These rides were fewer, smaller, shabbier, and in bad need of a wire brush and fresh paint. Cracks in vinyl cushions had been mended with duct tape.

Nevertheless, there were enough neon tubes and chasing lights to put stars in children's eyes and make their grandparents remember their own first carnivals. Barkers with hand-held cordless mikes or makeshift megaphones stood before colorfully lit stands, exhorting people to step right up to the best game around—"A winner every time, folks!"—and bluegrass music with a heavy, toe-tapping beat blared from a speaker above Dwight Bryant's head where he was trying to knock over the milk bottles with two softballs.

There was no way he could have heard Portland's catty remark, but she subsided anyhow. Advancing pregnancy had tied my best friend's hormones in such knots that her normally happy disposition had degenerated into wildly erratic mood swings. Sylvia Clayton's giggles were enough to grate on anyone's nerves, but we all like Dwight and wouldn't hurt his feelings for the world, even though it depressed us to think he might be getting serious about Sylvia and that we'd be stuck with her for the rest of our lives.

She'd been wished on us by my brother Andrew's wife. April teaches sixth grade in the same school with Sylvia, and she had decided that Sylvia would be perfect for Dwight. Most of my sisters-in-law, both past and present (I have eleven older brothers, some of whom have been married more than once), have tried to fix Dwight up ever since he resigned from Army Intelligence and came back to Colleton County to be Sheriff Bo Poole's right-hand man.

Came home to lick his wounds, my sisters-in-law decided after Jonna divorced him and got custody of their little boy. "He needs somebody to make a new home with so he can have Cal down more often," they said as they pushed their unmarried friends at Dwight.

Hell, they even push me at him whenever I'm between men and that hasn't worked any better than their other candidates. This time around, though, April was starting to preen herself on her success. Dwight and Sylvia had been seeing each other on a fairly regular basis since June and here it was a week away from October.

To be fair about it, Sylvia Clayton's a perfectly nice woman.

Which is part of the problem, of course.

Ever since the two of us got kicked out of the Junior Girls' Class at Sweetwater Missionary Baptist Church for less than sanctified behavior, Portland and I have never been real comfortable around perfect women. It's not that we smoke like wet bonfires, drink like the crappies in my daddy's pond, or curse like farmers trying to hitch a set of forty-year-old plows to a thirty-year-old tractor, but everybody in our crowd indulges in one or the other on occasion.

Sylvia doesn't smoke or swear and while she's never actually said anything about the evils of alcohol, we're acutely aware of *her* awareness if any of us order a second round while she's still toying with her first glass of wine as if it were the threshold on the doorway to hell. Not that Por orders anything stronger than ginger ale these days. (We only get rowdy, not reckless.) But Sylvia's hair is always perfect, her nails look as if they've just been manicured, and she seems to have discovered a lipstick that never wears off because it's usually as fresh at the end of an evening as it was at the beginning and we never see her touch it up.

("Bet you a nickel she does it in the stall," Por says.)

Dwight's first ball hit one of the bottles and pushed it back but not over and my cousin Reid groaned in sympathy.

Like Portland and Avery, Reid Stephenson's an attorney here in Dobbs, and like me, he's not seeing anyone special these days, so I'd invited him to come along to the carnival tonight to even the numbers.

Dwight pessimistically gave the second ball a sidearm pitch almost level with his belt buckle and over went all the wooden milk bottles with a satisfying clatter.

Sylvia squealed with excitement, and when the concessionaire told her to take her pick of the big stuffed animals at the top of his canvas wall, she said, "Oooh, Dwight, honey, I can't decide!"

She finally settled on a black-dotted white plush Dalmatian that would have been sticky with elephant ears and corn dogs by evening's end if it were mine, but would probably arrive at her house as pristine as it began. The thing was the size of a real Dalmatian sitting up on its hind legs and just as cumbersome to carry. I figured Dwight would wind up with it on one of his broad shoulders as soon as Sylvia tired of cooing at it. She'd already decided it would be a perfect guard dog by the door of her bedroom.

"That's right," I said pleasantly. "It's all white, isn't it?"

I knew for a fact that it was. April and I had stopped by her rented townhouse one day back in July and it hadn't been hard to get the fifty-cent tour.

(Okay, so I'm nosy, but Dwight's like another brother and I wanted to see what he was letting himself in for.)

Sylvia's bedroom reminded me of the inside of an eggshell. Carpet, curtains, rocking-chair cushion, and bed linens were white. Bed, chests, and chair were a pale oak. The coverlet and lampshades were ruffled white eyelet and the bed was piled thickly with white ruffled pillows of various sizes. April told her it was just lovely. I had trouble keeping a straight face and Por had whooped when I described it to her later.

"That was the bedroom my mother decorated for my twelfth birthday," she said, laughing. "Poor Mama."

(For her thirteenth birthday, while her mother was out, we striped the walls silver and midnight blue and screwed black bulbs into the dainty milk-glass lamps.)

"More to the point, poor Dwight," I'd said, and we'd both laughed again, trying to imagine Dwight's muscular six-foot-three body taking its pleasure amid fluffy white ruffles. Dwight? Who'd once described himself as looking like the Durham bull in a pea jacket? Imagination faltered.

"I'm sure it'll look darling there," Portland said with such wicked innocence that Dwight gave her a suspicious glance.

"What about you, Avery?" I said hastily. "Don't you need to win a teddy bear for the baby?"

"Hey, I won us a goldfish. What else you want?" Avery asked, holding aloft a plastic bag. The bag held about a quart of water and a confused-looking little black-and-orange fish that he intended to add to his koi pond. It'd only cost him about four dollars to win the thing.

"Every baby needs a teddy bear," said a husky voice behind us. "Guess your age, guess your weight, guess the baby's due date?"

We turned, and there, standing a little apart from the others, was a head-high hinged set of shelves stuffed with small pastel bears beside a large step-on scale. In front was the woman who'd been in my courtroom earlier this month—tall, blue-eyed, dressed tonight in a white shirt tied under her bare midriff and cutoffs that showed long, tanned legs.

Aines? Tampa Aines?

No, not Tampa or Miami. Tallahassee?

Yes, that was it. Tallahassee Ames. And she had recognized me, too.

"Hey, Judge! Guess your weight?"

As if I'd step on a scale anywhere except in a doctor's office.

My horrified expression made her laugh. "How about your birthday, then? Get it within two months or any bear's yours, okay?"

I peeled off two dollars, and she eyed me up and down as she added my money to the wad of bills in her pocket, then said, "Virgo, right? End of August?"

"On the nose!" said my nephew Reese, who'd suddenly appeared at my elbow. He's one of my brother Herman's sons. The one that hasn't finished growing up. The one who owns nothing but a white Ford pickup and the contents of a trailer he rents from my brother Seth. An unfamiliar young woman hung on his arm.

"Aren't they just the cutest little bears?" she cooed. "See if you can win me a pink one, Reese?"

"Guess your age within two years, your weight within three pounds, your birthday within two months. Only two dollars," Tally Ames chanted.

Reese handed over the money. "Weight," he said.

She walked around him, talking trash as she eyed his tall Knott build. "Muscles in those arms. Skinny backside, but a coupla beers too many in that belly. Let me see your hands. Umm, hardworking hands, but slow, right?" She winked at Reese's girlfriend, who giggled in agreement.

She scribbled a number on the tiny pad in her hand. "A hundred and eighty-seven pounds, okay?"

Reese grinned, handed his foot-long chili dog to his girlfriend, and stepped confidently toward the scales. "I ain't weighed but a hundred and seventy-five since—"

His grin turned to disbelief as the needle swung back and forth, then settled at 188.

"Better cut back on the beer and hot dogs, Reese," I teased.

But my nephew was peeling off another two dollars. "So how old you think I am?"

She peered deeply into his eyes, then wrote the number on her pad. "I've written it down. What do you say?"

"Twenty-eight," said Reese.

She showed him the pad where she'd scribbled twenty-eight.

"Damn!" said Reese, and two more dollars changed hands. "When's my birthday?"

More scribbling. "I'm ready."

"July," Reese said.

She showed him her pad where she'd abbreviated "Jly."

Reese swung around and glared at our laughing faces. "Y'all are telling her!"

"No, they're not," said Tally Ames, her bright blue eyes sparkling from the roll she was on. "Son, I can even tell you what beer you drink!"

She took his two dollars and wrote *Bud Lite* on her pad.

"I know y'all're telling her," Reese insisted.

"Tell you what," said the guesser. "For two dollars, I'll make 'em stand behind me and I'll tell you what kind of car you drove here tonight, okay?"

"Now here's where I get you your teddy bear, Patsy," Reese told his girlfriend as she joined us behind Tally Ames.

Once more, the woman looked Reese up and down, then started writing on her pad. Patsy peered over her shoulder and began to giggle. "She's got you, babe."

I looked, too. *Ford pickup.*

"Now, how the hell you do that?" Reese asked, totally amazed. As if everybody in the world couldn't look at him and know that he drove a truck and that the only chancy thing would be whether it was a Ford or Chevy. She'd had a fifty-fifty chance of getting it right.

"You're a good sport, son," she said. "I'm gonna give you a free teddy bear, okay? You deserve it."

My eyes met Dwight's above Sylvia's head. He winked at me and I knew I wasn't alone in figuring out that Reese's "free" teddy bear, a fuzzy little blue thing no bigger than my hand, had cost him ten bucks.

But Patsy was happy as she and Reese wandered away and Tally Ames turned back to us.

"Guess your weight, guess your age, guess how long that goldfish is gonna live?"

Avery and Portland laughed and Dwight held up his hands in surrender. "You're too good for us."

She laughed and called to one of the women standing at a Bust the Balloon concession. "Hey, Lia, mind the Guesser for me a few minutes?"

"Sure," said the woman.

Past the midway and one row over, I saw a large and colorful slide that undulated as people slid down the rainbow arc.

"Is that your Pot O'Gold?" I asked.

"That's it," Tally Ames said.

As she led us toward her slide, I heard the woman behind us chant, "Guess your age, guess your weight, guess if you're gonna get lucky tonight? Two bucks to play, win a bear if I'm wrong."

Along the way, our tour guide paused at a Cover the Spot game, where the object was to drop five flat metal disks so that they completely covered a large red dot. It was being tended by a lanky teenager who exhorted passersby to give it a go. "A game of pure skill, folks. All it takes is a steady hand. A dollar tries and you choose your prize."

Even if I hadn't heard Mrs. Ames's courtroom testimony, the boy's height and coloring would have told me he was her son Val. He fanned the metal disks, then dropped them one by one almost casually on the target. Not a smidgen of red could be seen. Avery couldn't resist. He immediately handed the boy a dollar. Four dollars later, he admitted defeat.

Reid asked to see it demonstrated again. Five dollars, no prize.

"Sorry, guys," said Mrs. Ames. "Val? This is the judge I told you about."

He smiled and said he was glad to meet me, but the smile didn't quite reach his eyes and he didn't stick out his hand to shake mine.

He did offer me the disks, though. "Want to try? No charge."

"Sure," I said. I'd watched his demonstration and I was doing just fine till I dropped the last disk and left a tiny arc of red no bigger than a fingernail clipping exposed.

"Not bad," said Mrs. Ames as we moved on through the crowd to the Pot O'Gold.

"Just two tickets to ride," chanted the wiry man taking tickets and handing out ride sacks. "Land in the pot, win a prize or a free slide."

"Hervé," said Tally Ames, "this is Judge Knott."

All the warmth lacking in Val's was in his smile, even though several of his teeth were missing. "You the lady judge took care of those jerks that tried to wreck this ride?"

I nodded.

"Want to try it out?" Mrs. Ames gestured toward the opening in the vinyl "tree" that led to the stairs. "On me," she added, brushing away my string of tickets. "You and your friends, okay?"

I was game since I, too, was wearing cutoffs and sneakers, but Sylvia wasn't about to risk her pale pink slacks. "Besides," she said, reaching for the big stuffed dog, "somebody has to hold Mr. Dots."

Portland patted her thickened abdomen and blandly said she'd hold Mr. Tuna, so Avery handed over the goldfish. The air was stuffy inside and smelled like warm plastic as I climbed the spiral iron staircase ahead of the three men.

From below me, Dwight asked, "Hey, shug. When was that woman in your courtroom?"

"A few weeks back. Some jerks put a knife in this slide."

We emerged through the painted cloud doorway atop the thirty-foot-high arch and could see the whole carnival spread out below us. Above the colored neon and flashing lights, the moon floated in a cloudless sky. I don't have a great head for heights and the ground looked a lot further away than I expected.

We positioned the burlap sacks we'd been given, then pushed off, aiming for that very small pot of gold sponges at the bottom. As we slid down, the bow twisted and rippled beneath us. My legs got tangled with Dwight's, then we both crashed into Reid and ended up in a heap at the bottom. Only Avery managed to slide into the pot. When the number on the bottom of the sponge he'd picked was matched to the prize board, he'd won a fluorescent yellow kazoo, which he immediately put to his lips and began blatting out "Ding-Dong! The Witch Is Dead."

While we were climbing and sliding, more customers had plunked down tickets and I heard myself called from above. Four young men had come through the clouds and were getting their slide sacks in place. One of them was yet another nephew, Haywood's Stevie, home from Carolina for the weekend, and his friend Eric Holt, who's at Shaw. Eric's Uncle Cletus and Aunt Maidie work for my daddy and I'd heard Maidie say she was expecting Eric for Sunday dinner. Eric and Stevie had graduated from West Colleton High together, but I didn't recognize the other kids who were with them.

We watched them push off, then try to maintain direction as the vinyl rainbow undulated like a drunken horse, rolling them off to the side troughs like gutter balls in a bowling alley. Eric was the only one to make it into the winner's pot for a bright green yo-yo with tiny lights at the center that twinkled like little flames as it spun up and down.

"Remember how to walk the dog?" asked Dwight, who's known Eric since he was a baby.

Eric laughed and with a flick of his wrist made the yo-yo "sleep" so he could walk it along the ground.

I collected hugs from Stevie and Eric both before they and their friends drifted on to the next attraction.

Tally Ames showed me the place where Victor Lincoln had sliced the vinyl with his knife, but the mend was so good I could barely see it.

"Take another slide?" she asked.

We thanked her, but we were ready to try out the swings and the Tilt-A-Whirl.

After that came a rather tame haunted house, although the fake spiderweb felt uncomfortably real when it brushed my face in the pitch blackness of the maze. And okay, yes, I jumped when my shoulder set off one of the sensors and an eerie flash of green light unexpectedly revealed a grotesquely lifelike rubber face only inches from my own. Sylvia squealed and tucked herself under Dwight's arm.

We hit some of the food carts for nourishment—elephant ears, cotton candy, and popcorn—then stood and watched the action on the kiddie rides as we ate. Events like this graphically illustrate just how fast our Hispanic population is growing here. Knots of immigrant Mexican workmen paused to watch as Mexican parents guided their children through the ride gates. Spanish was almost as prevalent as English.

Reid spotted his son there with his ex-wife and her new husband, and he and young Tip went off together to ride the Ferris wheel.

"Cal would love this," Dwight said with a sigh as he shifted the stuffed Dalmatian to the shoulder Sylvia wasn't leaning on. I saw Portland's hand reach for Avery's and knew she was probably imagining their own child here in two or three years.

And where would I be by then?

Still alone?

I'm independent enough to know that no man is better than the wrong man and God knows I've had my share of those, beginning with the one I ran off with when I was eighteen. After two back-to-back fiascoes in the spring, I had taken a vow of chastity which I had kept all summer, but dammit all, I *like* men. I like kissing and touching and waking up with a stubbly face on the pillow next to mine. If it's for keeps and Mendelssohn, though, it'll have to be someone who'll do more than just warm my bed. I want someone who'll share my life and let me share his, someone who'll be there through PMS and bad hair days and who'll give me a chance to do the same for him.

I've made so many bad choices in the last few years that I've started doubting my own judgment everywhere except in the courtroom. What if I'd already met the man who could have been perfect for me and bobbled my big chance? Gone chasing after the sexy one and missed out on the steady one?

Like Bradley Needham, for instance. Brad and his wife had stopped to speak to Portland and Avery, with nods for the rest of us. Janice is one of our better courtroom clerks and Brad's director of marketing for Longleaf, a sausage- and meat-packing company headquartered here in the county. I realized I hadn't seen Janice in the courtroom since early summer.

"You haven't been sick, have you?" I asked.

"Oh, no," she said, plucking a stray hair from the collar of my shirt.

Janice is a picker—hair, threads, bits of lint. She can't seem to help herself, and we either pretend not to notice or stay out of arm's reach.

"Bradley had a temporary assignment with Longleaf's West Coast distributor and we've been in California since the end of June. It was only supposed to be for a month, but everything was such a mess, it took twice as long as they thought for him to straighten everything out." She picked a gnat off my bare arm. "We didn't mind, though. Longleaf put us up in a residential hotel with a swimming pool, maid service, everything. Didn't cost us a cent. It was like a second honeymoon."

"Y'all been back long?" Portland asked politely.

"Tuesday." Portland's nubbly blue shirt had picked up so much fluff from Dwight and Sylvia's plush dog that Janice didn't seem to know where to start. Her thin fingers darted in and out. "We decided to take the rest of the week off, give us time to unpack and get the house in order. I really ought to be there right now—you wouldn't believe the dust!—but Bradley just had to come see the carnival. Like we hadn't been to Disneyland twice while we were out there in California. He doesn't even enjoy it all that much. But he thought he ought to come out tonight to support the harvest festival, and as much as he has to travel, I don't like him to have to go places here by himself. You know how husbands are."

Her fingers moved compulsively toward Portland's shirt.

"Yes, I know," said Portland, and moved out of reach. If I'd been less choosy, I probably could have had

Brad Needham for a husband. He called me at least a half-dozen times when I first came home to Colleton County several years ago, but I didn't have much enthusiasm for sausage back then or for Brad, either, though he'd been considered a good catch. A little dull maybe, but cute, decent, hardworking, no bad habits. His best features were his dark brown hair and eyes. He had thick eyelashes and even thicker curly hair that still fell boyishly over his forehead and almost touched his collar in back. Probably made a comfortable living back then, too. But I was still getting over someone in New York in those days and I never even let Brad buy me a cup of coffee.

Of course, there was also that matter of height. Every man in my family's at least five-ten and most are over six feet. It would have been cruel to bring in someone a good six or eight inches shorter, no matter how sexy his eyes.

Hadn't bothered Janice. She's three inches taller than Brad and four or five years older, a house-proud woman who wears silky pastel dresses and holds her long hair back with headbands that match. Tonight she wore pale coral and the color looked good against her dark hair and the tan she'd picked up in California. No children, but they seem happy together and there's been no courthouse gossip about their marriage, even though Brad's on the road a lot, from what I hear.

By ten-thirty, parents with small children had drifted toward the gates, noticeably thinning the crowd so that walking the midway was a little easier. We'd tried almost every game and had acquired more prizes — a purple-and-green

plush snake (Reid), an eight-inch pink teddy bear (Portland), and a poster of Richard Petty, which I'd probably
wind up giving to Reese to liven up the bare walls of his
trailer. (I'd actually been aiming for Willie Nelson, but
someone jiggled my arm just as the dart left my hand.) We
were at that point of debating whether to call it a night and
go find a quiet watering hole, or just call it a night, period.

Even though she can't drink now and was already
yawning, Portland insisted that it didn't matter to her.
"Whatever y'all want to do."

Sylvia, who hadn't yet won a thing on her own, was
still anxious to try something called the Dozer, which sat
slightly apart from the other stands beneath its own red-
and-white-striped tent. The tent's two end walls acted as
a divider from the kiddie duck pond next to it on one side
and a cotton candy wagon on the other side. The other
two flaps were tied open so that players could enter from
either side of the midway.

As for the Dozer itself, picture a rectangular box on
wheels with its four sides hinged at the top so they could
be folded up out of the way. Interlocking red *A*'s were
stenciled around the bottom. It had been too crowded the
first time we passed it. Now there were more than enough
places to accommodate all six of us and we reached in
our pockets for quarters.

"I used to be pretty good at this," Sylvia said. "Wait till
the pusher goes back before you put your quarters in so
they'll land behind the pile."

The setup reminded me of an old-fashioned candy
counter. Each station was a separate glass box. Just at eye
level was a shelf heaped with quarters and poker chips
that could be redeemed for prizes or cash. A pusher blade

like the blade on a bulldozer came forward and the pile of quarters seemed to teeter on the edge. Then the blade went back and I quickly reached up and pushed two quarters through the slot while the blade was still retreating. The two coins rolled down to the empty part of the shelf and lay flat. As the blade came forward, it pushed my quarters toward the pile accumulated at the front edge. The pile quivered and a single quarter tumbled over and down into a cup at waist level. I immediately retrieved it and fed it back into the slot. When the blade came forward, though, that coin slid harmlessly to the side. I fed in two more quarters with no better luck than before. One landed on the pile, the other rolled off to the side and disappeared.

A tiny hand-lettered sign there read COINS THAT FALL INTO THE SIDE SPILLS ARE RETAINED BY OPERATOR. (Like anyone really thinks the operator would give them back?)

I could see the logic of Sylvia's instructions, though. I needed to lay down a carpet of quarters at the back center so that when the blade pushed them forward, they in turn would push that front pile of quarters over the edge and into my cup.

Unfortunately, I was out of quarters.

I fished a couple of dollars out of my pocket and called, "Change, please."

There was no response from the well behind the boxes. I stood on tiptoes to catch the eye of the person who should have been standing ready to make change or redeem the poker chips for prizes.

"Excuse me," I called again. "I need some change down here."

"Good luck," growled a black man a few spaces away. "I don't think nobody's working this place."

"We've not seen anybody anyhow," said the woman with him.

Across the way, strobe lights suddenly flashed and a siren wailed as someone won at the Bowler Roller stand. A guy there was high-fiving his friend, and everyone in eyesight turned to watch till the lights and siren turned themselves off.

"I've got quarters," Reid called from the woman's far side. The others were around on the other side of the setup.

"That's okay," I told him. There were two steps leading up into the wagon and the wooden flap that led to the dim interior was unhooked. I put my foot on the bottom step, pulled back the flap, and stuck my head in. "Anybody he—"

The words died in my throat.

A white man lay crumpled on the wooden floor. Blood clotted his nose and had oozed down the side of his face. His eyes were open and unblinking.

His mouth was open, too, but it had been stuffed to overflowing with bloody quarters.

CHAPTER
3

I backed out quickly and bumped into Dwight, who was holding dollar bills in his own hand.

He grabbed my arm to steady me, took one look at my face, and said, "What's wrong, shug?"

I swallowed and pointed to the space behind me.

He squeezed through the narrow opening, then immediately stepped back out and reached for the phone clipped to his belt to call for backup.

As Reid came over to see what was going on, Tally Ames darted out of the midway crowd with a frown on her face.

"Hey," she called. "No customers in the hole, okay?"

Her eyes ran across the top of the game as if expecting a head to pop up from behind the glass boxes with their endlessly moving blades. "Braz!"

With an exasperated sigh, she said, "I swear I'm gonna kill him, sneaking off again and leaving the store to run itself. Here, y'all need change? I'll get it for you."

She tried to move past Dwight, but he held his ground

in front of the opening. "Sorry, ma'am." To Reid, he said, "I saw a couple of town officers around here earlier. Run see if you can find them."

While my cousin for once went off to do as he was told without asking why, Tally protested. "Officers? Hey, wait a minute, Mister. You got a problem with Braz or this store, you talk to me, okay? I'm the owner. And if I can't fix it, I'm sure our patch—"

"Wassup, Tal?" asked a man who was working the duck pond next door, an idle pond now since all his little customers seemed to have gone home to bed.

She turned to him gratefully. "Is Dennis still on the lot, Skee?"

"Yeah, I saw him up at the gate a few minutes ago. Want me to get him?"

"Would you? And if you see Braz, tell him to get his tail back here right now, or he can just keep on going, okay?"

She swung back to me and said, "Look, Judge, can't you tell your friend here—"

"I'm sorry, Mrs. Ames." I was almost positive that it was her older, missing son who lay just beyond the hinged flap, and even though Dwight was shaking his head at me, I couldn't not start preparing her for the worst. "There's been an accident. And this is Dwight Bryant of the Colleton County Sheriff's Department."

"Accident? Sheriff's department?" She glared at us suspiciously. "What sort of accident?"

The African American couple who'd been feeding quarters into the machine next to Reid started to edge away, and Dwight said sharply, "You two! Wait right there, please."

"Hey, this ain't nothing to do with us," said the man.

"Woods, isn't it?" asked Dwight. "Vernon Woods?"

I couldn't quite remember the charges—DWI? Possession of an illegal substance?—but I was pretty sure that he'd stood before me in a courtroom in the last year or so. From the way he was scowling, he seemed to remember me, too. The woman tugged at his sleeve, and he subsided.

Not Tally Ames, though. She was getting more and more upset, yet, curiously, the vibes I was getting were not because she feared something had happened to her son, but more as if she feared he'd instigated whatever it was that required the law.

Happily, Reid soon returned with two of Dobbs's finest close at his heels, one black officer, one white. And from the opposite direction came help for Mrs. Ames in the form of a good-looking white man in jeans and a short-sleeved white polo shirt. A little shorter than Dwight, he was slender, with a small gray moustache that was as neatly trimmed as the salt-and-pepper hair beneath his gimme ball cap. Without the least hesitation, he instantly deduced who was in charge here and held out his hand to Dwight.

"Dennis Koffer, Officer. I'm the show's patch. They tell me there's a problem?"

At the time, I'd never heard the term "patch," but Dwight clearly had. He shook the man's hand and said, "I'm afraid so. Someone's been hurt here."

"Dead?" Koffer asked shrewdly.

Dwight nodded.

"Who?"

"We don't know yet."

Koffer nodded almost imperceptibly toward the door flap and lifted an inquiring eyebrow.

Dwight nodded again.

"Want me to take a look?"

"Maybe in a few minutes, after my people get here."

By now, Portland and Avery had begun to realize that something was wrong and had come around with their fish and teddy bear to join the group. Sylvia trailed them with a happy smile on her face and both hands so full of quarters and prize tokens that she could hardly keep from dropping some. She hadn't been bragging. She really was good at this game.

Abruptly, she realized that the fun and games were over. "Dwight?"

"Someone's been hurt," he said. "Looks like I'm going to be tied up for a while. Reid? You mind driving her home? I'll call you tomorrow, Sylvia."

Reid nodded and Sylvia said, "Sure thing, honey."

I was surprised and, okay, yes, a little impressed that she didn't fuss or exclaim or make a big deal of it. Of course, this couldn't have been the first time one of their evenings was cut short. Goes with the territory when you're seeing a sheriff's deputy.

"We'll head on out, too," said Avery. "Deborah?"

I glanced at Dwight, thinking he'd want to question me about what, if anything, I'd noticed, but he'd turned back to Dennis Koffer and was conferring in low tones.

"Thanks, Avery," I said, "but my car's here and I'll be okay."

"You're sure?" asked Por. "You know you're welcome to crash with us tonight."

It wouldn't have been the first time. We each know

where the other's house key's hidden and we run in and out as freely as sisters. Now I patted her arm and said I'd be fine. "You need a good night's sleep and Avery needs to get that fish in your pond before it dies."

Several squad cars arrived, followed by the county's crime-scene van and an EMS truck. They drove straight down the midway. The crowd had been thinning, but all the people still there now surged toward the flashing blue, red, and orange lights, ready to gawk at this new attraction. I hung off to the side, hoping none of my family was still around, or, if any were, that they wouldn't connect this with me.

Around the lot, flaps were being closed and secured on the various games, lights were turned off, and several of the concessionaires, including the man called Skee, the woman we'd met earlier at the guessing booth, two younger women from the cotton candy wagon, and presumably the Polly of Polly's Plate Pitch, opposite the Dozer, gathered in a protective clump around Tally Ames. I'd heard that carnival people form a tight-knit community and now I was seeing it in action.

Someone pulled the plug on the upbeat country-western music that had pounded through the loud-speakers all evening just as Tally's teenage son from the Cover the Spot game came running up and the boy's question was audible to everyone. "Mom? What's wrong? What's Braz done now?"

She shrugged, then said something to him in a low voice that sent him loping down the midway to eel through two concessions at the end where he disappeared from my view. A cluster of travel trailers and eighteen-wheelers were parked out there beyond the line of game booths—"stores," in Tally's usage.

The newly arrived officers immediately began stringing yellow tape to establish a perimeter around the tent, and Dwight told two of them to start collecting garbage bags from all the trash containers.

"I don't know if a weapon was used, but if it's been dumped, I want it found. Any bloody rags or paper napkins, too."

Normally, Dwight's so slow-talking and laid-back that most times you'd never know he spent several years in Army Intelligence. He makes it easy to forget that they don't take just anybody and they don't give rapid promotion just because they like your looks.

"Hey, Deborah," said my nephew Stevie. "What's happening?"

"Somebody at the Dozer get hurt?" asked Eric Holt.

"Looks like it," I said noncommittally. "Did y'all play it tonight?"

A glance passed between them.

"Yeah, for a few minutes," said Stevie. "Then we decided to do more rides."

"Was there someone here making change?"

"Yeah, a guy about our age, maybe a little older. Is that who got hurt?"

Before I could answer, Dwight borrowed the hand mike from the game next door and addressed the crowd. "Anybody who played this game tonight, we ask you to speak to the officer over here to my left. The rest of you can go on home. There's nothing more to see here."

Even before he spoke, I'd noticed several don't-want-to-get-involved types melt away toward the entrance, but

Dwight had already posted someone there at the gate to take down the names of everybody still on the lot. He wouldn't be able to catch them all, of course. The place was too porous. But with close questioning and cross-checking, I was willing to bet he could come up with the names of ninety-five percent of the people who'd come to the carnival today and surely one of them would have seen something.

I looked around for Stevie and Eric but they were gone.

Without telling the deputy they'd played the Dozer.

All this time, there was an eerie glow from the flood-lights aimed at the floor inside the wagon, and now the photographer stepped out to let a colleague start collecting any physical evidence. He handed one of the instant prints to Dwight, who showed it to Dennis Koffer, who confirmed my original guess.

"It's Braz, Tally."

"Braz?" At first she seemed incredulous. Then her head began to shake back and forth in denial. "No! Oh God, no! How? What happened?"

She tried to duck under the yellow tape, but was held back.

Across the lot, I saw Val Ames returning with a wiry man of middle height and a receding hairline.

Pushing through the stragglers who probably wouldn't leave till they were chased with a stick, he roared, "What the hell's going on, Dennis?"

Tally Ames had been watching for him, and now she burst into tears, rushed to him, and buried her head on his shoulder. "It's Braz. He's been hurt bad, Arn. He's dead."

"Arnold Ames," Dennis Koffer told Dwight. "Tally's

husband. Arn, this is Major Bryant of the Colleton County Sheriff's Department. He and the judge here were playing your Dozer when they found Braz in the hole."

Colleton County's in the process of switching away from the old coroner system, and the doctor who's acting as interim medical examiner came over and told Dwight that he was ready to have the body transported to Chapel Hill for autopsy as is required in cases of violent death.

Uniformed officers of the Dobbs PD moved people back even further so that the boxy EMS truck could move in closer. The techies had draped the still form before lifting him out onto the gurney. As they transferred him into the ambulance, Tally Ames's low sobs were the only sound until the ambulance drove slowly away and murmured speech returned to the onlookers.

The crime scene technician went back inside in case there had been anything under the body that he'd missed the first time. When he came back out, he extinguished the floods, packed up the van, and told Dwight he was finished for now.

"I'd like to come back tomorrow morning, though. In the daylight."

Dwight nodded, then asked the Ameses if there was someplace private where they could sit down and talk.

Tally Ames looked around. "Dennis?"

"You could use the cookhouse," he suggested, pointing toward the one food stand that offered places to sit down and eat. Four wooden picnic tables with attached benches stood beneath a yellow tent. "We can close the flaps so you can be private."

"What about the Dozer?" asked Mr. Ames. "We got close to five hundred dollars in quarters there."

"I'm going to leave a guard here for tonight," said Dwight, "but if it'd make you feel better, you can let the sides down. I assume they lock? I'll ask you not to go inside till we're finished tomorrow morning."

The man nodded and looked around for some of his help. "Binga? Hervé? Raggs?"

The three men slipped under the tape. Inside their glass boxes, the Dozer blades moved back and forth until one of the men disconnected the power cord that snaked from the back side.

As the men lowered the sides of the game and locked them in place, the carnival's patch asked Dwight, "What about tomorrow? Saturday's usually our biggest day. You're not going to keep us from playing tomorrow, are you?" He glanced at the Ameses. "No disrespect, Tal, Arnie, but you know we can't afford to close tomorrow."

"We know," Arnold Ames said grimly.

"We'll get someone to cover for you," said Koffer, and murmurs of agreement from the other carnies backed him up.

"There's no reason you can't open the rest of the carnival," said Dwight. "If we keep these tent flaps shut, we can come in and out without anybody hardly knowing we're here."

I realized that Dwight probably wasn't going to get to me tonight and that I might as well go on home, but thinking of how the Ameses were strangers in a strange town, I slipped over to them and said, "If there's anything I can do to help with the legalities—"

Before either adult could speak, their son glared at me with hot, resentful eyes. "We don't need the help of any damn Knotts. Just leave us the hell alone!"

The boy's hostility was like a slap across the face, and I could feel my cheeks flushing.

Arnold Ames glared at him. "Shut your mouth, Val! Now! Help the others close up, then get to the trailer and stay there. You hear me?"

The teenager nodded with matching anger, then stomped off toward his game stand.

"I apologize for our son," said Tally Ames, and her voice broke again as the mention of one son seemed to renew her grief for the one so newly dead. "He's— We're—"

"I understand," I told her, even though I didn't. Unless it was because I was the one who found his brother's body, so let's kill the messenger?

"We do appreciate your offer of help, though," said her husband. He put his arm around Tally's shoulders to guide her toward the tent with picnic tables. "Come on and sit down, Tal. Kay's getting you something to drink."

As I started to walk away, Dwight called to me. He was holding out that stupid stuffed Dalmatian. "Sylvia forgot her dog. Could you stick this in my truck for me on your way out?"

"You sure you don't want to forget it yourself?" I was only half joking.

"And find myself in the doghouse tomorrow? Not hardly. Course, if you don't want to be bothered—"

"Don't be silly," I said. "Hand it over."

With the thing hoisted on my shoulder, I walked on down to the main gate. The patrol cars and emergency vehicles had effectively closed the carnival for this night. Most of the gaming concessions were shuttered tight and looked shabby and forlorn with but a scattering of unflattering security lights to illuminate their gaudy fronts. Deputy Mayleen Richards had rigged herself a flat surface for her laptop and was typing in names and addresses so efficiently that only a few people were still in line when I got there, and the line moved briskly.

She smiled at the dog on my shoulder. "Oh, hey, Judge. I see you got lucky."

"Not me, your boss."

As she entered my name and numbers on the glowing screen, I made my voice casual. "Many of my relatives here tonight?"

Her sturdy fingers manipulated the keyboard and the list she'd compiled obligingly sorted itself in alphabetical order. Haywood and Herman and their wives had been there along with Robert and Doris and some of their grandchildren. Several of my nieces' and nephews' names were starred like mine to indicate they'd played the Dozer. As I'd feared, Stevie's name wasn't there at all, which made it a safe bet that Eric Holt's wasn't either. I made a mental note to look into it, but not tonight.

"You wouldn't happen to know where Dwight parked his truck, would you?"

Mayleen stood and shaded her eyes against the bright headlights of cars and trucks streaming from the parking area. There were still quite a few vehicles back there in the darkness and more than half were pickups.

"Is that it down yonder towards the end?" she asked, pointing in what was also the general direction of my own car.

Shifting Mr. Dot to my other shoulder, I told Mayleen goodnight and headed across the gravel and grass lot. Dwight's truck was there all right, but both doors were locked. I considered slinging the dog in the back to let it take its chances, but I know that enough of my fellow citizens would think this ridiculous object was something worth stealing, so I lugged it on over to my car and crammed it in the front seat, where it sat looking through the windshield as I fastened a seat belt around its bulk.

I wondered what Blue and Ladybelle would think if they caught sight of a dog like this in my car. Those two hounds belong to my daddy, but they like to lope across the fields and visit me, and they're always trying to hitch a ride in my car if I start to leave while they're there.

My brothers keep offering to get me a dog of my own even though I don't want to bother with one just yet.

"You need you a good loud barker," says Haywood.

"Protection," says Herman.

"After all," says Will, "you *are* living out there all by your lonesome."

I should be so lucky.

My so-called lonesome is only an illusion of isolation and nothing more. Daddy cut me off a few acres of the farm when I built out there, and while my plat's surrounded by fields bordered in trees and brush so that no other house is visible, I wouldn't have to yell loud to have half my family there in a heartbeat. The farm is crisscrossed by tractor lanes and somebody's always passing by my place at any hour of the day and night, either one of the boys or one of their children. *I* say they're being nosy, *they* say they're just taking the shortcuts they've always taken.

Whichever, there are so many watchful eyes that only complete strangers or total fools would risk coming onto Knott land with evil in their hearts.

The lights of Dobbs dimmed in my rearview mirror as I drove westward under the three-quarter moon. I knew my surface thoughts of dogs and busybody brothers were just a stalling effort to keep my mind from playing an endless loop of that young man crumpled on the floor of the Dozer, his face like raw steak, those bloody quarters spilling from his mouth.

Blood money?

Money to keep his mouth shut?

Surely his killer intended some sort of symbolic statement with that grisly touch?

And why had his brother been so hostile? At the Pot O'Gold, even before I found Braz's body, he hadn't taken my outstretched hand when his mother introduced us. I'd ruled in favor of Ames Amusement Corporation and had put a judgment on those vandals that would repay any monetary loss they'd suffered. Was he mad because I hadn't sent them to jail instead?

Or was he simply acting out some sort of adolescent angst with his parents and it wasn't about me at all? And for that matter, why wasn't that boy in school instead of traveling with a carnival?

"Not your problem," said the pragmatist who lives in my head and tries to keep me from messing with things that aren't my business.

From the other side of my head came the preacher who tries to keep me from acting only in my own self-interest. *"The Ameses are poor wayfaring strangers."*

"With plenty of friends to comfort them," said the pragmatist.

But there had been something odd about Val Ames's words: "We don't need the help of any damn Knotts." As if it weren't just me he was angry at, but other members of my family, too.

Had some of my nieces or nephews insulted him since the carnival came to town? Or gone down to Widdington last month and caused trouble? None of my brothers' children are bad kids, but they aren't Sunday school saints, either. Andrew's son A.K. spent a couple of weekends in jail last summer for vandalism and Herman's Reese has brawled his way into overnight lockups a time or two. Some of the others, including the girls, have collected DWIs and misdemeanor possession of marijuana before settling into respectability. And let's not talk about the times I've danced with the devil myself.

Haywood's Stevie has always stayed out of trouble, though. So why had he and Eric Holt sneaked away from the carnival without telling Dwight's people that they'd played the Dozer?

I wasn't crazy about any of the possible answers.

Maybe it was time to listen to the pragmatist for a change, or as Daddy's housekeeper Maidie would say, "Don't trouble trouble till trouble troubles you."

Nevertheless, blood-smeared quarters troubled my dreams all night, only they were blue beneath the blood, not silver.

CHAPTER
4

Saturday dawned hot and sunny. My calendar might say this was the last weekend in September, but nobody had told the thermometer that it was no longer summer. Cutoffs and sneakers had been fine last night; unfortunately, today's obligations called for more formal wear.

A policeman's lot is not an 'appy one, according to Gilbert and Sullivan. The same might be said of a judge's. Most of the time, we're called upon to pass judgment on society's offenders "who'd none of 'em be missed." But at least there's dignity in the courtroom. So why are we always being asked to judge things outside the courtroom?

Which is to say that rather than catching up with laundry and all the household chores I tend to let slide during the week, I was due to spend this Saturday morning judging the Some Yam Thing or Other contest at the harvest festival.

Sweet potatoes are a big money crop in Colleton

County, and farm kids have always had fun with some of the oddities to be found when digging potatoes in the fall. I still remember one in which the root end was so forked that it looked like a man on tommy-walkers. If the contest had existed back then, I'd have painted that yam in a red, white, and blue Uncle Sam suit with a cotton beard and entered it. Today I could expect anything from yams shaped like cell phones to Elvis look-alikes. The only rule is that the base potato has to remain uncut. Contestants can augment, but they're not allowed to carve.

A silly event to get involved with (thank you very much, Minnie), but when you have to run for elective office, it's politic to show that you can be a good sport.

I settled on a two-piece blue chambray dress that does good things for my eyes and sandy blond hair, thick-soled straw espadrilles that would help keep my feet out of the dust that was sure to be churned up around the exhibit hall, and silver dangles for my ears. As I rummaged in my jewelry box for an elusive earring back, I had to move several bags made of treated brown flannel that keep my silver pieces from tarnishing. Before I had a house of my own, inexpensive silver jewelry was a popular Christmas or birthday gift from my sisters-in-law. Now they're into sheets, towels, and cookware.

Earrings in place, I rooted around for a silver pin I hadn't worn in ages. It didn't seem to be there. I pulled open my lingerie drawer and poked around at the back where I keep odd pieces I don't really like but hate to throw away. No luck.

I'd just about given up on the pin when my fingers felt an unfamiliar shape inside another of those tarnish-resistant bags. I opened it and there was the silver charm bracelet my mother had started for me when I was a toddler.

Dangling from the first link was a calendar page for August with a tiny little peridot marking my birthday. Next came a doll, a teddy bear, an ABC, a pair of scissors, a dog—

Tricksy!

Lord God in glory. How long was it since I'd last thought of Tricksy? I was nine when he ran under a tractor wheel and had to be put down. I cried for two days, yet I'd almost forgotten buying this charm, which I swore would keep him in my heart forever and ever. As I had forgotten this Empire State Building and a domed Capitol, souvenirs of my first trips to New York and Washington with Mother and Aunt Zell—"Just us girls," Mother had said.

She adored Daddy and was crazy about her sons and her stepsons, but sometimes all that maleness got overwhelming and then she'd call her sister and it was off to the beach, off to a big city, off to the mountains for a long weekend of purely female indulgence.

The bracelet was so bound up in memories of her that I hadn't worn it since I was eighteen, since the summer she died.

Yet here it was, hardly tarnished at all, and thick with tiny objects whose symbolism I could barely recall. It reminded me of the gold charm bracelet Tally Ames had worn when she testified in court, the delicate jingle when she placed her hand on the Bible.

I clasped the bracelet around my wrist and looked at the effect in the mirror. It echoed the gleam of my silver earrings. Festive, but not flashy. And time to get another haircut, I noted. I like to keep it right at chin line, not brushing my shoulders.

A little eyeliner, a touch of blusher, lipstick and I was almost ready to go as soon as I found my car keys.

I had just picked up my straw shoulder bag when a truck door slammed outside and Dwight's voice called, "Anybody home?"

"Two minutes later and the answer would have been no," I told him as he pulled open the screen door and came in.

Like me, he had on his working clothes this morning: olive chinos, dark blue jacket, a soft white shirt with small blue figures. The end of a blue knit tie trailed from his pocket. Dwight cleans up real good, if I do say so. No wonder Sylvia seems so taken with him.

"I was out this way and thought I'd have breakfast with Mama, but she's off somewhere, so I was hoping maybe you'd give me a cup of coffee."

Dwight has two younger sisters. You'd think that would be enough for any man. (Mine usually say that one's too many and that I wrecked the perfect dozen Daddy was aiming for.) But he's always walking in and out as if I were Beth or Nancy Faye.

"I guess you want Sylvia's dog, too?"

He had the grace to look sheepish. "Sorry about that. I could have sworn I left the truck unlocked."

"The dog you can have," I said. "It's still in my car, but I have to judge the yam contest at ten, so it'll have to be a quick cup."

"I was wondering why you were so dressed up. That dress looks real nice on you."

"Don't start," I said. "Daddy's always fussing that he

never sees me in anything but shorts or jeans and am I sure I'm a girl?"

He put up his hands in mock surrender. "Hey, I wasn't sniping. You can wear gunnysacks for all I care."

I thought about Sylvia, always so neat and feminine in dresses or pastel slacks. No cutoffs for her.

As I refilled the coffeemaker and spooned fresh coffee into the basket, Dwight noticed my bracelet. "When did you start wearing that again?"

"Today. I found it in the dresser just now. I'm surprised you remember it. I hadn't thought about it in years myself."

"Does it still have the scissors?" he asked, his big hand reaching out to touch the small charms till he located it. "I was with Will and the little twins when they bought it for your birthday. I forget how old you were. Six? Seven?"

(Even though Adam and Zach are a couple of inches taller now than Herman and Haywood, they'll always be called the "little" twins because they're younger.)

"Why scissors?" I asked.

"You don't remember?"

I shook my head.

"Miss Sue used to put your hair in pigtails in the summer. She said it was cooler and neater. But you hated the way it pulled, so—"

I burst into laughter as memory flooded in. "—so I took her sewing scissors and whacked them off!"

"And then tried to get Zach to even it out before Miss Sue saw it, but she came in and caught y'all and thought at first that he was the one who'd done the whacking."

We both smiled, remembering Mother's dismay. Fortunately, her sense of humor had kicked in and she decided that my butchered looks were punishment enough.

"Daddy was the one that grumbled the most," I said. "Mother took me to the barbershop and had it clipped almost as short as you boys, remember?"

Dwight grinned. "Yeah, Mr. Kezzie wasn't one bit happy till it grew back in."

As the coffee finished dripping, I asked how things were shaping up with Braz Ames's death.

"Brazos Hartley," he said, pulling out a chair at my kitchen table. "He was from Mrs. Ames's first marriage."

"Brazos?"

"Born when the carnival played Texas," Dwight explained. "And Val is for Valdosta, Georgia. I guess it helps keep track. I didn't ask."

"Does that mean she was born in Tallahassee, Florida?" I sliced a bagel, slid it into the toaster, and set out cream cheese and a jar of strawberry jam that my sister-in-law Mae gave me this spring.

"You might say. It's where she joined the carnival, anyhow. You toasting that thing for me? You don't have to feed me."

"Right," I said sarcastically. "Like you didn't tell me about Miss Emily not being home just so I'd feel sorry for you."

I poured coffee for both of us, not bothering with cream or sugar since we both drink it black. The toaster popped up with the bagel nicely browned, and I slid it onto a sandwich plate.

Bagels instead of biscuits. What's the South coming to? Smelled wonderful, though. After last night's indulgence, my breakfast had been half a grapefruit. Without sugar.

"So what's the story with Brazos?" I asked. "From the way his mother was acting before she knew who was hurt, it was like she thought he was the perp instead of the victim."

"Yeah, I picked up on that, too. That's why I had Mayleen run his name through NCIC as soon as we got back to the office." He smeared cream cheese and jam on both halves of the bagel. "Don't you want some of this?"

"Couldn't eat another bite," I lied as I sipped my coffee. "Mayleen find anything on him?"

"Juvenile records were sealed, of course, but there's been an incident or two these last eight years, ever since he turned sixteen."

"He was twenty-four? But Mrs. Ames can't be forty yet."

"Your point being?"

True. Children with babies turned up in my court every week. Since her son Val was so clearly no more than fifteen or sixteen, I'd just assumed the other son was a teenager, too.

"What sort of crimes?" I asked.

"Breaking and entering. A little possession of stolen property. Nothing major yet. Did six months on one of those possessions. Only crimes against property, though. No assaults. None that show up in his records anyhow and, oddly enough, no drugs or alcohol, either. According to his mother, he didn't smoke or drink beyond an occasional beer. She sounds a little proud of that."

"Maybe there's not much to be proud of where he's concerned. Sad." I capped the jam and put it back in the refrigerator. "They have any idea who killed him? Or why?"

"If they do, they're not sharing it with me. Jack and Mayleen are going to search the semi this morning and—"

"Semi?"

"Yeah. Best I can tell, he camped out in the eighteen-wheeler when they're on the road. The Ameses live in a trailer with the younger kid; then they've got a couple of travel trailers they use as bunkhouses for their hired help, a large one for the men and a smaller one for the women. But Hartley slept in the truck van, so we sealed it last night before we left."

I glanced at the clock. "Speaking of leaving—"

"Yeah, I need to get moving, too." Dwight swallowed the last of his coffee, wiped his lips on a paper napkin, then carried his plate and cup to the sink.

As we walked out to our respective vehicles, Dwight said, "Tell me again your connection with Mrs. Ames?"

"She was the complainant in a vandalism case I heard three or four weeks ago."

"That's all?"

"Yes. Why?" I opened my car door so he could take Sylvia's stuffed dog.

"She wants to see you. Asked me to ask you if you'd stop in if you were going to be at the festival today." He unbuckled his prize Dalmatian and tossed it onto the seat of his truck.

"Me?"

"Well, you did tell her to let you know if there was anything you could do to help, didn't you?" He grinned at the look on my face. "Didn't expect her to take you up on it, did you?"

The small Ferris wheel was already turning and music was playing beyond the Agricultural Hall when I came skidding up at five past ten. I thought Dwight's visit had made me late, but I soon learned that I'd confused the time of my event with the barbecue contest and wouldn't have to face any yams till eleven. That gave me a chance to visit with Herman and Haywood and to see how they were faring in the blind tastings.

A dozen or more black steel cookers were lined up under the huge oak trees that shaded the rear of the hall. The big twins had been there since midnight, slowly grilling a hefty pig on their gas-fired cooker and taking turns catching catnaps in the back of Herman's van.

"Just like setting up with a 'bacco barn," said Haywood, who really wasn't quite old enough to remember those days when tobacco was cured with wood fires that had to be fed all through the night. He liked to think he was, though.

Two of my sisters-in-law, Haywood's Isabel and Herman's Nadine, were seated nearby in folding chairs. Herman's an electrician here in Dobbs, so Isabel and my niece Jane Ann had spent the night with Nadine and her Annie Sue rather than drive back to the farm. Evidently, they'd brought breakfast for the twins because Herman was munching on a homemade biscuit.

"Where are the kids?" I asked.

"Oh, those girls were still talking when we went to bed," said Nadine. "We won't see them before noon."

"What about Stevie? Didn't he stay over, too?"

"He had laundry to do," said Isabel with a comfortable chuckle for her un-motherliness. "If he wants to wear cotton shirts, then he's gonna be the one to wash and iron them. Same with Jane Ann."

"Just what I tell my kids," Nadine chimed in. "You get good polyester and you can't tell it from cotton 'cepting you don't have to iron it."

She gave my chambray dress a critical look. "Is that cotton?"

"Well, I like cotton for my work shirts," said Haywood. "You'n heat to death in them synthetic shirts. You got any more of them ham biscuits, honey?"

Isabel reached into a cooler at her feet and waved a somewhat depleted but still fragrant basket of cholesterol and carbohydrates beneath my nose.

"Don't you want one, too, Deb'rah?"

Well, of course, I did—Isabel makes her buttermilk biscuits big as bear claws and she'd sliced the salt-cured dark red ham with an equally generous hand—but somehow I dredged up the willpower to resist.

"Just finished a big breakfast," I said, hoping they wouldn't hear my stomach growl in protest above the music coming from the midway. "I'll be back for some barbecue later if there's any left."

"We'll save you some, honey," Haywood promised, biting into pure succulence before getting on my case.

Even though Herman's still in a wheelchair, there had been plenty of opportunity between catnaps and hands of gin rummy for the big twins to visit the other cookers and catch up on all the gossip around the county. Haywood's never seen a stranger and has never been shy about asking questions or giving advice and Herman's not far behind him.

"Heard you was the one found that boy that got hisself killed," Haywood said disapprovingly.

"Ought you to be doing such stuff and you a judge?" asked Herman.

"You need to remember to be a little more dignified," Haywood said. "Don't look good for you to be messing around with trouble like that."

"I promise you it wasn't something I'd planned on," I told them.

Nadine and Isabel wanted to hear every detail, and they were disappointed at how little I could tell them. I gathered there were much more interesting speculations making the rounds of the cookers—"You know what carnival people are like. All them tattoos? Steal you blind if you take your eyes off 'em"—and they were prepared to share those speculations with me, but Seth and Minnie arrived about then just as someone with a microphone called for our attention.

"The first round of tasting has been completed," he announced. "The final four are numbers one, four, seven, and eight."

There were whoops and cheers from the spectators and a couple of good-natured boos from the eliminated cooks.

"We're number seven," Haywood confided in a bass whisper that could've been heard in Raleigh if the music from the merry-go-round on the other side of the fence hadn't drowned him out.

They had placed second last year, he reminded me, and while second "won't real shabby considering the competition, this year me and Herman's got us a secret ingredient."

"Oh?"

"Yes, ma'am! This year we soaked some oak chips overnight in ginger ale and we sprinkled them on the bottom to get that extra flavor in the smoke."

But for all his pretense of complacency, he and Herman watched closely as the judges sampled the four finalists and marked their scorecards. Then, after a whispered conference, they each went back for yet another taste of numbers four and seven. I saw Haywood's big hand clench Herman's shoulder.

A final huddle with the judges, then the list of winners was handed to the announcer. Honorable mention went to number one, a team of Shriners from Dobbs. To everyone's surprise (and more than a little chagrin), third place was awarded to number eight, a couple of newcomers from Michigan who've really taken to our style of barbecue. Last year's winners, the men's Sunday school class of Mt. Olive A.M.E. Zion, started high-fiving each other, confident that they were about to carry home the blue ribbon again.

The announcer milked the suspense for all it was worth, then cried, "The red ribbon goes to number four, and number seven is this year's blue-ribbon champion! Let's give 'em all a big hand, folks."

Haywood grabbed the handles of the wheelchair and pushed it so fast across the uneven ground toward the announcer that Herman said later he thought he was taking a victory lap at Rockingham rather than accepting first place at a little old barbecue contest. "The way Brother

Haywood was taking them curves, I needed me a seat belt."

The other ribbon winners crowded around to congratulate them.

"What'd you say you soaked your oak chips in?" asked one of the Michiganites.

"Grape Nehi," Herman answered blandly.

"Now, why'd you go and tell 'em that?" Haywood scolded when they returned with their ribbon. "That's liable to taste real good."

Leaving the big twins to fasten that blue rosette to their cooker and bask in their glory, Seth and Minnie walked into the Ag Hall with me for the Some Yam Thing or Other contest. Seth is five up from me and the brother who's always cut me the most slack. Minnie is my self-appointed campaign manager and she's the one who volunteered me to judge today. She believes in keeping me in the public eye. (At least, she believes in keeping me there as long as there are only positive things for the public eye to see.)

Since last night's murder hadn't come up in front of her, I could safely assume she hadn't yet heard of my involvement. I was hoping to keep it that way for the time being.

As I glanced around the hall, I noticed other family members and looked at Minnie suspiciously. "I thought we agreed that none of the kids would enter."

"What makes you think they have?" she parried.

"Oh, come on, Minnie. Why else are Doris and Robert

here? And there's Jess, your own daughter. And Zach's Emma."

"Now, don't worry about it, honey. There's no names on anything. You just judge it like you would if you didn't know they were in it."

It was a good thing that I had two colleagues to help with the judging or rumors might have started that the fix was in.

"Yoo-hoo, Deborah!" my sister-in-law Doris called. When she caught my eye, she shifted her own eyes significantly from her grandson Bert to the table that held entries for the under-sixes.

"I saw that," said Luther Parker. Luther is tall and gangly and looks sort of like a black Abe Lincoln without the beard. He's Colleton County's first African American district court judge and has a dry sense of humor. "No playing favorites, now."

I looked around the hall and saw his wife Louise. We exchanged waves as a bright-eyed little girl ran up to her and tugged at her hand.

Luther and Louise's first grandchild.

"May we assume Sarah's entered in the first category?" I asked sweetly.

He gave a sheepish shrug.

"And what about you?" I asked our third judge, Ellis Glover, who's Clerk of Court.

"I don't have a dog in the first fight," he laughed, "but my sister's son's in the six-to-sixteen bunch."

"I probably have some nieces there, too," I told them. "Shall we all recuse ourselves and go home?"

"Not unless you know which entries are which," said Luther.

I admitted I didn't and the same held true for Ellis and him, so we got down to it.

The object, of course, is to give out as many rosettes as possible to the younger children. Neither Bert nor Sarah won first, second, or third, but they each carried off one of the ten green ribbons for honorable mention and were too young not to be pleased with their success.

In the second group, I was pretty sure that the wagon-load of yam children pulled by a remarkably horse-shaped yam was Jess's entry. She's crazy about horses and it would have taken something serendipitous like this for her to enter when I'd asked the family to skip the contest this year. Ellis and Luther had marked it as a possible winner on their first ballots, so I didn't feel bad keeping it in the first round, too. The yam baby had a natural indentation that made it look as if it was bawling its head off.

It was cute enough to win a unanimous second place, but the blue ribbon went to a Hispanic boy's tableau that featured space yams walking on the moon along with some yam aliens. When Jess bounced up to accept her award, we both pretended we didn't know each other. Wouldn't have looked good for a judge to hug one of the winners.

That didn't stop Minnie and Seth, though, and while they were distracted, I slipped back to the pig cookers. The Ladies Auxiliary of Colleton Memorial Hospital had brought coleslaw, spiced apples, hushpuppies, and various desserts to augment the meat and were now selling plates of the donated barbecue to benefit the children's wing. I asked Isabel and Nadine if I could have a foam take-out box of barbecue and another of slaw and apples.

"Not that you're not welcome, Deborah, but what're you going to do with so much food?" they asked me.

"I thought I'd take it over to the family of that boy that got killed yesterday," I said. "They'd probably like something a little more substantial than corn dogs and elephant ears."

That's all I had to say. I don't know if it's genes or something in the water, but death or sickness always triggers the female impulse to provide food for the afflicted, and the next thing I knew, Nadine and Isabel were cutting into the serving line to fill more foam boxes with hushpuppies and banana pudding, too. They divided the boxes between two shopping bags and I set off down the midway like someone making a delivery from a Chinese restaurant.

When I reached the compound where all the carnival vehicles were parked, I saw Dwight standing beside the open back end of a tractor-trailer van with Arnold Ames and a couple of uniformed town officers. I didn't have to ask him which travel trailer belonged to the Ameses. There was a small spray of white carnations wired to the lamp beside the door.

CHAPTER
5

I tapped on the metal door, and eventually Tally Ames opened it. Like me, she was wearing a long blue skirt and her charm bracelet. Her eyes were red rimmed and bloodshot, and she stared at me a moment as if trying to think why I was there.

"I thought you were another reporter."

"Have they been bothering you?" I asked.

"Not as much as you'd've thought. Carnies are like migrant workers far as the local newspapers ever care." Her tone was bitter as she held the door wider for me to step inside. "They're always so sure it's one of us whenever there's any trouble, and as long as we're killing each other . . ." She shrugged in resignation.

Those first few minutes of a condolence call are always awkward. Anything I say sounds so trite in the face of such loss and it's even worse when it's the death of someone young.

I held out my shopping bags of food cartons. "My

sisters-in-law thought maybe you and your family might be able to eat a little something."

"That's nice of them." She took the bags with a wan smile and set them on the kitchen counter that probably doubled as a snack bar.

This travel trailer was fairly big, designed to be pulled by a two-ton truck. The master bedroom was two steps up over the flatbed, and there was a pop-out bedroom at the back end. In the middle were a bathroom, a tiny kitchen, and a surprisingly roomy dining room/den combination. The deep blues, turquoise, and amethyst of the furnishings had been chosen with a knowing eye for her dark hair and blue eyes, and the space was brightened by September sunlight that spilled through a line of skylights in the ceiling.

Except for a drink cup of clear purple plastic on the shelf beside the plaid couch and an ashtray with three cigarette butts, there wasn't a paper or thread out of place. Janice Needham would've been hard-pressed to find something to pick at here.

I glanced around as we sat down in the chairs at opposite ends of the couch. The doors to both bedrooms were open and she seemed to be alone. A house of bereavement is normally crowded with relatives, friends, and neighbors. In this case, though, relatives and neighbors were probably back in Florida, and friends here would be out working the carnival. This sunny Saturday had brought out lots of people and profit margins were probably too small to let natural sympathies take precedence till after hours.

She noticed my glance. "Arn's over at Braz's trailer with your deputy friend. And we're so shorthanded, I told

Val he might as well help keep the stores going. Nothing else for him to do right now till they release Braz's body. I guess that sounds sort of mercenary to you?"

I shook my head. "My mother died near the end of barning season. The neighbors did what they could, but they had their own fields to harvest. So I know a little bit about what it's like for you."

"Yeah, I was sorry when I heard she'd died."

That surprised me. "You knew my mother?"

She abruptly reached for her glass and stood up. "I'm going to have another glass of tea. Can I fix you one?"

I stood, too. "Let me get it for you. You're the one who should be sitting."

"Trust me, I'm not, okay? If I sit still for too long, my mind keeps going over and over all the thing I might've done different, things that might've kept Braz safe."

"Mrs. Ames, how did you know my—"

"Call me Tally, okay? Unless you mind if I call you Deborah?"

"No, of course not."

"Or is it Deb?"

"Never," I said firmly. "Too many Little Debbie jokes when I was a child. Dwight—Major Bryant said you wanted to see me?"

She put ice cubes in a second glass and poured tea from a jar in the small refrigerator. As she handed it to me, both our bracelets tinkled and she gave me a wan smile. "You *do* remember, don't you?"

"Excuse me?"

Now it was her turn to look puzzled. "Isn't that why you wore your bracelet to come here today?"

"Because I saw yours in court? No, I came across

mine by accident this morning. I'd almost forgotten I even had it."

"Pure coincidence, huh?"

Her tone was flatly skeptical and I didn't understand why.

She held out her wrist and said, "Take a good look at mine."

From the weight of the charms as I touched them, I was sure they were solid gold and worth a lot more than my sterling ones. And yet, there amongst all the little gold totems was a single silver one, a tiny teddy bear identical to mine.

A silver teddy bear?

I could almost hear Mother's voice. "Just like yours, Deborah. You were only three, though. That's probably why you don't remember."

"Olivia?"

Her smile was half-defiant. "Or should I call you Aunt Deborah?"

I couldn't believe it. But here were those blue, blue eyes that I had noticed that first day in court.

Cornflower blue.

Knott blue. Like every one of my daddy's children.

Like all his grandchildren, too, it would seem. And on some visceral, subliminal level, my subconscious had picked up on Tally's eyes—on Braz's as well—and sent me a dream of blue quarters.

"I had just turned five," Tally was saying. "You weren't quite three. My mom had dumped me on my Hatcher grandparents that summer, and you and your mom came out to the farm. She gave me a bag of choco-late candy and a silver charm bracelet just like yours. I forget what all was on mine besides the teddy bear. It came loose and I kept it in a little box by itself or it'd be gone now, too."

"She told me about that visit right before she died," I said. "What happened to the rest of the bracelet?"

She gave a rueful shrug. "Who knows? Mom probably hocked it to buy another bottle of gin, okay?"

"She was an alcoholic?"

"Oh for God's sake, Deborah. You think our mothers were anything alike? That I ran away from her because I hated algebra or was having a bad hair day?"

"How old were you when you ran?"

"Fourteen."

"I was eighteen."

"*You* ran away? With all that you had? Why?"

It was my turn to shrug. "Bad hair day?"

She gave a small, disbelieving snort. "How long did you stay gone?"

"A few years. Long enough to learn that bad hair's not the end of the world."

"Get pregnant?"

"No, I managed to sidestep that."

"Must've been the difference between fifteen and eighteen," she said. "Or maybe you weren't looking for love in all the wrong places."

"Oh, I did a little of that, too."

When Mother died, everything else seemed to fishtail out of my control as well. I fought with Daddy and most of my brothers, left college at the end of my first semester, ran off with a redneck car jockey, damn near stabbed him through his sorry heart, and didn't come home again for several years till I finally got my act together. But hard as it might have been in patches, it was hardship of my own choosing and probably an eiderdown featherbed compared to the life led by Tallahassee Ames, aka Olivia Knott.

"Was Braz's dad with the carnival?"

"He was a roughie even greener than me. It was my second summer of washing dishes and working one of the grab joints and I knew how hard carnies work, okay? He thought it was going to be blue skies and cutting up jack-pots. He made two jumps with us, then he was out of there. But not before I'd played possum belly queen for him. I never even knew his last name, and he was gone before I missed my first period. Sounds like my own daddy, doesn't it?"

"Andrew married your mother," I said mildly.

"With my grandpa riding shotgun all the way to South Carolina's the way I heard it."

Well, yes, there was that aspect of it, I suppose. I tried to talk to Andrew about Carol and Olivia right after I first came home, but he told me it was none of my business and to shut up about them.

"It wasn't my baby" was all he'd say.

But Mother had said differently that last summer. "Andrew doesn't believe the child was his, but I only had to take one look at her, Deborah. Olivia was him all over again. Same eyes, same smile. Your daddy's tried to find her, but Carol's never come back again, at least not that we've ever heard. Amanda and Rodney Hatcher aren't the friendliest people you'll ever meet. He's Old Testament righteousness and she's under his thumb with no more backbone than a squashed beetle, so there's no learning from either of them where Carol and Olivia are."

The very next day, out of curiosity, I'd driven over to that eastern part of the county. The land's a little flatter there, more coastal plains than sandhills. The soil's easy to tend but everything leaches through so quickly that it needs a constant supply of fertilizer and water. I found the Hatcher farm and drove slowly past it two or three times. It was a depressing sight. The crop rows were cleaner than a preacher's jokes. Not a weed, not a blade of unwanted grass. The outbuildings were modest, but in good repair. The house itself sat in a grove of oak trees a couple of hundred feet back off the road, and if it hadn't been for the barns that surrounded it, I would have thought it was the sharecropper shack of a tightfisted land owner. The paint was peeling, the tin roof was rusty, a few of the windowpanes had been replaced with cardboard, and there was no indoor plumbing if that outhouse behind the barn was any indication.

A cheerless, loveless place.

The only spot of color was a rusty washtub full of red petunias that bloomed by the front steps, and as I drove past the third time, an old white woman came out and poured water on them from her dishpan.

Everything for the land, nothing for the woman who helped tend it. Probably nothing for the daughter, either. I could understand why Carol had shrugged off the reins and tore loose. It all happened before I was born, but I knew the rough outlines.

Andrew, nine brothers up from me and going through his own wild teen years, had gotten a Widdington girl pregnant.

Or so she claimed.

Andrew swore he wasn't the only one having sex with

her at the time, but her father had literally pointed a shot-gun at him and asked him what he meant to do about the situation. There had been a hasty drive to Dillon, South Carolina, where underage kids could get married without a waiting period or blood test, and he'd moved into this shabby old house with her parents, prepared to "do the right thing," even though he roiled with anger at getting trapped. That's when he started drinking heavily.

The arrangement lasted till two or three months after Olivia was born, when Carol told them all to go to hell and she'd lead the way. That was the last time anyone in my family ever saw her again. Daddy let it be known around the Hatcher neighborhood that he'd be mighty grateful if anybody heard tell of a girlchild being there, but it was five years before someone sent him word.

The summer she was dying of cancer, Mother told me all sorts of things she thought I ought to know, things she trusted me to keep to myself till the knowledge was needed.

Olivia was one of those things.

"Your father was set to run right over there as soon as he heard," she had said, "but he and the Hatchers had al-ready had so many hard words between them by then that I said I'd go for both of us and I'd take you as my shield. Rodney Hatcher's a foul-mouthed old man, but I sus-pected he'd behave in front of a little girl like you. Lucky for both of us, he wasn't even home that day. As soon as I saw the child, though, I knew she was Andrew's. I should have just gathered her up and brought her home with me then and there, but I was waiting for the right time to speak to Andrew. That was barely a month or so after he married Lois, remember?"

Well, certainly I still remembered Lois. Andrew's second marriage only lasted about two years longer than his first one, but the wedding itself had been a big splashy circus. That may have been the first time I was pressed into service as a flower girl. After a while, all the weddings ran together, so there must have been something special about Andrew's.

"You were so cute," Mother said nostalgically.

As if there's ever been a three-year-old flower girl who wasn't.

"What happened when you told him?" I'd asked.

"He still claimed Olivia wasn't his daughter, but he went with me to see her. When we got there, though, the child was gone. Carol had taken her again." Her eyes had glistened with tears then. "I'll never stop blaming myself that I didn't do something quicker. If she ever comes back, you make sure she's part of this family if she wants to be, you hear?"

"I hear."

"Promise?"

I promised.

"Should I call you Olivia or Tally?" I asked her now.

"Tallahassee's my legal name, okay? They called me Tally when I joined my first carnival in Tallahassee and I made it official when I married Arnold Ames the day I turned twenty-one."

"And Carol—?"

"Dead."

She took a long swallow of her tea. "And my father's

married for a third time with some hell-raisers of his own."

I wasn't as surprised as she seemed to think I'd be. "You've kept tabs on the family?"

She nodded. "Every time we come through Colleton County, I stop at the library and the courthouse. I'm real good at searching legal documents."

For the last few minutes, she'd been fiddling with a pack of cigarettes. "Will it bother you if I smoke?"

I shook my head as she lit up, hungrily drawing the smoke into her lungs. "You should have contacted us."

"Why? Y'all never contacted me, did you?"

"But we tried," I said. "Least Daddy did. But it was as if you and Carol had vanished off the face of the earth. Then after your grandparents died and the farm changed hands, I guess you just slipped out of our memory."

Saying those words jarred a more recent memory. "In court you said you owned property here in the county. The farm?"

"Yeah. Ironic, isn't it?" She flicked ashes into the tray beside her. "My Grandpa Hatcher wanted to make sure we'd never get a penny out of him and he willed the place to his only sister, who willed it to her son Mack. Mack got killed in a car wreck about a week after she died and guess who was his last living relative? So, yeah, I've been paying taxes on it for three years now."

It occurred to me that Daddy must be starting to lose it a little. In years past, he'd have known about this the minute Tally took title to the farm. Anything that touched his family touched him, and since Mother had been so sure that Carol's baby was his granddaughter, he'd have tried to keep his feelers out. Somehow, this had slipped past him.

"We've been fixing the place up a little every time we pass through," said Tally. "The house isn't much, but at least Aunt Nancy put in plumbing. And the outbuildings are solid, okay? We're using some of the barns for storage."

"Storage?"

"Yeah. Arn and Braz? They buy up stuff when we're on the road and we cart it back to Gibtown when the season's over. We sell it on eBay or flea markets in the wintertime." She sighed. "Every time Braz went off and bid on a storage locker or bought something at a salvage auction, he thought he was going to hit the jackpot. Score big. Poor kid. He wanted to be rich so bad."

As she spoke, I remembered that she'd said she never knew the biological father's name. "Major Bryant told me your son's name was Hartley?"

"My first husband," she said. "He sort of took me under his wing the week I joined the carnival. He owned a couple of grab wagons, okay? Let me wash dishes for my keep and made me go to school in the winter. When I got pregnant, he already had the colon cancer. Told me if I'd stay and nurse him, he'd marry me and say the baby was his so we could have his name and Social Security. I was eighteen when Hartley died. His Social Security and his grab joints kept us going till I met Arnold and I earned every penny of it, okay? But he was good to me. Gave me books. Made me get my GED."

"I'm really sorry I never got to meet your son," I said. "I wish you'd called us, let us know when you were here."

She shrugged. "I didn't see the point."

"But you're family."

"Yeah?"

The skeptical look she gave me was so like Andrew or A.K. that even if Mother hadn't made me promise, I'd have had to say it. "Can I tell the rest of the family who you are? Andrew? My daddy?"

She was clearly torn. "I thought I would one of these years, but now . . . What with Braz and all . . ."

Tally stubbed out her cigarette and lifted her anguished blue eyes to me. "I don't want him left by the side of the road somewhere. That's why I asked your deputy friend to ask you to come. Do you think I could bury him in your family graveyard?"

I leaned over and gave her a hug. "Of course, you can. It's your family, too. Honest."

As if things to do with family are ever that easy.

"What about Andrew?" asked the pragmatist.

"Andrew can damn well lump it," said the preacher.

CHAPTER
6

SATURDAY AFTERNOON (CONTINUED)

   I stayed with my arm around Tally till the worst of her sobs eased off, then wet some paper towels with cold water so that she could soothe her reddened eyes.

"Tell me about Braz," I said. "Why was he killed?"

"I don't know. I can't *think*." My newfound niece pressed the wet towels to her eyes even as she shook her head in frustration. "Nobody that really knew him would hurt him." She hesitated, choosing her words with care. "I mean . . . he's had his problems. All kids do. And he wasn't any angel, okay? I know that. I did the best I could, but hell, I was still a kid myself when I had him. If it hadn't been for Irene Matusik, I'd have probably dropped him on his head the first week."

"Who's that?"

"Irene? She and her husband had the doublewide next door to Hartley's trailer in Gibtown. Maybe you saw him last night? Skee Matusik, okay? She started with the duck pond he's still running. Had a couple of other hanky-panks, too. She loved children, but couldn't have any on account of her bad heart. All the same, she's the one showed me how to take care of Braz when he was born. What does a fifteen-year-old know about being a good mother if you had a tramp for your role model?"

I started to protest, but she brushed away my words with an impatient wave of her hand.

"You think I don't know why Andrew Knott claims I'm not his? With my grandpa yammering at me how she was the whore of Colleton County? Maybe your brother's right. Maybe I'm *not* any kin to you."

"With those eyes? That mouth? What's your real hair color?"

"Dirty blond. Even duller than yours," she said with the same tell-it-like-it-is bluntness of some of my younger brothers.

"You're kin," I said firmly.

There was a framed snapshot on the ledge behind the couch of her family standing in front of a gleaming new Pot O'Gold. There were palm trees in the background and a bright blue Florida sky. Tally was in the center, her husband had his arm loosely around her shoulder, and her younger son leaned against her other shoulder. A young man with long sandy hair pulled back in a ponytail stood slightly apart from them, his face in a shadow. His arms were tightly folded across his chest to make his muscles stand out, and there were tattoos running up both arms.

"Is that Braz?" I asked.

"He didn't like to have his picture took, but we'd just got that ride and we were so proud of it. First brand-new one we ever bought. You know the smell of a new car? It's not half as sweet as the money smell of a brand-new ride. This is the only picture I have with all four of us in it together."

Her eyes filled again as she looked at her dead son. Never mind that his shadowed face was indistinct. I knew she was seeing every feature as sharply defined as the others in the photograph. To me, though, there was no mistaking that lanky build.

"Throw them both in with the rest of my nephews and you'd be hard-pressed to say which boy belonged where," I said. "Did Braz have any cowlicks?"

Her smile was wobbly as her hand went unconsciously to her nape. "He and Val both got mine. Reason I can't wear my hair real short."

"Me too," I said, lifting my hair so she could see my version of the cowlicks most all of Daddy's descendants have on either side of their necks. "Daddy says his grandfather had them there, too."

"I wish I had a better picture to show you, but everything's back in Gibtown. Wait a minute, though."

She got up and went into her bedroom. I heard a drawer open and close, then she was back, carrying a red billfold thick with credit cards and photographs.

"Here's his graduation picture."

For some reason, that surprised me. Carny kids graduate from regular high schools? But there he was, a head-and-shoulders shot in a cap and gown that hid his tattoos. He had a senior's usual pimply chin and goofy, self-conscious grin, but there was a gold stud in his nose, two rings through his left eyebrow, and another three in the visible ear. His face was more oval than square, and while his eyes were Knott blue, all right, they were closer together than Tally's.

"He was very good-looking," I said. In truth, though, head piercings anywhere except the earlobes are so distasteful to me that I have to bend over backwards to stay objective in the courtroom whether it's the plaintiff or the defendant who sports a lot of metal through his face. "His mouth and chin are different, though. He must have taken after his father."

Tally shrugged. "Couldn't prove it by me. I barely saw that guy in daylight, okay? I always thought Braz looked more like the pictures I've seen of my mother and grandmother when they were young."

She took back the photograph and shook her head as she slid it into her billfold. "He was supposed to've taken out the rings and stud before he got to the photographer's. When the proofs came back . . ." She shook her head. "Kids."

"Yeah," I said, both of us conveniently forgetting for the moment our own teen years of acting out.

From where I sat, I could see the whole length of the trailer and into the back bedroom. With the front wall popped out, it wasn't much smaller per person than the spaces my brothers had shared growing up, but it appeared to hold only a single bed.

"He didn't actually live with you?" I asked.

"Not when we're on the road. He needed his own place. We fixed him like his own little room in a corner of the van. Mattress and box springs. A desk for his computer. A hookup for electricity. He'd shower over here, eat with us whenever he wanted, but most of the time he was pretty much on his own. It was what he wanted."

I wondered how he and the younger boy had gotten

along. An eight-year age difference with no linking siblings in between?

"It was the usual," said Tally. "Val thought Braz picked on him. Braz thought we babied Val." She shrugged and lit another cigarette. "And there were girls, of course. He was twenty-four, okay? A grown man. What could I say?"

Indeed.

"Dennis told me his face was smashed in. That his mouth was full of quarters. You're the one found him like that, weren't you?"

I nodded. "Why would anyone do that to him, Tally?"

"Polly said she saw a black guy hit him. Maybe he came back later."

By the sudden set of her jaw, I knew there were things she wasn't telling. Dropping the sodden paper towels into a nearby wastebasket, she went over to the refrigerator and pulled out more ice cubes to replace the ones that had melted while we talked.

"You said he wasn't an angel," I reminded her as she closed the refrigerator door. "They've already run his record, you know. It's standard procedure."

She dumped her ashtray and rinsed it out. "Your deputy friend tell you what they found?"

"Yes."

Her back was still to me as she tore off another wad of paper towels, dried the ashtray, wiped a few stray drops off the counter, then wiped it a second time.

"He took against being on the road for a while, okay? Once he hit high school, he wanted to stay in Gibtown year-round. My friend Irene lived down the block from the new place Arn and me bought after Val was born. She said she'd keep an eye on him. She was like his grand-mother, so I gave in and let him. Tell you the truth, it seemed easier than having him with us and listening to him bitch all the time, okay? He wasn't a bad kid, but he could be a real pain in the butt when he put his mind to it."

"Most teenagers can," I said. "You've got a bunch of cousins who are living proof."

"Yeah? Anyhow, Braz was a follower, not a leader, and even though he was my son, he couldn't seem to read people the way you need to be able to read them if you're in the life. So he started running with some wrong kids, broke into some pawnshops, and they left him holding the bag. Twice. He was a slow learner, okay? And I guess you know he served a few months for trying to sell a dig-ital sound system a so-called friend of his gave him to pay off a debt. He forgot to tell Braz the stuff was stolen, and with his record, the judge didn't believe him."

She turned to face me and the sadness in her smile made my heart ache for her. "But he's been clean for the last eighteen months, ever since he got his own laptop and started buying and selling online. He got along all right with everybody here this summer, our crew, the other agents. You ask any of them. 'Course, he did like to stick his nose in everybody else's business, like he was the boss, not Arnie. And other times he'd get on that com-puter when he was supposed to just be going to the don-niker."

"Donniker?" I asked.

"Toilet," she translated.

I remembered her exasperation last night when she thought he'd deserted his post.

"Somebody probably had too much to drink and got pissed off about something. Braz could mouth off without thinking and sometimes he'd let the marks get under his skin. A couple of times—if Arnie hadn't been there . . . ? You'll see. If it wasn't that black kid that hit him the first time, it'll be something as stupid as a drunk cake eater punching him out because the Dozer took all the rent money."

I didn't know whether to say "Oh, surely not" or "I hope so," but it didn't really matter. She was back to beating up on herself again.

"Oh God! If I'd only let him go to the auction last night instead of making him work!"

"What auction?"

"One of those self-storage places was having an auction down in Makely but we were shorthanded and I told him if he went, he could just keep on going 'cause we were counting on him here."

"Storage lockers like the one the Lincoln brothers had their tools in?"

"Those guys that put a knife through my ride? Yeah, I told you. People don't pay the rent on them and they get put up for auction. A lot of time, it's just junk. Old clothes. Ratty furniture. You'd be amazed at the garbage people'll pay thirty-five dollars a month to hang on to. Sometimes, though, you can wind up with some interesting things. Braz took the bid on a locker last year stacked with books. None of them were all that old, but they were all first editions, okay? He bought them for like two-fifty, and by the time he sold the last lot on eBay, he made almost four thousand clear profit. The first year we started doing it, Arnie found an antique pocket watch with a solid gold chain. It was just crammed into a box full of buttons someone had cut off old shirts. That locker cost us seventy-five dollars, okay? He and Braz put a picture of that watch on eBay and the bidding went to just shy of eight thou.

"Braz thought Arnie ought not to sell it so fast, get it appraised first. But Arnie always says that a quick dime's better than a slow dollar. He'd rather make his profit and move on to the next lot. Braz, now, he always put a reserve on his stuff. He didn't mind sitting on it till he got the price he thought it ought to bring."

I listened to her talk some more about the odd things people abandon in self-storage lockers, everything from bicycles and surfboards to clothing and family photo albums, even wedding gifts still in their original gift boxes. All the time, though, I couldn't help noticing her likeness to other members of my family—the way she held her head like Robert, the unconscious hand gestures Reese and Lee always use, the curve of her lips when she smiled and the sweep of her eyelashes that were both like Herman's Annie Sue and Haywood's Jane Ann.

Several of the kids were probably out there on the midway right now, squealing on the Tilt-A-Whirl, throwing darts at a balloon board. I wasn't sure if all of them knew that Andrew had fathered a child before he married April, that A.K. and Ruth had a half-sister none of them had ever seen. Hell, I wasn't even sure A.K. and Ruth knew.

And to learn that she existed in one breath and then hear in the next that it was her son who'd been murdered last night?

One thing was certain. I couldn't tell any of them till I'd talked to Daddy.

As I stood up to go, Tally said, "You sure it's going to be cool with your dad if we put Braz there?"

"I'm sure. We'll have to tell the others, though. And as soon as they hear, they're all going to want to meet you."

"Do you have to do that right now?"

I couldn't blame her for hesitating. It's one thing to spend an hour or two in the courthouse uncovering paper facts about a grandfather, father, stepmother, half siblings, ten uncles, one aunt, and a yardful of first cousins who are no more than names in a database. It was quite another to think of meeting that many kinfolks in the flesh.

"How about we start with Daddy, Andrew, and April?" I said.

She took a deep breath. "I've handled drunks and crazies, even talked a cokehead out of trying to rape me after Hartley died, but I gotta tell you, Deborah, this scares me more than anything else."

"You'll be fine," I said. "Any thoughts of when you want the funeral?"

"Well, we're booked here through next Saturday night and it'd cost us a bunch to breach the contract. We were planning to tear down that night and lay over at the farm a couple of days, then jump to Kinston. We don't open till five on weeknights, so maybe one day this week, okay?" Tally looked suddenly bereft. "Only I don't know when they'll let us have him—his body back."

I told her the name of Duck Aldcroft, the funeral director in Cotton Grove. "And I'll call him, too, if you like. He'll tell you what to expect."

"We're not religious," she warned. "Arn and Val and me, all we want's a graveside service, okay?"

"Duck'll do whatever you want," I assured her. I gave her my phone numbers. "Call me anytime. I'll be in court here Monday. And what about you? Is there a number where I can reach you?"

She gestured to the cell phone plugged into its charger on the shelf behind me, and while she was writing down the number for me in my address book, there was a tap at the door.

It was the man who ran the duck pond next to their Dozer, the guy who'd found the carnival's patch for her last night. Shorter than me, he was one of those wiry little white men who reach a certain age and then time stops. They look the same at eighty as they did at forty: wispy gray hair, weather-beaten face with deep lines around the eyes. Although his arms were free of tattoos except for a band of small red spiders around his scrawny wrist, the head of a bright green dragon peeked up past the neckline of his dark blue T-shirt. He wore dirty jeans and even dirtier white sneakers and carried a cardboard tray that held hamburgers and two capped drink cups.

"Arnie asked me to bring you something to eat, Tal," he said, proffering the tray. "He said he'd be along in a few minutes. You heard any word yet on how it's going? If they caught the guy who did it?"

His eyes were bright with curiosity.

"Hey, you're the lady found Braz, right?"

"Right," I said.

I knew Dwight or some of his people had probably already talked to him and it really wasn't my place to ask, but I couldn't resist.

"You worked next to Braz all evening, didn't you?"

The man looked from me to Tally.

"It's okay," she told him. "Deborah, this is Skee Matusik. He's known Braz since before he was crawling. His wife Irene's the friend I told you about that used to babysit for me. Deborah and me, we're kin to each other, Skee."

"Yeah?" His face cleared but his eyes were still wary. "Yeah, I was there all evening, but there's canvas between my store and the Dozer, and I was pretty busy till about nine."

"Polly told Arn that he and some black guy were mixing it up. Braz wasn't a fighter. What happened, Skee?"

"It was over before I knew it was happening," he said with a shrug. "All I saw was some black and white kids pulling another black kid away. I looked around the corner of the tent and saw Braz sitting on the step of the Dozer with his nose all bloody, so I wet a towel in my pond and gave it to him. Polly came over, too. We asked him if he was all right and he said he was. Next time I looked around the corner, I didn't see him. Figured he was taking a break."

"No loud voices? Nobody running away?"

"Lady, this is a carnival. It was Friday night. Loud voices? Running? Who'd notice?"

"Who's Polly?" I asked.

"Runs the plate pitch across the way from the Dozer."

Through the open door, I saw Tally's husband heading toward us.

I patted her shoulder and told her I'd be in touch soon.

As I threaded my way across power lines and cables that snaked through the grass, past the trailers and back to the midway, Dwight fell into step beside me.

"Buy you a chili dog?" he offered.

I kept on walking. "She didn't have anything to say that you probably don't already know."

"Hey, did I ask?"

"No, but you were fixing to, weren't you?"

He smiled down at me ruefully. "Well . . ."

"Fortunately for you, I'm starving, so yes, you can buy me a chili dog."

"Unless you'd rather have barbecue?"

"That would mean the big twins and Isabel and Nadine," I reminded him.

"Right. Chili dogs, then."

Not that Dwight doesn't enjoy their company, but he knew perfectly well that if we joined my brothers, there would be four conversations going at the same time and none would be the one he clearly wanted to have with me.

The murder didn't seem to be affecting either the festival or the carnival. The beautiful weather had brought out a big crowd, and we had to wait in line several minutes for our dogs and drinks. I got bottled water, Dwight got something in a drink cup with ice.

"So what did she want?" he asked when we were settled with our food on a low wall out of the flow of foot traffic.

"Oh, this and that," I said vaguely.

Normally I can tell Dwight anything. In this case, though, I didn't feel that Tally's true identity was something I could talk about to anybody till I'd told Daddy and Andrew.

"She was worried about the legalities of getting her son's body back. And funeral arrangements. I gave her Duck Aldcroft's number."

A drop of chili landed on his blue tie and I wet my napkin with water and leaned over to wipe it off before it could leave a spot.

"She did tell me that he hadn't been in any trouble with the law since he got involved with buying up storage lockers and selling the stuff on eBay and at flea markets."

"Yeah," said Dwight. "The van he's been sleeping in looks like a thrift shop. Furniture, books, clothing."

"Find anything useful?"

"I doubt it. The place had been tossed before we searched it."

"What?"

"Yep. Least that's what his stepdaddy says. Says Braz took after his mother. Place for everything and everything in its place. And it was still sealed from last night, so that means whoever tossed it probably did it between three o'clock when he took a computer break and the time we sealed it." He took a swallow of his drink and frowned as he looked into the cup. "These damn things are more ice than drink."

"I don't suppose Ames knew what the tosser was looking for?"

"Says not."

"Remember I told you about Tally Ames being in my courtroom this month?"

"Yeah. Someone vandalized her slide. So?"

I recapped the case for him in more detail. Since he'd been the one who arrested the Lincoln brothers on the larceny charge that sent them away two years ago, he listened intently.

"Don't you see? They were so mad at Arnold Ames for buying their tools when they defaulted on the storage locker fees that they tracked him down and slashed his ride. What if Braz Hartley bought the locker contents that belonged to somebody who was even more violent than the Lincoln boys?"

"You reckon?" Dwight said thoughtfully. "Mayleen and Jack have been hearing that he and his brother didn't get along. Don't forget that more people are murdered by family members than by strangers."

"So who was the stranger that punched him in the nose the first time last night?" I gibed.

"Who told you that?" he asked sharply. "Mrs. Ames?"

"No, it was the guy running the Lucky Ducky duck pond. Skee Matusik is his name. Said he didn't see it actually happen, but a woman across the way did. A woman named Polly? Runs that game where you try to land coins on a plate?"

"We're looking into it," he said. "Leave it alone, Deb'rah."

Usually when he's warning me to mind my own business, there's a blend of exasperation and amusement in his voice. This time I heard something different there. A real No Trespassing sign.

And suddenly I remembered Stevie. Who hadn't given his name to either deputy last night.

And Eric Holt. Who could fit the description of some young black guy whose friends had pulled him off Braz and hustled him away.

CHAPTER
7

As soon as I got back to my car, I took out my cell phone and called Daddy's number. Not surprisingly, Maidie answered. Technically, she doesn't work on the weekends, but nobody ever put up a time clock for her to punch at the kitchen door, and since she and Cletus live just down the lane from Daddy's shabby old farmhouse, she's in and out whenever it suits her. If she happens to be in when the phone rings, she answers it automatically because my father doesn't like talking on the phone and won't pick up if he knows she's around.

"Is Daddy there?" I asked.

"Him and Cletus just got back from the long pond with a mess of brim for supper," she said. "Don't you want to come eat some? They's plenty."

"Sure," I said promptly, knowing that pond fish meant Maidie's crispy cornbread and a medley of late-summer vegetables, including the best fried okra in North Carolina. "And while I have you, are Eric and his parents still coming out for dinner after church with y'all tomorrow?"

"Far as I know they are. Why?"

"I just thought that maybe you'd tell him to bring his swimsuit and he and Stevie can go swimming off my pier."

"I bet he'd like that," she said. "I'll call him right now before I forget it."

"Be sure and tell him I'm particularly looking forward to seeing him. I haven't had a chance to talk to either of them in a long time."

"I'll tell him," she said. "You want to speak to your daddy a minute?"

"Has it ever been more than a minute?" I asked.

She laughed. "Hang on, honey."

A moment later, I heard Daddy say, "Yeah?"

No *How you doing? How've you been? Everything all right?* He expects us to state our business and get off the phone.

And much as it pains him to take a local call, long distance makes him crazy, even when he's not paying for it. My brother Adam, one of the little twins, will deliberately call from California and see how long he can keep Daddy on the line before he says, "Well, less'n you got something to say worth ten cents a minute to say it, I'm gonna get off 'fore you go broke."

Adam hasn't yet made it to five minutes.

"You going to be there for the next hour?" I asked.

"Yeah."

"Good. I'm just leaving the festival here in Dobbs. I'll run past my house and change clothes and then I'll be over," I said. "I need to talk to you."

"Yeah?"

"It's—" I hesitated. No point in just blurting it out.

Better to wait till I could soften the news with words and judge his reaction as to how much to tell.

"Never mind," I said. "I'll tell you when I get there."

"Fine," he said, and hung up.

Next I called Haywood's house. I didn't really expect Stevie to answer, so I wasn't disappointed when he didn't. I left a message on the machine that I hoped would sound innocuous to Haywood or Isabel but would let my nephew know I meant it when I said I really wanted to catch up with everything that's been happening to him lately.

Dwight should know by now that I won't leave trouble alone when it involves my family.

As a teenager, I used to make the drive from the farm to Dobbs in just under twenty minutes. With all the new housing developments and population growth, the speed limit's dropped to forty-five miles an hour and it now takes me closer to thirty, which means that there was plenty of time for Daddy to drive down the lane past Maidie's house, through the cut, and around the fields to my house.

His truck was parked at my back door when I pulled into my yard, and he was sitting on the steps smoking a cigarette.

Ladybelle came over and nuzzled my hand in greeting as I got out of the car, but Blue continued to sprawl with his head on Daddy's workboot and merely thumped his tail in welcome.

"He's getting lazy," I said.

"Naw, just getting old," said Daddy. "He'll be twelve, come Thanksgiving."

He's partial to those two hounds, but like most farm people, he's realistic. Over a long lifetime, he's watched a lot of puppies turn into good dogs, then grow old and die.

He stubbed out his cigarette and stood up so I could hug him. "You look mighty pretty in that blue dress, shug. Real ladylike."

"Looks can be deceiving," I said lightly, not looking to pick a fight. "Come on up on the porch and let me get you some tea."

I opened the screen door and stepped inside to switch on the ceiling fan above the circular glass-and-metal table. I don't like air-conditioning any more than he does. Long as the air's stirring and I don't have to do stoop labor out under a hot sun, the heat doesn't really bother me. Oh, I'll complain about it right along with my friends, but that's only pro forma. In actuality, I love our hot, muggy summer days unless they drag on and on through early fall without a break. Makes our winters more special.

Daddy pulled out a chair, took off the white straw planter's hat he wears from April till October, and hung it on a nearby peg. His hair has been snow white since before I was born and was still thick across the crown.

"Better bring another glass," he said off-handedly. "Andrew'll be along directly."

I about dropped the pitcher.

"Andrew?"

"That *is* what you wanted to talk about, won't it?" he

asked. "Andrew's girl being back and her boy getting hisself killed?"

"You know who she is? How? Who told you?"

He gave a half smile. "Well, now, shug, you ain't the only one knows people at the courthouse. I been keeping an eye on the Hatcher farm ever since old Rod Hatcher died. Watched the farm go to his sister, then to her boy, then back to the boy's cousin three years ago, and he didn't have but two cousins. Carol and Olivia. Tallahassee Ames won't old enough to be Carol, so I figured she had to be Olivia. Had somebody backtrack on her and sure enough."

"Somebody?" I asked suspiciously. "Dwight?"

"Naw, not Dwight."

"Terry Wilson, then?"

"I ain't saying."

He didn't have to. Terry's an SBI agent and would do anything for Daddy, long as it was halfway legal. I was the one introduced them when he and I were hanging out together a hundred years ago. They bonded over a bass right out there on that pond, long before I built a house in this pasture, and they stayed tight even after Terry and I moved on to other relationships. Veteran lawmen and old reprobates are just two sides to the same coin, which is probably why Terry and Dwight are so crazy about my daddy and why he's right fond of them, too.

"She tell you how come her to change her name to Tallahassee?"

"That's where she joined the carnival," I said.

"Real sorry to hear about her boy. Just wish you won't the one had to find him. You okay? He was messed up pretty bad in the face, I heared."

But I was still reeling. "Why didn't you tell us?"

"What for?" he asked. "She knowed who we were and where we were. When she didn't try to sell the farm, I figured she'd come looking us someday when she was ready to know us. We hadn't done nothing for her growing up, so we didn't have no claims on her now. Figured it was her choice."

My brother drove into the yard about then, parked his truck beside Daddy's old Chevy, and got out. There was a puzzled look on his face.

"Does he know?" I asked.

Daddy shook his head. "You want to be the one to tell him?"

"Tell me what?" said Andrew as he came up on the porch and joined us at the table.

Of my eleven older brothers, Andrew's third in the birth order after Robert and Frank. He's the one that looks the most like Daddy. His thick brown hair is fast going gray and will probably be all white in another year. He's also the one that seemed to have the hardest time of it as a child. Didn't get a chance to be a baby long before the big twins came along and pushed him out of his mother's lap.

"Andrew was wild as a ditch cat," Aunt Zell says whenever she talks about the houseful of boys Annie Ruth left behind, which explains why she always had a soft spot in her heart for him.

Although he eventually came to love my mother, it was hard for him to show it, especially since he was the one who initially resented her the most after Annie Ruth died and Daddy remarried. Took him a long time to find his way in life, to find April, who gentled him and brought him back to the farm and a settled life.

"Tell me what?" he asked again, beginning to get an apprehensive look on his face. "What's wrong? A.K.? Ruth?"

"No, no," I assured him. "I saw both of them when I was leaving the carnival and they were fine. Enjoying the rides."

He didn't relax. "What then?"

There was no easy way to say it, but I couldn't help trying.

"Andrew, I heard today that Carol's dead. She's been dead for years."

He looked at me blankly, trying to think who I was talking about.

"Carol Hatcher," said Daddy.

Carol was more than half a lifetime behind him, and nothing I'd ever heard made me think there'd been anything other than sexual attraction between them.

"Olivia too?" he asked.

"No. She's alive and she's here."

He swiveled in his chair abruptly as if he expected her to come walking from my kitchen onto the porch.

"Not here in the house. Here in the county," I said. "She's with the carnival over at Dobbs."

"Yeah?"

"You heard about the young man that was killed over there last night?"

Andrew nodded.

"That was your grandson, Andrew."

"The hell you say, Deb'rah!"

"Watch your tongue," Daddy said mildly. He never likes it when the boys use language around me.

"Well, tell her to watch hers." His jaws were tight with anger. "Olivia ain't mine! How many times I got to tell y'all that Carol gave it out to every guy in three counties?"

"You can tell it till you're blue in the face," I said, "but it won't change the fact that you're the one got tagged fair and square. She's yours, kid."

"And how would you know? You won't even born then."

"Because Mother said so, remember? She was so sure that she took you over to the Hatcher farm right after you and Lois were married, but Carol had gone off with Olivia again."

"You were just a baby," he said. "How could you know that?"

"I told you. Mother said so. Just before she died, she told me all about it. Besides, I've seen her, Andrew. I've talked to her. She looks more like you than A.K. or Ruth."

"What's she doing back here?"

"Right now, she's part owner of the carnival, but she did wind up getting the old Hatcher place and she and her husband have been fixing up the house."

"So what does she want?"

He was radiating so much resentment and suspicion that I wanted to slap him for his self-centeredness.

"From you? Not a d—" I caught myself just in time. Much as Daddy doesn't like anybody cussing in front of me, he likes it even less when I cuss. "Not a blessed thing, Andrew. Just put her out of your head and don't give another thought to what kind of a life you let your daughter have and what she's going through right now."

I turned back to Daddy. "Her boy's dead and she wants to bury him at the homeplace."

He looked at Andrew and his voice was courteous. "That all right with you, son?"

Andrew stood up, jammed his John Deere ball cap back on his head, and pushed open the screen door. "Do what you think you need to, Daddy. You and Deb'rah both, since it looks like y'all've adopted her. Just keep me and my family out of it, okay? Them carnival tramps is nothing to do with me or mine and that's how I aim to keep it."

"She's no tramp," I called to his retreating back. "And you tell April or I'll do it for you."

He never looked around, just got into his truck and drove off with a great spray of dirt.

I guess I must have given an involuntary sigh because Daddy reached out and patted my hand.

"Don't let him get under your skin, shug. He's got to huff and blow about it awhile, but he'll come 'round. Don't forget, he did try'n do the right thing back then." He cut his eyes at me. "Just the way you did with Allen Stancil."

Like Carol for Andrew, Allen Stancil was a part of my past I'd just as soon not talk about and certainly not with Daddy, so we sat silently for a few minutes, sipping our iced tea and watching a pair of wood ducks dabbling out on the pond. It's still pretty peaceful here. Without the occasional beep-beep-beep that drifts in on the wind during the workweek as dump trucks back and haul, one could almost forget the pile of houses that are being built across the creek a half mile away. On this quiet Saturday afternoon, all we could hear at the moment were birdsongs and the hum of insects.

"I reckon Sue told you a lot of things there towards the end," Daddy said finally.

I nodded.

"Things you still ain't talked about?"

"A few."

"I won't much use to her there for a while, was I? To you, neither, the way I put it all on you like that."

No denying that it had been hard. I was the only child still at home that summer. The boys were all busy building careers or getting their crops in, getting married, getting divorced, getting babies. And Daddy was gone half the time, too. All of them were unnerved by her dying and the intensity of her need to talk. Daddy was hurting so bad and in such deep denial that he couldn't—*wouldn't*—listen until it was almost too late.

"She understood," I said, taking his big, work-roughened farmer's hand between my own. "You were there when she needed you the most. And she knew that you would be. She told me so."

He squeezed my hand tight, then pulled out his handkerchief and blew his nose. "Durn ragweed," he muttered, as if I didn't know that he's never been allergic to any plant. "I believe I could drink another glass of that tea if you're offering it."

As I refilled his glass, he said, "Tell me about Olivia. Or Tallahassee, I reckon I ought to say."

So I told him as much as I knew, omitting the circumstances of Braz's conception and the fact that Tally's first marriage had been in name only. And yes, I sort of glossed over Braz's record so that it didn't sound too much worse than Reese's and A.K.'s. Or Andrew's and Will's.

Or his, either, for that matter.

"A lot of people look down on carnival people, think they aren't much good," I said, "but—"

"Yeah, I know," he said. "Like that Cher song."

"Excuse me?"

"Don't you remember? Your mama used to like it. I learned how to play it for her to sing. 'Gypsies, Tramps and Thieves.' That was the name of it."

He hummed the chorus, his fingers tapping out the rhythm on the glass tabletop, and for a moment, I could hear Mother's throaty voice as she sang the line about the hypocritical men who hurled insults at the carnival folks and then came around every night eager to buy tickets for the kootch show.

"I don't know if Tally ever did any dirty dancing," I said, "and I'm sure there's a lot she's not telling me, but for somebody who had to bring herself up, looks to me like she's done a pretty decent job of it."

"What's her other boy like?"

"Val? He's about fifteen or sixteen, same build, same coloring as all your other grandsons. Prideful," I said, remembering his outburst to me last night. "Mindful of his parents, I think. But I only spoke to him briefly."

He listened to the silence behind my words and nodded. "When does she want to do it?"

"She doesn't know. When I left, Chapel Hill still hadn't called her. And that reminds me. I need to call Duck Aldcroft. He's going to handle things for her."

"Good." He stood and reached for his hat. "I'll go along then. Maidie says you're coming for supper?"

"If you'll have me."

"Always room for another pair of legs under my table, shug. You know that."

CHAPTER
8

TALLAHASSEE AMES
SUNDAY MORNING

Tally Ames awoke a little after six Sunday morning. Even though she was still tired, she was so wide-awake that she knew she'd bother Arnie if she stayed in bed. Carnies can sleep through blaring loud-speakers, the clatter of roller coasters, noisy crowds — anything except a restless bunkmate, and he'd worked hard till after midnight. She eased out of bed, slipped on her clothes, and tiptoed out for life-restoring coffee and cigarettes.

At the other end of the trailer, Val's door was still shut, of course. He wouldn't roll out till much before noon, either. Braz's murder had made yesterday doubly rough on the two of them.

Braz had been a pain in the butt all summer: undependable, moody, and quicker than usual to feel sorry for himself. She kept threatening to kick him off the lot and Arnie, always more easygoing, kept giving him one more chance.

"He's a pair of hands that can take tickets, make change, help us make our nut," he kept reminding her, and yesterday only underscored the loss.

She herself had been absolutely useless. Short two more people, Arn and Val had scrambled to redistribute the tasks and take up the slack when they were already strained to keep all the spots covered. Worse, with police officers all over the place, one of their mechanic's helpers had taken off, not wanting to be where there was any possibility of someone running his fingerprints.

Tally had no idea what his trouble with the law in south Georgia was and didn't really give a damn long as he helped Raggs keep the rides going. Besides, half the people on the midway had things in their past they'd just as soon didn't get dug up again. Too, you never knew what law officers might notice about the games themselves, gaffs that might get their stores shut down, so everybody was on edge even without all those questions about who saw what and who Braz might've pissed off.

Take a number, Tally thought wearily.

The coffeemaker finished doing its thing, and she stubbed out her cigarette, filled a large mug, and stepped outside into the cool September morning. The sun was just coming up, a rare sight for her. Also rare was the quality of the air, fresh and clean, blown free of the smells of carnival foods. Most days, by the time she reached the midway to open up the Guesser, the fry vats were already bubbling with hot grease, the cotton candy makers were going full tilt, and spicy sausages were sizzling on the grill—smells so familiar and pervasive that she never noticed them until they were no longer there. Like now. Here at sunrise, it was only the smell of dew rising from the grass and dirt beneath her feet. No music either, just the sound of birds twittering in the tall oaks that ringed the Agricultural Hall and an occasional car passing beyond the fences.

Carrying her oversized coffee mug and sipping as she walked, she passed the trailers of sleeping friends and employees. No one stirred or called her name, and she was glad to have this time alone. They had rallied 'round last night after closing, and she was grateful for their sympathy, but she wasn't ready for more speculation as to who could have killed Braz or why, or unasked questions about her connections here. Polly was the only one besides Arn and the boys that she'd actually told about being born in this county, but several of them knew about the farm and had heard that she was related to the judge who tried those guys with the knife. Since Polly wasn't one to chatter, Tally put it down to Braz running his mouth to Skee Matusik, who could never keep his mouth shut, either.

Whereas Val wanted nothing to do with a North Carolina family that had ignored her existence almost from the beginning, Braz had been scheming how to exploit the relationship ever since she told them that the judge in their vandalism case was actually her father's sister. Sooner or later, Braz would have made one of the Knotts aware of who he was, despite her expressed desire to remain anonymous and unrecognized.

Not that it mattered anymore. Not now that Deborah knew who she was. Not when she'd be meeting her grandfather and God knows who else day after tomorrow. When she telephoned Duck Aldcroft at the funeral home yesterday, he'd told her that the medical examiner would be releasing Braz's body either today or tomorrow, so they could hold the funeral Tuesday morning if that's what she wanted.

"Tuesday will be fine," she'd said.

"Ten o'clock?"

"Ten o'clock. About the cost, Mr. Aldcroft. I hope you won't mind an out-of-state check?"

"You don't need to worry about that, Mrs. Ames. Mr. Knott's already taken care of everything. All we need you to do is come over sometime before Tuesday and select the casket."

She had protested in sudden anger, but the funeral director had been gently adamant. "I'm sorry if this is a problem, Mrs. Ames, but Mr. Knott is an old and valued customer and he's already paid me. You'll have to discuss it with him."

"Which Mr. Knott?" she'd asked, abruptly remembering that Andrew was hardly alone in possessing that name in this county.

"Mr. Kezzie Knott," he'd answered.

"Oh," she'd said, confused by such conflicting emotions.

If Andrew wanted to pay for the funeral, it could mean he accepted that she was his daughter. Unless, she thought angrily, it meant he thought he could make up for a lifetime of denial with a one-time check. But that it was her grandfather . . . ? Well, Deborah did say he'd tried to find her for years.

As she slipped between Polly's Plate Pitch and the Rope Climb to get onto the midway, Tally realized that she was smiling at the thought of having a moonshiner and a bootlegger for a grandfather. Over the years, passing through Dobbs on the way to gigs further north, she'd always made Arn stop here. While he loaded up on cheap cigarettes for bribing ride jockeys and greasing Yankee palms, she would spend the afternoon in the courthouse. Once she discovered that the library directly across the street also housed genealogical data, she started dropping in there first. The Colleton County Heritage Center on the second floor was just full of goodies. Its staff of volunteer genealogists seemed maniacally dedicated to documenting everything from obituaries and gravestones (which is how she learned that Susan Knott had died years earlier) to clipping news articles and filing them in folders that were open to anyone who wandered in.

A catchall Knott family folder was like dipping into a family scrapbook. Any time any Knott made the newspapers, someone had filed the article. Here was where she'd read about her stepmother ("April Knott Named Colleton Teacher of the Year"), her uncles ("Knott Brothers Pool Labor and Equipment to Control Rising Farm Expenses"), and her cousins and half siblings ("Cotton Grove Man Has Truck Damaged by Deer" and "Area Youths Charged with Vandalism"). Judge Deborah Knott had recently acquired a folder of her own with clippings about her career.

Finding a folder for Keziah "Kezzie" Knott had interested her the most, though. It held yellowed clippings that went back to his arrest, trial, and eighteen-month incarceration for income tax evasion forty-five or fifty years ago. It didn't take much reading between the "alleged" and "rumored" lines to understand that this was the only way the Feds could get at a man everyone knew controlled the making and selling of illegal whiskey in the area. The crossroads gas and grocery store he'd bankrolled had been the equivalent of a game so slickly gaffed that nothing could be pinned on the agent. The later expunging of his record was just butter on the popcorn.

Ever since she'd read that, Tally had wished she could have known him while she was growing up instead of Grandpa Hatcher. Unless Kezzie Knott was a huge hypocrite, he wouldn't have cursed her birth or scorned her for the life she'd made for herself.

Directly across from Polly's was the Dozer. The flaps of the red-and-white tent had been tied down, and now she carefully set her coffee mug out of the way to untie the flaps and fold them back on both sides till the Dozer was open to the midway on both sides again. She unlocked the sides of the wagon itself and snapped out the hinges that held them up and away so that customers could get to the stations. Then she retrieved her coffee and stepped up into the well of the wagon.

The police had removed their yellow tape late yesterday afternoon, and she knew that Arnie had seen to having the floor scrubbed clean by one of the townies they'd hired on for the week. Today the Dozer would go back into operation.

"You sure you want to do this?" Arnie had asked her when she said she'd work it.

He thought she wouldn't want to stand in the spot where Braz had been killed, but she certainly didn't feel up to working the Guesser. Talking trash to the crowds as they streamed onto the lot? No way. Anyhow, the Dozer took less concentration than any of their other stores, which is why they'd put Braz on it. All you had to do was make change and occasionally explain which game pieces could be exchanged for which prizes. Besides, it was always too much temptation to green clerks. All those shiny quarters tumbling off the side spills into the baskets? For her to lay out another day would mean a serious financial drain.

Now she stood where her firstborn had died and drank a long steadying drink of her coffee. She was neither superstitious nor religious nor even particularly sentimental, but if anything remained of Braz, surely it would be here?

Incoherent thoughts crowded through her head. Images of Braz the first time they'd put him in her arms all red and screaming with colic that had gone on and on and on for what seemed like four solid months without a break. Braz as a toddler underfoot in Hartley's grab wagon, curled up under the counter for an afternoon nap while she tried to be careful that no hot grease splattered on him. Braz at six hysterical with rage because she wouldn't let him come on her honeymoon with Arnie. They were only gone two nights and he adored Irene Matusik, who babysat him and spoiled him rotten, but he'd never gotten over that sense of abandonment and hurt. She had spent the next two years trying to convince him that he was still loved and valued, but when Val was born—Val, whose sunny disposition and easy ways endeared him to everyone—it was like a huge empty hole had opened up inside of her first son and there wasn't enough love in the world to fill it.

A low stool stood next to the end wall, and she sat down on it and rested her throbbing head against the cool metal ledge. Here in the morning dimness of the Dozer well, her eyes filled as she thought about his life.

"I'm sorry, Braz," she whispered. "I'm so, so sorry."

And even as her heart ached for his loss, she knew that part of her grief was guilt because Braz had been right.

"Tally? You okay?"

She opened her eyes, disoriented for the moment, then realized Dennis Koffer was peering in at her over the swinging flap. The show's patch wore a ball cap with "East Bay Raceway" stitched across the front and his usual cigar poking out the side of his mouth beneath his neat gray moustache.

"Yeah, Dennis. Thanks." She fumbled in the pocket of her shorts for a tissue and blew her nose.

"You sure?"

"Yeah. What are you doing up so early?"

"Just getting my ducks in a row about today. You opening the Dozer?"

She nodded.

"You do remember that we're a Sunday schooler this evening, right?"

"Oh, God, I'd forgotten."

"You might want to narrow the side spills a little and add more prize chips, okay?"

"Okay."

Sundays in the South were usually big-dollar days, and today would be no exception, especially since the

Fall Festival Committee had decreed that tonight would
be church night. This meant everything had to be squeaky
clean so that Sunday school classes and youth groups,
their parents and chaperons, could come out to the carnival, enjoy the lights and the rides, buy fried candy bars
and chili dogs, and play for charity without being led into
temptation. They would have money in their pockets, too,
because many of the groups would come to "play for
Christ" and to donate their prizes to toy drives for under-
privileged children.

All evening, gospel and Christian rock would blare
from the speakers strung through the lot, totally indistin-
guishable from soul and secular rock unless you listened
carefully to the words.

For hanky-panks, it would be just another evening, but
the gaffed games would have to be played fairly straight,
which meant stashing the expensive plush and electron-
ics that no one was ever allowed to win and scrambling
to restock their stores with "slum," cheap prizes that
wholesaled at less than it cost to play the game. The alibi
agents and flatties always griped when required to turn
the midway into a Sunday schooler, but it was good public relations. Made the town fathers look on you a little
kinder.

The patch smiled at her. "And you'll remind Val no
tricks with the Spot?"

Against her will, Tally had to smile back. "Now, Dennis, what are you suggesting?"

"Just be sure he loses the gaffed set tonight, okay?"

"Okay."

If the flat metal disks were less than a certain propor-
tion to the red spot, it would become impossible to cover

every bit of the red. If a sharpie stepped up too confidently to the counter and Val was getting close to having thrown twenty-five percent of his plush already, he would palm the regulation-sized disks and slip the mark a set of microscopically smaller ones.

All in a day's work.

As Dennis moved on, Tally finished her coffee and looked around, seeing what Braz would have seen on Friday night.

Arnie had laid out the midway. Since this was their first time playing Dobbs, they didn't really know how big the crowd would be—festival committees were notorious for lying about average attendance—and he'd deliberately kept it on the narrow side so that people would have to brush up against the stores. Nothing was worse than a wide midway and sparse crowds. When that happened, the marks hewed to the middle of the walkways and resisted the impulse to lay their money down.

Across the midway on the south side was Polly's Plate Pitch, with the Rope Climb on the left and the Balloon Race on the right. On the north side was Windy Raines's Bowler Roller, a shooting gallery, and the Bottle Setup. All six stores were easily visible. Skee Matusik's Lucky Ducky was next door to the west and the ears-and-floss wagon was on the east, but the tent walls would have blocked Braz's view of them.

Normally she or Arnie would have been checking around every hour or so to make sure everybody was in the flow, but one of their ride jockeys had quit and one of their cooks was stoned in the bunkhouse about to get his ass fired. There had hardly been time to let anybody even go to the donniker till after the marks with young kids had started to clear out. So it wasn't surprising that neither Polly nor Windy had noticed what was going on over here at the Dozer. But why hadn't one of the marks?

CHAPTER
9

"Deborah left a message for you on the answering machine," Isabel said as her son got up from the table and headed for the dishwasher with his empty plate. "Wants you and Eric to go swimming this afternoon."

"Yeah, I heard it," said Stevie. "Thing is, I've got some stuff to look up in the library for my history class tomorrow, and Eric said he wanted to get back to Shaw early, too."

"Well, give her a call so she'll know not to expect you," Isabel said.

"Yes, Mama." He spoke in exaggerated resignation and his teenage sister giggled.

"Mom's still not sure you know enough to wipe your own—"

"Here now, that'll be enough of that kind of talk," said Haywood. When it came to proper language for a daughter, Haywood was his father's son.

"—nose," Jane Ann finished. She looked at her father in all innocence. "What's wrong with nose?"

"Never you mind."

"What did you think I was going to say?" she persisted, laughter dancing in her blue eyes.

"Bel?"

"Jane Ann, help Stevie clear the table and stop picking at your daddy," Isabel scolded.

Obediently, the girl rose and lifted the meat platter. "All the same, Mom, I still think Dad has a dirty mind."

Haywood laughed and told Isabel he believed he could eat just another small slice of that coconut pie if she'd cut him off one.

Out in the kitchen, Jane Ann set the remains of a pork roast on the kitchen counter. "Come for a ride?" she asked her brother. She slid soiled tableware into the dishwasher basket. "It's been ages since you and I took the horses out together."

"Sorry, kid, I really did tell Eric I'd pick him up before two. Maybe next time."

"Sure," she said, trying not to whine.

A CD she'd borrowed from Annie Sue lay on the counter where she'd left it when they came home last night. Drops of water had splashed on the cover, and she carefully blotted them away with a paper towel, then set it atop the refrigerator out of harm's way.

"It's just that I never get to see you alone. Now that you're at Carolina, you're gone most of the time. And when you do come home, you're either hanging out with Gayle or your friends. It's like the older you get, the less I see of you. Like you're not part of the family anymore."

"You and I spent the whole morning together," Stevie protested.

"In church? Here with Mom and Dad? I don't count that being together." She went back to putting away the leftovers.

"Well, what about yesterday? You were at the carnival with your friends all day while I was out here alone with the ironing board and washer." Stevie held the refrigerator door open for her. "Things change."

He grinned and draped a dishtowel over her head. "But you're always going to be my doofus sister, no matter how old I get."

Jane Ann crumpled the towel into a ball and aimed it at his head; he ducked and caught it just before it hit his tea glass on the counter.

"Good hands," she said. "I still wish you'd come riding, though."

"I wish to hell I could, too, kid." He sounded so sincerely regretful that she was mollified.

"Well, don't let it wreck your life. Actually, I've got homework myself. Two more acts of Shakespeare to read."

"Miss Barnes's class?"

"Yeah, and she expects us to know the meaning of every single word."

"I know. I had her, too, remember?"

So okay. Yes, thought Jane Ann as they shared groans over the toughest teacher at West Colleton High. *He will always be my brother.*

Twenty minutes later, Stevie was helping Eric throw his duffel bag in the back of the Jeep.

"This is crazy, you know that, don't you?" he said when they were on the road and heading east, not north toward Shaw in Raleigh.

"When else'll we have this chance?" Eric said logically. "Sunday afternoon? The place should be deserted. You don't think it's fair Lamarr should get cheated out of what's rightfully his, do you?"

"No, but—"

"Besides," he argued, "if we get caught and you're with us, Deb'rah and Mr. Dwight won't let them do anything to us."

"Don't count on it," Stevie said darkly. "She let A.K. sit in jail three weekends last summer, remember?"

Brad Needham sighed and clicked off the television. Hard to concentrate on anything under the circumstances, and while he enjoyed watching public television (or enjoyed the idea of watching it), lap quilting and cooking shows just weren't doing it for him this afternoon.

On the floral couch where she had been drifting in and out of sleep since lunchtime, Janice roused herself with a yawn. "I was watching that, Bradley."

"Sorry." He clicked it back on.

"You coming down with something, hon?"

"No, why?"

"I don't know. Ever since we got back, you've been sort of blue. And like your mind's elsewhere." She looked up into his dark brown eyes. "You're not worried about work or anything, are you?"

"As a matter of fact, I am," he said, gratefully seizing on her suggestion. "In fact, I was thinking about running over to the office to work on my report for a couple of hours."

He took his stockinged feet off the pale blue velvet hassock that matched his pale blue velvet lounge chair and slipped on the sneakers that were neatly tucked beside the chair.

"Oh, hon!" She sat up in protest. "Can't you do it here? I thought you finished that thing before we left California."

"I did. But there are a couple of facts I want to check before I print it out—some data I need to get off the mainframe—and you know me. I won't rest easy till I get it done."

Janice smiled at him indulgently as he stood and hitched up the jeans he always wore for Sunday chores. "Oh, you! Always worrying about one more detail that needs doing."

As he stood up, she leaned back on the couch and looked around their pretty living room with deep satisfaction. "Isn't it wonderful to be back home, Bradley? California was great, but three months was much too long, don't you think?"

God, did he ever agree with that, thought Brad, but he merely nodded.

"Sandwiches for supper okay with you?" she asked.

"Fine," he said. "I'll try not to be too long."

Once in the car, though, he hesitated about which way to go. The office first, he decided, brushing back the strands of dark hair that fell across his forehead. Janice didn't exactly keep tabs on him, but it wouldn't hurt for the guard on the desk to be able to tell her he'd been in if she should call.

And then?

He had been so careful over the years. Never a single slip. And then there was the extra precaution he'd taken when he married Janice, a precaution that worked so well he'd come to rely on it and eventually take it for granted. It never once occurred to him that those extra weeks in California that the company had tacked onto his original assignment could be his undoing. He should have read the fine print, but who knew? And where did he go from here? He'd made himself face that guy Friday night and where had it gotten him? He should have stayed away.

But maybe it was going to be all right. It was almost forty-eight hours and no one had come looking for him. No reason for Dwight Bryant or anyone else to connect him to a sordid little carnival murder.

Reason said to just leave it alone, but fear made him remember the fingerprints, the pictures, and all the other details that could bring his world crashing down.

"How'd Lamarr find this place anyhow?" Stevie asked Eric as they drove slowly past the deserted-looking house and its collection of outbuildings, set down in the middle of nowhere.

"Aw, you can find anything on the Internet. He looked up Ames Amusement Corporation and found their sched-ule. So last week, when the carnival was over in Rocky

Mount, he got tight with one of the brothers that helps set up the rides, got him talking over a couple of beers after hours. The guy'd been here to help pick up a generator. He remembered the road because it was such a dumb name, and Lamarr checked it out. Only place on the road that fit the description."

They came to the end of Fannie Feather Road.

"Probably somebody's sweet old grandmother," said Eric.

"Or somebody's favorite stripper," said Stevie as they circled around the stop sign.

They hadn't met a single car the whole length of the road. Things might be booming in the western part of Colleton County, but here on the eastern edge, it was still pretty much untouched farmland and third-growth wood lots.

Lamarr Wrenn was in the white van in front of them. The plan was that they'd cruise past twice, and if they didn't see anyone, they'd drive into the yard and honk the horn. If anyone came to the door, they'd pretend they were lost and ask for directions to a nonexistent friend's house.

"There he goes," Eric whispered as the van turned into the long drive, through scraggly bushes that almost hid the place from the road.

With heavy misgivings, Stevie followed.

They had been speaking in such low voices that the sudden horn blast made them jump.

"Jesus!" Stevie said.

"Amen!" Eric agreed fervently.

Lamarr sounded the horn again and still no one appeared in the door. No curtain twitched. There wasn't even a dog to bark.

With that, the van moved forward, down the rutted sandy lane that led to the sheds out back. This, too, was part of their plan: get the Jeep and the van out of sight behind the barns and then reconnoiter till they found what they had come for.

Lamarr drove in behind the furthermost structure, through thick weeds that looked as if they hadn't been mowed all summer, and when Stevie swung around him, pointing the Jeep out for a quick exit if needed, Lamarr gave him a thumbs-up and repositioned his own vehicle. Built like a linebacker, Lamarr got out of the van and handed them each a pair of latex gloves like the ones he was already wearing.

Eric rolled his eyes. "You been watching too much television, man."

"No, he's right," Stevie said as he slipped them on. "No point leaving them a business card."

They fanned out, each checking the open or unlocked sheds that held gaudily painted signs and boards, boxes of stuffed toys, a popcorn maker with the glass missing from its sides, and bits and pieces of old carnival games and stands. At one locked door, all they had to do was tap the pin from the hinges to peek inside. The space behind was stacked with crazy mirrors from a fun house, so they carefully replaced the pins.

Finally, nothing was left but the shed they'd parked behind, the one shed with a hefty padlock. It stood a foot off the ground on rock supports. The windows were too high to look through even standing up in the Jeep and balancing on the roll bar. Worse, the door was hinged from the inside.

Lamarr reached into the back of his van and pulled out a tire iron.

"I don't know, guys," said Stevie. "So far, all we've done is trespassed. This knocks it up to breaking and entering."

"No pain, no gain," said Lamarr, sliding the flat end of the tire iron up under the hasp.

Before he could put some muscle into it and lever the hasp right out of the wood, Eric said urgently, "Somebody's coming!"

Out on the road, a car slowed down and they heard it enter the brush-lined drive. As one, they dived back behind the barn and crouched motionless in the weeds to peer through the rocks that supported the building. The car stopped out of sight, and whoever was driving had cut the motor.

Silence for a long moment; then they heard the car door open and close, and soon a pair of sneakered feet and jean-clad legs came into view. The legs hesitated, then came straight on toward the locked door.

Because they had been waiting subconsciously for the jingle of keys, the next sound, a wrenching of metal from wood, was so unexpected that it took them a moment to comprehend.

Lamarr got it first.

"Shit! The bastard's a fucking thief!" Tire iron still in hand, he came roaring up out of the weeds. "Hey! You! What the hell you think you're—"

With Stevie and Eric uncertain whether to follow or try to hold him back, he bulled his way between the van and the shed wall, started to turn the corner, stepped into a mole run, twisted his ankle, and went down so hard the ground around them shook.

By the time the other two got around Lamarr to look, the thief, if that's what he was, had already jumped back in his car and was halfway down the long dirt drive, kicking up clouds of dust. Between the dust and the glare of the late-afternoon sun in their eyes, the only thing they could be sure of was that the vehicle appeared to be a dark midsize sedan.

Lamarr limped around the corner and pointed in outrage at the lock and hasp that now lay on the ground. A few feet away was a claw hammer the guy had dropped in his flight. The open door was swinging on its hinges.

Lamarr quit cussing and beamed at Stevie like an innocent black angel. "We didn't do the breaking. All we're going to do is the entering."

CHAPTER
10

🦆 Even though we were almost into October, Sunday lived up to its name — a day of hot sunshine that kept the pond water warm.

I knew that both Stevie and Eric would be going to church this lovely morning, then big dinners with their respective families would occupy them till long past one, so I didn't expect to see them much before three o'clock.

I probably could have used a session in church myself. Instead, I spent the first part of the morning packing away most of my summer clothes and air fluffing some of my lighter fall clothes in the dryer.

At ten o'clock, I figured Tally would probably be awake so I called to let her know Braz could be buried at the farm.

"I know. I talked to that Mr. Aldcroft last evening. He says your dad's taken care of all the expenses and he won't accept our money. That wasn't necessary. We can take care of our own, okay?"

"Believe me, Tally, it's necessary for him. Let him do this. Please? And he wants you to know that anyone you want to be there, any of your friends from the carnival, will be welcome."

"That's good," she said stiffly.

The silence grew awkward.

"I guess you haven't heard from Chapel Hill yet?" I asked.

"No, but Mr. Aldcroft called them and they said either today or tomorrow, so we're thinking, say ten o'clock Tuesday morning, okay?"

"Tally, you do understand that the rest of the family's going to have to be told? They'd never forgive us if we don't. We'll try to keep them from stampeding you, but—"

"What about Andrew? What'd he say when you told him?"

I took a deep breath, trying to find the words.

"Bad as that, huh?" Cynicism tinged her voice.

"I'm sorry, Tally. But he'll come around. I know he will."

"For what? I'm a little old to be looking a daddy, Deborah. But thanks for calling. I guess I'll see you Tuesday, okay?" she said and hung up.

I gave Andrew a mental smacking and went back to cleaning out my closet and dresser drawers.

At midday I diced green peppers, onions, and mushrooms and made a western omelet with fresh tomatoes on the side. Not much of a Southern Sunday dinner, but probably healthier than some that would be eaten on the farm today.

While sorting clothes, I chatted on the phone with

Portland, who told me that our mutual uncle (hers by blood, mine by marriage) had finally decided to retire and why didn't we throw him a party? I called Aunt Zell to see if she thought Uncle Ash would want one, but only got their answering machine.

I restrained myself from calling April to see if Andrew had talked to her about Tally yet. If he hadn't, how would I broach it? If he had, surely she'd call me if she wanted to talk? Better to leave it for now.

I checked my e-mail, deleted the three inspirational messages forwarded by Robert's wife Doris without reading them, chuckled at a bawdy joke from Isabel, answered the most urgent messages, then surfed the Net for a while. Out of curiosity, I went to my favorite search engine and keyed in "carnival." Most of the results either had to do with Mardi Gras–type carnivals or cruise ships, so I reset the parameters to exclude those. As I followed the links from one site to the next, an interesting picture of carnival life and carnival culture emerged from the electronic ether. I found myself wishing I could call Tally and ask her at least a dozen frivolous questions based on what I was finding.

When I eventually surfaced, it was almost three o'clock. I put on my bathing suit, pulled an old T-shirt on over it and, since boys are always hungry, laid out a bag of nachos to go with a jar of salsa I'd unearthed from the back of my refrigerator. (There was just the teensiest bit of mold around the lid, which wiped right off. And don't tell me you've never done that yourself.)

Three o'clock came. The boys didn't.

At three-thirty, I started calling. Isabel answered the

phone, sounding sleepy. "Stevie? He went on back to Chapel Hill right after dinner."

"Didn't he get my message?"

"Yes, but he said he had a paper to work on or something. Didn't he call you?"

I punched the speed-dial button for Maidie and it rang eight times before she answered. "Sorry, Deb'rah. Him and Stevie left here before two o'clock. They said they had to get up with a friend or something before going back to school. Eric did tell him you was hoping to spend a little time with 'em, but Stevie said you'd understand. Maybe next time, honey."

Understand? Oh, yes. I understood all too well. Question was, what could I do about it?

Since coming to the bench, I've gotten a little spoiled. If I want someone in my courtroom at a certain hour on a certain day, they damn well show up or risk a contempt of court. And if that doesn't scare them into appearing, there are bailiffs and deputies to go out and find them for me, whether in jail or at large.

Unfortunately, bad as I wanted to at that moment, I couldn't sic a bailiff or a deputy on either of those two boys.

To cool off, I walked out on my pier, stripped off the T-shirt, and jumped in. It took a few minutes of serious swimming before the water did its job and let me look at the situation objectively.

There was a reason they hadn't left their names with either deputy Friday night, a reason they were deliberately avoiding me now. All the same, Stevie and Eric are two of the most laid-back kids I know. Did I honestly

think that either of them would let a carny's casual trash
talk get under their skin?

Of course not.

And even if Braz *had* managed to slip the needle in,
wouldn't they both just walk away from him? That didn't
mean they didn't know something or that they hadn't
been there when punches were thrown. And they could
well have been the friends seen pulling the puncher away.

I swam out to the boat mooring that marked a tangle
of old tree roots left behind on the bottom when this pond
was dredged. Bass liked to lurk down there, and it was
one of Daddy's favorite fishing spots. Nobody was out
fishing today, though. I had the place completely to myself.

The late-afternoon sun edged down behind the pines,
casting long shadows across the pond. Floating on my
back, gazing up into the sky, I watched the fluffy clouds
above me go from snowy white to gold and pale, pale
pink with streaks of deep blue in the crevices.

Drifting lazily on the still water, I let myself think
about Kidd Chapin and gradually realized—the way you
realize that a sprained ankle or sore knee has finally
stopped hurting even when you put your full weight on
it—that I was, at long last, completely over him, even
though this breakup had hurt more than any time since
Jeff Creech dumped me back in college. I no longer
missed Kidd himself, but I sure did miss being in love,
missed having my pulse quicken at the thought of someone, missed looking forward to seeing, kissing, being
held. All the same, I had spent the whole summer learning to live without all that, and if I never had it again, at
least I'd had it once.

(*"More than once,"* came the preacher's stern reminder.)

(*"More than twice,"* leered the pragmatist.)

The gold-and-pink clouds above me deepened to orange and purple and I was beginning to think about food when something big landed in the water off the pier fifty feet behind me with an enormous splash. I was so startled that it was as if a featherbed had been yanked out from under me, and I sank beneath the surface to come up spluttering as I saw someone swimming toward me.

"Jesus, Dwight!" I said when he pulled up close enough to hear. "I thought you were an alligator or something."

"Alligator?" Treading water, he grinned at me. "There's no alligators for a hundred miles."

"All the same, you should've hollered or given me some warning."

"I really did scare you? Sorry, shug, but I did call. You must have been a million miles away."

"Just running through the backwoods of memory. Clearing out some old underbrush."

"Say again?"

"Never mind. What're you doing here?"

"I thought maybe I'd get up with Eric and Stevie, but they'd already left. Maidie and Isabel both said you'd asked them to come swim this afternoon, so I figured you wouldn't mind if I came in their place. I stopped by Mama's, picked up a bathing suit, and here I am. Didn't mean to scare you, though."

"Just yell louder next time, okay? Race you around the mooring and back?"

I was a third of the way there before Dwight got his bearings and headed after me. My form's better, but he's got a longer stroke and stronger kick and he finished up at the pier at least three strokes ahead of me. That was all right. Gave me a chance to get my thoughts in order before we talked. Not that I knew anything more about Stevie and Eric than he did.

The air was starting to get cool as the sun settled further in the west and I climbed onto the pier and wrapped a towel around me.

"Did you hear from Chapel Hill yet?" I asked.

Dwight continued to bob around in the water. "They've released the body, and Duck was supposed to send someone for it this afternoon."

"What was the cause of death?"

"I didn't get the official report yet."

"Unofficially then. And don't say you can't tell me when you know it's going to be public record soon as the DA's office gets hold of it."

Dwight pulled himself out of the pond, and water streamed from his body. He hadn't brought a towel, so I handed him mine and slipped my T-shirt back over my damp suit.

"Okay, unofficially," he said as he dried off. "He drowned in his own blood."

"Really?"

"Truth. The ME thinks that somebody either knocked or pushed him down and then stomped him in the face while he was on his back. Most likely, he was unconscious at that point and his nose was smashed so badly he'd have had to breathe through his mouth."

"Only that was stuffed full of quarters," I said, shivering at the memory as a light breeze blew across the pond.

We walked back up to the house and I gave him first dibs on the shower.

While he dressed in my spare room, I sluiced off all the pond water, dried my hair, and pulled on fresh jeans, a white shirt, and a blue cotton cardigan. When I got back to the living area, Dwight was thumbing through my collection of old videos.

"We've watched them all," I said.

"So I see. I thought you might've broke down and bought something new."

"Sorry."

It was still light outside, but fast heading for dusk. Dwight roamed the room restlessly, picking up a framed snapshot of my parents, then one of a gang of us at a cookout over at Robert's house.

"Is something bothering you?" I asked.

"No, why?"

"I don't know. You look uptight about something."

Dwight's normally as comfortable as an old faded T-shirt, but this evening he seemed edgy, unable to light, almost as if he were annoyed at me over something that he knew was none of his business but was working up to blasting me about it anyhow.

"What dorm's Stevie in?" he asked abruptly.

"Old East," I said.

"Is that one of the ones next to the Old Well?"

"Yes. Why?"

"Oh, come on, Deb'rah. You know why. Why else did you try to get him and Eric over here this afternoon? You know they didn't leave their names with Jack or Mayleen. Just like you know that Eric could've been the one to punch Braz Hartley."

"No, I don't!" I said hotly. "And neither do you. He wasn't the only black kid at the carnival Friday night."

"Maybe not, but I've got to start somewhere, and it might as well be with the one who's acting suspicious. Or his friend. The one who has an aunt who can make him talk. Ride with me over to Chapel Hill?"

"This evening?"

"Why not?"

"Aren't you seeing Sylvia tonight?"

"Nope. I'm seeing Stevie. Or I will if you'll help me find him. You're the one went to school there."

"You could've," I reminded him tartly.

Dwight looks more like a football player these days, but there was a time when he was so fast and could shoot a basketball from outside with such accuracy that Dean Smith had sent scouts to his high school games. For some reason, though, Dwight had joined the Army right after graduation.

He was driving his pickup this evening instead of a patrol car and he didn't look very official in jeans and a long-sleeved green knit shirt with a navy blue collar.

"Shaw's closer," I said.

"Yeah, but you're not Eric's aunt. I thought I'd try to get Stevie to talk to me, off the record. Tell me what he saw, then go from there. We can stop for supper on the way home at that Mexican place you like. You want to come or not?"

With the odd vibes he was giving off, I wasn't sure. On the other hand, I didn't want him hassling Stevie without me there.

"Okay," I said, "but only if I drive."

"What's wrong with my driving? Just because I keep to the speed limit—"

Dwight's actually a good driver. When expediting with blue lights flashing and siren blaring, he can safely cover as much ground as any other officer in the county, but put him behind the wheel when he's off duty and he becomes an automotive ambler, moseying along at five or ten miles below the speed limit. The drive to Chapel Hill takes me about fifty-five minutes. It would take him at least ninety.

"Just give me your keys," I said. "I'm too hungry for you to drive."

On the way over, Dwight let go of a few more details. There had been a bloody shoe print on the floor of the Dozer, and they'd found tissue samples and nasal mucus around the heel area.

"No distinctive tread, though," said Dwight.

They were going to look into Braz's auction buys and eBay sales. "The mother says they've got a place this side of Widdington and he's been storing some of his buys there till they head back to Florida next month. We'll go out with her tomorrow, and I may send Mayleen or Jack around to any self-storage units in the area where he's bought stuff, but I still think we're going to find the killer right there in the carnival. You do know the speed limit's forty-five through here, right?"

"Why in the carnival?" I asked, ignoring his question. No trooper pulls you if you're doing less than eight over the limit.

Okay, so I was doing ten. I eased off the gas a hair and Dwight relaxed a little, too.

"Most homicide victims know their killers."

"To know is not to love?"

"Familiarity sure does breed contempt," he agreed. "Carnies don't usually want to talk to lawmen, but we've found a couple who say Braz Hartley was a liar and a petty thief, a blowhard and a coward. They say he used to bully his brother till his brother got old enough to kick ass back. Always full of big schemes to make a million dollars and leave the carnival, yet every year he was back on the road with the Ameses, who, incidentally, seem to be pretty well liked and respected."

"You may not like the idea of strangers like the Lincoln brothers," I said. "All the same, money's a big motive, and Tally told me they've had some high-dollar finds in those self-storage lockers. A watch worth thousands, for instance. I haven't read the statutes lately, but as I recall, if the operator of a self-storage facility follows the procedures for notifying the owner, then it's a good-faith sale and neither the operator nor the buyer has any obligation to the owner."

The forty-five gave way to fifty-five and Dwight's truck obligingly moved right on up to sixty-three.

"Think of how the Lincolns reacted over a few tools worth a couple of hundred at most," I said. "If someone with the same sort of faulty logic lost something worth thousands, especially if they lost it over a technicality like missed rental payments, don't you think they could get violent if the buyer wouldn't give it back?"

"But he hadn't bought anything particularly valuable this time out," Dwight objected. "Just four lockers. Two were some old furniture and a couple of gilt-framed pictures."

"Antiques?"

"Not that kind of old. More like made-ten-years-ago old that's falling apart. And the pictures are the kind you see in motels. Then there was one locker that only had used cans of paint and pieces of plywood that look like somebody's kid painted them for a Halloween party. Lots of skeletons and devils, Ames told us. Hartley bought them cheap, and Ames took them off his hands for twenty or thirty bucks and hauled 'em out to their place near Widdington. He's going to nail them around the outside of the haunted house that he's planning to rebuild. Oh, and one funny thing—two racks of expensive nightgowns and bathrobes in all colors of the rainbow. Satin and lace. All on fancy padded hangers. Matching bedroom slippers, too. Hartley had to bid pretty high for that. Stuff is good quality and barely been worn, according to Mayleen. Who would store stuff like that in a locker?"

"Maybe it's from a lingerie store that was going out of business?"

"Mayleen says it's all the same size."

I merged onto I-40. The speed limit here was seventy, and the truck seemed pathetically grateful to get a chance to stretch its horses.

Mischievous thoughts occurred to me. "Maybe it was a gift from a secret lover and the only time she could wear it was when she was meeting him? Or maybe she's a catalog model for Victoria's Secret."

Dwight wasn't amused. "So why let the rental payments lapse?"

"Well, jail time did it for the Lincoln boys. Sickness?

Death? The storage facility has to send a certified letter, but letters get tossed. Or lost. Especially during crisis times."

Before I could speculate further, the car in the lane beside me misjudged my speed and started to cut in front of us without signaling. I had to swerve to avoid hitting him, and I gave a blast of the horn that sent him back into his own lane as I accelerated to get away from him.

"Jesus H, Deb'rah!" Dwight yelped. *"Eighty-eight?"*

"Oops," I said, and kept the speedometer on a sedate seventy till we hit the Chapel Hill exit.

🦆

Visitor parking's almost nonexistent on UNC's north campus around the Old Well that actually furnished water for the first students back in the 1700s. I stopped beside Old East, slid out, and told Dwight to circle the block while I went looking for Stevie. "There's his Jeep, so he shouldn't be far."

I had no qualms about disturbing the scholar. He'd had at least four hours to study if he'd gone straight to the library after dropping Eric off in Raleigh.

"Steve Knott?" asked the first student I saw when I entered his stairwell. "Yeah, he just went up. Next floor. First room on the left."

The lights were on and the door was ajar, and when I pushed it open, Stevie was hanging freshly pressed shirts in his closet. He was, shall we say, surprised to see me. Indeed, his first words of welcome were "Oh shit, Deborah. What're you doing here?"

"Dwight wants to talk to you."

"Dwight *Bryant*? He's here?"

"Yep. Wants to know why you and Eric decided not to leave your names Friday night. Since you wouldn't come talk to me this afternoon, you can talk to him now."

"You sicced him on us? I don't believe this."

"Nobody sicced him on you, honey. Nobody had to. We talked to both of you at that Pot O'Gold slide, remember? When Dwight looked over an alphabetized list of attendees, you think he wouldn't notice which Knott wasn't on it?"

"Did y'all talk to Eric yet?"

It occurred to me that he might be more forthcoming if he thought we knew something he didn't, so I merely shrugged. "Dwight's keeping an open mind. He wants to hear your version."

"Oh Christ!"

"So why don't we get on downstairs before he gets tired of driving around in circles?"

Dwight was slowly making his way up Cameron Avenue when we got out to the sidewalk. At least a dozen cars were stacked up behind him. I pulled Stevie around to the driver's side, told Dwight to shove over, pushed my nephew in, and moved smartly down the street.

At the stoplight at South Cameron, I leaned across Stevie and said, "Don't worry, Dwight, I didn't tell him anything Eric said."

Dwight kept a poker face. "That's good," he said.

When the light changed, I continued on down half a block and turned left into the parking lot at the Carolina

Inn. It's got a Guests Only sign, but hey, we might've been planning to dine there that evening for all the inn knew. I pulled into an empty slot directly under one of the security lights and cut the truck lights. Both of us turned in our seats to look at Stevie.

He tried to brave it out. "So what did Eric tell y'all?"

"No, son," Dwight said gently. "That's not the way it works. I ask the questions. You give me straight answers, all right?"

"Yes, sir."

"Tell me what happened at the Dozer game that night when you and Eric and your friends were there? Was Braz Hartley in the well of the game wagon?"

Stevie nodded.

"Was he razzing y'all?"

"Is that what Eric said?"

"C'mon, Stevie," I said.

"No, he wasn't razzing us. But one of our friends was on his case."

"What about?" asked Dwight.

"I didn't hear," Stevie said cautiously. "All I know is that one minute we're putting in our quarters, playing the game, everything's cool. Next minute, Lamarr's yelling that Hartley's an effing thief. Hartley was standing by that swinging-door thing, and Lamarr just reached over, grabbed him by the shirt, and socked him smack in the face. Hartley was bleeding like a stuck pig and crying that his nose was broken. Eric and I grabbed Lamarr and got him away. Honest, Mr. Dwight. All Lamarr did was sock him one. He was sitting on the step of the wagon when we left and everybody else sort of scattered."

"Who's Lamarr?" Dwight asked.

"Lamarr Wrenn. He's from Dobbs, but he's tight with Eric and they room together at Shaw. He's majoring in economics, putting himself through school. A good guy, honest, Deb'rah."

"And this Lamarr was with you and Eric the rest of the evening?"

"You heard what Eric said."

"We want to hear what you say," said Dwight.

My nephew looked at me with misery in his eyes. "Don't I have a right to an attorney about now?"

"Are you serious?"

"I know I don't have to say anything that incriminates myself. I have the right to remain silent."

"He's right, Deb'rah," said Dwight. He handed Stevie his cell phone. "Here, son. You want to call your parents? Tell them to meet you in Dobbs with an attorney?"

I'm sure Stevie had the same image of Haywood and Isabel roaring into Dobbs as I had. "God, no!"

"Well, then? Were you guys with this Lamarr Wrenn or not?"

"Not," he said reluctantly. "Lamarr was pumped and still mad as hell and he said he was going home. Eric offered to go with him, but he said he needed to be alone. Needed to think."

"What time was this?" Dwight asked.

Stevie shook his head. "I don't know. I never looked at my watch till right as we were leaving."

"You're sure he left?"

"We didn't follow him, but he was heading for the entrance when we split up."

"And you didn't hear what he was mad at Hartley about?"

"I was around on the back when they got into it. All I heard was what I told you."

"And where was Eric?"

"Right beside me. It was over as quick as it started. A few words, one punch. That was it, Mr. Dwight. I swear."

"Who else was with y'all?" Dwight asked.

I didn't recognize either of the other two names, but Dwight jotted them down on a scrap of paper, then said, "Okay. Thanks, Stevie. We'll run you back to your dorm."

"That's it?"

"Unless you saw or heard something else I ought to know?"

"Nope, that's it." His face shone with holy innocence, but I'd seen his palpable relief an instant before.

He immediately turned to Dwight and said, "If you'll let me out, I'll walk back to the dorm."

"Stevie—"

But Dwight had opened the door and stepped out, and Stevie didn't linger. " 'Night, Deborah. 'Night, Mr. Dwight," he called, already halfway across the parking lot.

"Now what do you suppose he thought Eric didn't tell us?" I asked as we watched Stevie take a shortcut through the inn's lobby.

"Whatever it was, he'll probably be on the phone to Shaw in five minutes, getting their stories together."

CHAPTER
11

We stopped for supper at Las Margaritas in Garner, and the waiter, mistaking our relationship, seated us in a secluded booth made romantic by candlelight. I pushed the candle over to the side while Dwight ordered a Dos Equis for himself and a frozen margarita for me. There were years that I couldn't face them, but I tried one again last spring and it was so refreshing that it's back in the lineup now. Dwight likes burritos or chiles rellenos. I usually get the taco salad with extra guacamole. (I might not have been tempted had the serpent offered me an apple, but if it'd been an avocado, don't bet the Garden.)

I was concerned about Stevie, but he's a basically sensible kid and maybe when he'd had a chance to think about it, he'd realize that murder isn't a game where you get to decide what to tell and what to withhold, especially when it's the murder of a cousin. And even though he didn't yet know Brazos Hartley was a cousin, blood still counts for something in our family.

"So," I said to Dwight as our drinks came, "how come you're not out with Sylvia tonight?"

He shrugged. "Sylvia and I are finished."

"Really? What happened?"

He took a swallow of his beer and gave me a rueful look. "I guess she decided a divorced lawyer with monthly child-support payments was a better prospect than a divorced lawman with monthly child-support payments."

"*Reid?* She's seeing Reid now?"

That was so preposterous that I thought he had to be kidding. "Reid put the moves on her when he drove her home Friday night?"

"He was still there yesterday morning when I dropped that damn dog off."

"Oh, Dwight." Relieved to hear that his moodiness was due to Sylvia and not to anything I had or hadn't done, I reached across the table and patted his hand. "I'm so sorry."

"Don't be," he said. "It wasn't going anywhere with us. I was just waiting for her to realize it."

I had to smile. "A gentleman to the end."

He shrugged. "I learned a long time ago that things end better if the woman thinks it's her decision."

I can relate to that. I've dumped and I've been dumped and I know which hurts and humiliates more.

"Reid never could resist a challenge," I said, "but if Sylvia Clayton thinks she's going to get him to the altar . . ."

"I don't know," said Dwight. "Sylvia's a nice person. And maybe he's tired of window-shopping. I know I sure as hell am."

"Me too," I sighed.

Our food arrived and our talk turned to courthouse gossip and eventually back to the murder.

"I keep wondering why his mouth was filled with quarters." I dipped a piece of my taco shell into the guacamole. "What's the symbolism there? Put your money where your mouth is? Money talks?"

"Or keeps someone *from* talking," said Dwight.

"Money to keep his mouth shut forever?"

"The Ameses both say he was obsessed with money."

"Most carnival people are," I said, and told him about some of the bulletin boards I'd surfed that morning with their colorful language and blunt candor. "Their way of life almost demands it. They have from April till October to make enough to carry them through the rest of the year. Every day it rains, every day the thermometer goes much over ninety, every time the equipment breaks down, they're losing income. All they've got is a smile and a fast line of talk—"

"And a gaffed game," Dwight interjected cynically, referring to the dozens of ways a carny agent can keep you from winning if he wants to, despite the law's best efforts.

"—and a gaffed game, maybe," I conceded. "But you can't cheat an honest man, and anybody who expects to get something for nothing ought not to be allowed on a midway. It's a hard life out on the road for months—having to tear down all that gear and move it every few days, then set it up all over again. The real game, of course, must be dreaming up new ways to separate the marks from their money. Probably what keeps it from being a total grind."

I thought of how Tally's eyes had sparkled when she was stringing Reese along, keeping him in the game. "But it sounds like Braz Hartley took it a step further."

Dwight nodded. "He did try a little blackmail this spring on the woman who runs the plate game."

"The same woman who saw this Lamarr Wrenn bloody his nose? Polly somebody?"

"Polly Viscardi. She says this is the first time she's hooked up with the Ameses, so Braz didn't have a clue about her. She looks sweet and proper, doesn't she?"

"I suppose." I had a memory of bright red hair, a money apron tied around a thick waist, a smile for all who passed, and calculating eyes. And yes, she'd been one of those who offered support to Tally Friday night, but with her androgynous oil-stained leather work shoes, tight black slacks, and belligerent glares at all the gawkers, sweet and proper wouldn't have been my description. Unless it was the pretty-in-pink ruffled blouse she wore? Or the little bells on the tips of her pink shoelaces? I've noticed that ruffles and pink can cloud men's judgment at times.

"Sweet like a buzz saw," Dwight said. "He found her getting it on with one of the roughies in their haunted house back in May and threatened to tell her husband if she didn't pay him. Only he wasn't her husband. She had the roughie bust Braz's balls, then kicked the not-husband out and moved the roughie in."

Dwight's plate was empty and the waiter removed it. "Another drink?" he asked us.

We both shook our heads, and I gestured that he could take my plate, too.

"Coffee?" asked Dwight.

I still had some of my margarita left. "But you get a cup if you want it."

"No, we'll just have our check," Dwight told the waiter, who nodded and went away to fetch it.

"So if Polly Viscardi actually saw who came along and finished the job Eric's friend started, she doesn't have a real strong motive to tell, does she?" I said. "For her, it could be good riddance to bad rubbish."

"Your guess is good as mine, shug."

"A woman could have stomped Braz hard enough to kill him," I mused.

"Well, it's downward force," he conceded. "Enough momentum and determination, why not?"

"Might be why the Viscardi woman says she didn't see anything."

He wasn't convinced. "And her motive would be?"

"Oh, I'm not doing motive tonight," I said with an airy wave of my hand. "I'm just doing opportunity."

"Yeah? Well, let me know when you get around to motive," he said dryly.

"Did Tally hear about that blackmail attempt?"

"Not from Viscardi. She says she handled it herself. Didn't feel a need to involve the Ameses."

"What *about* the Ameses? Did you run background checks on them?" I wished I could confide in Dwight, but I couldn't see that Tally's identity had any bearing on the murder, and my first loyalty had to be to Andrew, even if he was acting like a horse's ass at the moment.

"The husband," Dwight said. "Just minor stuff. Traffic violations, license irregularities. And any juvvie records for the boy would be sealed."

Thinking of all we'd learned about Braz, I found myself hoping that Val was a decent son. I liked Tally, and on a purely selfish basis, I hoped she wouldn't have her heart broken again by her second child.

The check arrived in a black plastic folder, and Dwight tucked a couple of bills inside the cover as I finished my drink.

"Ready?"

I nodded.

Out in the parking lot, he jingled his keys and asked if I wanted to drive.

"It's still early and I'm not in any hurry now," I said.

As he pulled out of the parking lot, the radio was tuned to a country station, or what passes for country these days, and Dwight flipped up and down the dial before turning it off with an impatient growl. "Hell of a note when you can't find real country on the radio anymore."

My stabs at conversation went nowhere, and we drove south on Old Forty-Eight in deepening silence till the lights of Garner faded behind us. The moon kept slipping in and out of hazy clouds, and the comfortable easiness that had been present between us during dinner seemed to be evaporating with each mile we traveled. He had sounded okay about Sylvia and Reid, but I wondered if maybe he was more down about it than he wanted to admit. It's one thing to think a relationship's going nowhere, quite another to have a friend cut you out so abruptly.

"Deb'rah?"

"Mmmm?"

As if paralleling my thoughts, he asked, "Did you mean it when you said you were tired of channel surfing?"

"Oh, God, yes," I sighed. "I'm always clicking on the wrong guys. And now Minnie's after me about my image. She thinks Paul Archdale may be planning to run against me next time and that I'm vulnerable to a whispering campaign."

I'm a yellow-dog Democrat and Paul's a Jesse Helms Republican, but that's not the reason we dislike each other. We had a run-in over a dog once that could have gotten him disbarred and me reprimanded had we gone public with the situation. If he could get away with it, he'd smear me with the biggest creosote mop he could find.

"She keeps saying I need to just pick somebody respectable and settle down."

"How about me?" said Dwight.

"Oh, I don't think Minnie worries about your reputation. Men still get cut more slack these days. Even sheriff's deputies."

"No, I mean how about you and me get married?"

I looked at him in astonishment, expecting to see a big smile, hear a joking comment. Instead, the set of his jaw was serious in the glow of the dash lights and he kept his eyes fixed on the road.

"You're not kidding, are you?"

"Nope."

"Dwight—"

He still wouldn't look at me. "It's really not that crazy. Think about it a minute before you say no, all right? We've known each other since you were born. Our families like each other. We like the same old movies. We know each other's moods and bad habits. You like Cal. Cal likes you."

I was speechless.

"I just want to be married, Deb'rah," he said plaintively. "I'm tired of bars and pickup lines and trying to be funny. I'm tired of living in a bachelor apartment. I want a real home. I want to plant trees, cut the grass, buy family-size packs of meat at the grocery store. I want somebody beside me I can laugh with and enjoy coming home to every night, somebody who won't be jealous because I love my son and like having him here whenever Jonna will let me."

"But what about love?" I asked. "You're not in love with me, Dwight."

"So? You're not in love with me, either, but we like each other, right? I mean, you don't think I'm repulsive, do you? Or all that hard to be around?"

"Of course not. It's just that I've never thought of you that way before."

"Nothing will change. Except that neither of us'll have to go home after the movie's over." This time, he did shoot me a grin before turning his eyes back to the line of cars coming at us.

"But what about—?" Suddenly I felt shy. "What about sex?"

"I like it," he said promptly. "Don't you?"

"Well, yes, but—"

"Don't tell me you were madly in love with every guy you ever slept with."

"Maybe not to begin with, but I certainly meant to be or I wouldn't have. And anyhow, just how many do you think there've been?" I asked indignantly, mentally counting up even as I spoke.

They would all fit comfortably on the fingers of one

hand, so it's not like my bed's been a revolving door. All the same, Dwight had a point. In fact, he had several. He's decent and caring. Takes his obligations seriously and he's not exactly hard to look at either, not with that solid build and strong face. And yes, we *were* comfortable with each other . . . most of the time.

But marriage? Sex?

He kept glancing over at me as he drove, but now it was my turn to stare straight ahead as I considered the ramifications. My family would be over the moon, of course, but what about Cal? Dwight often brought him out to the farm when the child was down for a long weekend or for his summer vacation and he always seemed happy enough in my company. All the same, things would surely be different if his dad and I were married.

Married.

There was something awfully final to that word. Yet, wouldn't it be a relief to be done with all the games? Playing the field sounds glamorous at seventeen, amusing at twenty-seven, but at thirty-seven the field was getting pretty damn thin and a lot less amusing with each passing year. Did I want to be like the friends who were still hanging at Miss Molly's every weekend, hoping to get lucky, hoping not to spend the rest of their lives alone?

"How come you and Jonna really busted up?" I asked.

"No one big reason. She just didn't want to be married anymore. What about you and Chapin?"

"He *did* want to be married. Only not to me."

Again the silence stretched between us as we passed through Cotton Grove, along Possum Creek, and onto the road past the farm. The moon flicked in and out of the thick trees.

"Okay," I said at last.

"Really?"

I took a deep breath. "Yes."

"You're sure?" he persisted.

"Aren't you?"

"Yeah."

Dwight turned off the hardtop into the lane that ran up to my house. When we pulled in next to the back porch, he left the motor running and reached across me to open the door so I could hop out as I always did.

"Well," he said. "I guess I'll see you tomorrow. Want to—"

I turned off the key in his ignition.

"Hey, what are you doing?"

"Before we make it official," I said, "we need to find out if we're really as compatible as you think we are."

"Huh?"

"Don't play dumb, Dwight."

"Oh."

He doused the truck lights and followed me into the house. The moon followed, too, and we did not turn on any lamps.

After a lifetime of treating Dwight like family, I was afraid that sex with him would feel vaguely incestuous. Instead, once we got past the first awkward kiss, it felt normal.

Okay, better than normal.

All right, dammit! It felt wonderful.

Nevertheless, as the coital glow faded, a wave of sadness washed over me. Lying next to him in the moonsoftened darkness of my bedroom, I said, "We're just settling, aren't we?"

"Settling?"

"Settling for safe and comfortable because we're afraid the real thing's never going to come along?"

"You want an escape clause?" he asked quietly.

"Well, we ought to look at it logically."

For some reason, that seemed to irritate him. "Oh shit, Deb'rah Knott! You never looked at love logically in your whole damn life."

"But this isn't love, is it? I mean, we love each other. We always have. But this isn't romantic love. This is expedience. And I don't know why you're getting so huffy."

"Well, why wouldn't I? You no sooner say yes than you're looking for a way to bust us up. If we do this, I expect it to be for better or worse till death do us part. No more divorces."

"And what if someone comes along who makes you feel the way you felt when you and Jonna first fell in love?"

"Not going to happen," he said stubbornly. "And even if it does, I'll just remind myself where that feeling ended up the last time around."

His denial of love's importance made me so much sadder that I couldn't speak and his head turned on the pillow beside me.

"But if you want an escape clause, if that someone comes along for you . . . Well, then, I won't try to make you stay, okay?"

"Okay," I whispered.

He rolled closer and gathered me into his arms. "It'll all work out, shug. You'll see. It'll be fine."

His hand was gentle as he smoothed my hair away from my face, and his soothing words reminded me of someone trying to reassure a nervous filly that the saddle wouldn't hurt at all. Amused and comforted, I eventually quit nickering and took the carrot he offered on his open hand.

After a second test of compatibility (we needed to be absolutely certain, didn't we?), Dwight and I put our clothes back on and sat at my kitchen table to talk until after midnight.

Over coffee and some of Maidie's oatmeal cookies, we agreed that he'd move in with me after the wedding and we'd think about adding on to my small house in the spring.

We also agreed he'd tell his mother and I'd tell Daddy; then he'd drive up to Virginia to tell Cal himself. Until then, to guard against any rumors reaching the boy first, no siblings and no friends.

"Just Portland," I emended. We've always told each other everything and I knew I wouldn't be able to keep her from guessing that something serious was on my mind.

"That means Avery, too, you know."

I nodded. "It always has, but he's never talked out of turn that I know of." I looked at Dwight suspiciously. "Has he?"

"Well, maybe to me once or twice," he admitted sheepishly. "When he and Portland were worried about you out there messing in stuff that could get you hurt."

"So that's how you found out," I said, remembering a couple of those times when I'd have sworn there was no way he could know what I was up to. "Okay, Portland and Avery and nobody else till you tell Cal."

"You gonna want a big church wedding?"

"Not really. You?"

"Hell, no. I say we go stand in front of a magistrate. How about Gwen Utley next week sometime?"

"Be serious, Dwight. There's a lot of middle ground between a big church wedding and a magistrate's court. Part of this is PR—show the voters I'm becoming a respectable married woman, remember? That means pictures in the newspaper and some sort of church ceremony. And you know how hurt the boys would be if we didn't invite them to come. Or their wives if we didn't let them do the reception."

Dwight laughed and leaned back in the wooden chair till he was extended his full length. "In other words, the usual big, sprawly Knott family celebration with two pigs on the cookers and half the county invited?"

"It'll probably be too cold for a pig-picking," I murmured, sneaking a discreet glance at the fit of his jeans. My body still pinged and tingled like an overheated engine cooling down.

"Too cold?" he scoffed. "It won't get too cold till November."

"I was thinking the Christmas holidays," I said. "When Cal could be here."

"Christmas!" He sounded dismayed. "That's three whole months away."

"No, it's not." I pulled out a calendar and laid it on the table between us to count the weeks. "We're practically into October, see? So it's only ten or twelve weeks till Christmas vacation starts. We'll need that much time to get it together. You'll have to give notice on your apartment. I have to clear my court calendar and find a dress. Not white satin with a train and veil," I assured him, "and you won't have to wear a tux, but I think I ought to look a little bit bridal, don't you?"

There was a discreet glance of his own as he ran his eyes over my snug shirt. "I guess."

(Ping!)

"It won't be easy finding something for a matron of honor who's gonna be about nine months pregnant," I mused aloud, already making lists in my head.

"You're having bridesmaids?"

"Just Portland. To balance your brother. You'll want Rob to be your best man, won't you?"

He nodded. "Did you hear that he and Kate are expecting a baby?"

"No! When?"

"January or February."

Rob and Kate were already raising two children: her son, who was born after her first husband died, and her orphaned cousin, who was four or five when Kate married Rob. This would be their first child together.

January or February? Nice. That should help distract Miss Emily's attention from Dwight and me. I adore his eccentric mother, but sometimes she's a real force of nature.

We talked some more, then Dwight got up to go. I walked him out to the truck and he gave me a chaste goodnight kiss on the forehead. At least it started out chaste. We were both breathing heavily when we pulled apart.

"No," I said a little unsteadily, "not repulsive at all."

He laughed and stepped up into his truck.

I watched till his taillights disappeared through the trees, then went back to bed where I lay awake another hour thinking about where I'd landed myself this time. It might not be a great and burning romance, it might be settling for safe and comfortable, but it was certainly going to have its compensations.

(*"Ping!"* chortled the pragmatist.)

(*"Would you just quit that and go to sleep?"* the preacher scolded.)

(But I noticed he was grinning, too.)

CHAPTER
12

MONDAY MORNING

I had just dragged myself out of bed, put on the coffee, and was now going through the daily ritual of deciding how to retrieve my morning newspaper. I could jog the half mile to the box at the end of my driveway, or I could pedal down on the dirt bike I'd bought secondhand from a niece who recently acquired her driver's license, or I could cheat and drive. I'd about decided on the bike when I heard a car door slam. My back door stood open to the screened porch and April didn't bother to knock.

Automatically, I glanced at the clock. Seven-oh-five. Court didn't start till nine, and I'd showered last night, so I had plenty of time, but I was under the impression that April's school day started at eight so why was she over here in stained shorts and sneakers, no makeup, and a ravaged face? After Minnie, April's the sturdiest, most got-it-together of my sisters-in-law, but today even her short brown hair with its threads of gray stood up in uncombed tufts.

"What's wrong?" I asked as my heart froze. "Daddy—?"

Well past eighty now, he's always my first thought when someone obviously bearing bad news shows up at my door unexpectedly.

April shook her head mutely.

"The kids?"

"No, I sent them over to Seth and Minnie's to spend the night and go on to school from there." April was freckled all over, and now her face was red and splotchy as tears filled her hazel eyes and ran down her cheeks. She wiped them away with an impatient hand. "It's Andrew."

"What's wrong? Is he hurt? Sick?"

"You tell me, Deborah. What happened over here Saturday?" she demanded. "He came back from seeing you and Mr. Kezzie and went straight to the bourbon. He's been drunk ever since, cussing you and not too happy with Mr. Kezzie and sloppy maudlin over Ruth and A.K. He drinks till he passes out, then comes to just long enough to drink again. I haven't seen him like this since before we were married and I'm scared, Deborah. What set him off?"

"He won't talk to you?"

"No, and when I beg him to tell me what's wrong, he just gets mad and starts cussing."

Alarmed, I asked, "He hasn't hurt you, has he?"

"Hit me, you mean?" Indignation stiffened her back. "No, of course not. He'll never get that drunk."

All this time, I'd been getting her seated, pouring two mugs of coffee, and pushing sugar and milk at her in hopes that small routines might calm her down. Suggesting that Andrew might knock her around seemed to have done the trick. As Andrew's third wife, April's only got a few years on me and there's no submissiveness in that marriage. Not on her part anyhow.

I handed her a box of tissues and said, "April, you do know that Andrew was married before, don't you?"

"To Lois McAdams. So?"

"Before Lois."

Her brow furrowed. "Carol somebody. Carol Hatcher?"

"That's right."

"She claimed Andrew was the father of her baby and *her* father made them get married. But after the baby was born, she ran off with it and—oh my God!" Her face went white beneath her freckles. "She's back, isn't she? And the divorce was never legal, was it?"

"No, no, no," I said before she could follow that train of thought right on into the station and start worrying that her children were bastards. "Carol's dead. She died years ago. Before you and Andrew got married."

Having never met the woman, I could speak easily of her death.

"Really? Does Andrew know? Is that why Mr. Kezzie called him over here? To tell him that? But why would that make him—?" She heard herself jittering and broke off with the first semblance of a smile. "And if I'll shut up a minute, you'll tell me, won't you?"

I reached over and squeezed her hand. "Carol's dead, but her daughter's come back to Colleton County. Andrew's daughter. She owns her grandfather's farm over near Widdington, and she also has a share of the carnival that's playing at the harvest festival in Dobbs."

"Daughter? Olivia?" April was bewildered. "But Andrew said she wasn't his. He wouldn't lie to me about that."

"Maybe he's honestly believed that all these years, or maybe he's just talked himself into it, but trust me, honey. She's his. He can get a DNA test if it'll make him feel any better about it, but it'd just be a waste of money. She's his child."

"You've met Olivia? Talked to her?"

"I told you. She and her husband own part of the carnival that's playing Dobbs. Her name is Tallahassee Ames now and it was her son that got killed Friday night."

April sat there numb and speechless, and I could almost see her brain working under that thatch of wild brown curls as she processed the data I'd just given her. I poured myself another coffee and brandished the pot toward her half-empty mug. She nodded and drank deeply.

"If that's true, he'd be Andrew's grandson? My God! No wonder he's crawled into a bottle."

"The funeral's tomorrow morning at ten," I told her. "Over at the homeplace."

She was bewildered. "Does everybody in the family know about this but me?"

"No. Just Daddy and me. We were waiting for Andrew to talk to you before we told the others. Doesn't look like that's going to happen, though, does it?"

I described how Daddy had been keeping tabs on the situation all these years and how Andrew had gone into denial Saturday afternoon and told us to leave him and his family out of it.

"Well, that was pretty dumb of him," she said in exasperation.

"Maybe he feels guilty for not trying to find her in all these years," I suggested neutrally.

April is as practical as she is pretty and has more common sense than a farmer's almanac. "Now, why would he feel guilty if he's been sure all these years that the baby wasn't his?"

I shrugged.

Her hazel eyes narrowed. "Carol *told* him she wasn't."

"Yeah, but Mother told him she was," I said, and described the visit Mother had made to the Hatcher farm when I was too young to remember, and how, when she finally persuaded him to return with her, Carol and Olivia were gone again.

"In the end, which one do you think he really believed in his heart of hearts?" I asked her.

There was a long silence, then April said softly, "Poor Andrew."

"Yes."

"And poor Olivia, too," April said with returning briskness. "You say she calls herself Tallahassee now? That's sort of cute, isn't it? What's she like, Deborah? Is she nice?"

I shared with her my impressions of Tally Ames, her family, and her way of life and April listened intently while the clock edged closer to eight. When I'd finished, she said, "Use your phone?"

Her first call was to her school to tell them that she wouldn't be in that day and that the substitute would find today's lesson plans on her desk under her roll book.

Next, she called Robert, who lives here on the extended farm, too. He was on his way out to cut silage when Doris called him back in. April was concise. "Andrew's drunk as a skunk, Robert. I'm going to call Seth to come help you, and I'd appreciate it if y'all would take him out to the barn, throw him under that cold shower out there and see if you can sober him up."

Lastly, she called Seth, explained that Robert needed his help with Andrew, then asked him to put Minnie on. Years in the classroom had given April the ability to convey a lot of information in clear, short sentences, and she explained the situation to Minnie a lot quicker than I could have done it.

"So thanks for letting the kids stay over there last night and I'd appreciate it if you'd let all the others know about the funeral," she said as she hung up.

I admit that I was standing there with my mouth open.

"I'm going to go take a shower and get dressed and drive over to Dobbs," she told me. "Shouldn't you be getting dressed, too?"

"Yes, ma'am," I said.

When she'd gone, I called Daddy to give him a heads-up on April and how she'd told Minnie to get the word out. "And I talked to Tally, too. The funeral's scheduled for tomorrow morning at ten o'clock."

"Yeah, Duck Aldcroft's people are coming to open the grave this morning," he said. "Anything else, shug?"

"No," I lied. "That's about it."

"Fine," he said, and hung up.

Driving into Dobbs, my thoughts were focused on April, Andrew, and Tally, with forebodings about the funeral tomorrow, but as I started to get out of my car in the parking lot across the street from the courthouse, I saw Dwight heading toward the departmental lot diagonally across the street from where I was parked. The mere sight of him flooded all my senses and it was as if the bottom had dropped out of my stomach.

He had his back to me and was in deep conversation with three other officers. They stood there on the sidewalk talking for another moment or two before Raeford McLamb got into one of the squad cars with Jack Jamison, and Mayleen Richards went off alone in another. I saw Dwight check his watch, then he drove off alone, too.

Yesterday, I would have called to him or certainly waved. Today, I just sat motionless, half in, half out of the seat until he'd driven away and I could start breathing normally again.

Maidenly vapors or sudden misgivings?

(*"Get a grip,"* said the pragmatist. *"Think about last night. Remember compatibility? Remember Ping?"*)

(*"Gonna be a long time till Christmas,"* sighed the preacher.)

By the time the DA and I'd disposed of sixty or seventy cases of DWI, speeding violations (*I know, I know!*), seat belt violations, improper equipment, etc., etc., I was back to normal.

I recessed for lunch early, snagged Portland, and hauled her over to an end booth at the Bright Leaf Restaurant before the rest of the regulars came straggling over. Normally when the courts are in session, a table near the back is reserved for judges, and the waitress tried to seat me there, but I made her give us the most private booth in the place. Even so, the four elderly ladies two empty tables away looked at us as Portland squealed in a perfect blend of surprise, horror, and amusement.

"You and *Dwight*? I don't believe it."

"Will you keep your voice down?" I snapped. "This is for your ears only."

With black hair so curly she has to keep it short, Portland sometimes reminds me of a well-clipped poodle. Today, though, she was like a bright-eyed terrier on the scent of a weasel as she leaned forward conspiratorially. "So what's he like in bed? Tell, tell!"

"It was fine," I said.

"Only fine?" She gave me such a leer that I couldn't restrain my own smile.

"Actually, it was better than fine," I confessed. "He probably learned a lot while he was in the Army."

"Well, that's something anyhow. But marriage, Deborah? I mean, you know Avery and I are crazy about Dwight, but *marriage*? When you're not in love with him?"

"Isn't being in lust with him almost as good?" I asked lightly.

She wasn't to be deterred. "It'll be like one of those cut-and-dried arranged marriages."

I shrugged. "From what I've heard, a lot of arranged marriages were very happy."

Portland just sat there, shaking her head.

"Look," I argued. "If an Avery had come along for

me, I'd probably have three kids and be lending *you* maternity dresses right now. But one didn't. You know my track record, Por. Allen. Lev. Terry. Kidd. Not to mention Randolph Englert and at least a half dozen more that nearly made junior varsity. It's time to quit kidding myself. I don't *have* an Avery out there. He probably got run over by an eighteen-wheeler twenty years ago. Dwight's here and now and he's one of us. We have history together."

"But without love?"

"But we do love each other," I said, knowing I was using the same arguments to convince her that I was still using to convince myself. "We always have. So it's not thrills and chills. Big deal. That just means it's no spills, either. No letdown after the honeymoon's over. We're going into this with our eyes wide open and no illusions."

Portland sighed. "Sugar, you've done some crazy things in your life, but arranging a sensible marriage probably wins the jackpot. When do you two plan on getting this business deal notarized?"

"If you're not going to take it seriously," I said stiffly, "we might as well go on back to the courthouse."

"Oh, no, you don't. You invited me to lunch." She waved to the waitress. "Mary? We're ready to order now."

When Mary had taken our orders and gone away, Portland said, "You're really going to do this?"

I nodded solemnly. "I'm really going to do it. We haven't set an exact date yet, but probably over the Christmas holidays."

Portland laughed and patted the little bulge beneath

the jacket of her dark red suit. "My due date's the twenty-eighth. I'll come as the goddess of fertility."

"You don't get out of it that easily, girlfriend. You're gonna be my matron of honor. If I could wear bright pink satin for you, you can wear red velvet trimmed in white fur for me."

Her glee turned to horror. "I'm coming as *Santa Claus*?"

CHAPTER
13

DWIGHT BRYANT
MONDAY MORNING

As Dwight Bryant headed his squad car toward the carnival grounds, he caught a glimpse of Deborah's car in the parking lot across from the courthouse and in his rearview mirror, he saw her get out and lock the door. Any other day, he might have circled the courthouse and intercepted her with a teasing remark or the offer of a cup of coffee if she had time, but not today. Not after last night. He had loved her and wanted her for so damn long that the wanting had become a permanent ache in his heart, like a limp from a badly mended broken leg or a torn muscle that wouldn't heal, something you learned to live with but that could still leave you gasping with pain at unexpected moments. And now that ache was finally, cautiously, lifting.

He still couldn't believe that she'd actually said yes.

And hadn't changed her mind even after he made love to her.

Twice.

So until they both got used to the idea, he told himself, better not risk messing it up or making a fool of himself in broad daylight. Stick to business.

Marriage to Jonna had taught him to compartmentalize his feelings, a useful trick these last few years as he watched Deborah with other men—the willpower it had taken to keep his mouth shut and his hands off when she confided in him while watching some old World War II Van Johnson movie, or that time she wept on his chest after Herman had been poisoned, or any other time when she would touch him with casual, sisterly affection. If she'd ever suspected the intensity of his feelings for her, he knew she'd shy away. Every instinct warned him to keep it light, act as if nothing had really changed between them, compartmentalize.

He was halfway across town before he realized that he was whistling. So much for compartmentalization.

"Boss is in a good mood today," Raeford McLamb said to Jack Jamison as he pulled out of the Hardee's drive-through and turned onto the highway for Raleigh.

"Was he? I didn't notice," said Jamison, yawning widely as he uncapped his coffee. It was scalding hot, but the caffeine was a welcome jolt to his tired nerves.

"Jack Junior still keeping you awake?" McLamb asked sympathetically.

"He's seven weeks old," Jamison moaned, turning a plaintive face to his fellow officer. "Shouldn't he be sleeping through by now?"

As the voice of wisdom and experience, McLamb

said, "Well, Rosy was, but it was almost three months before Jordo gave up that two A.M. feeding."

"Three *months*?" Appalled, the tubby young detective
recapped the coffee and stuck it in a cup holder clipped to
the dashboard, then leaned back in his seat and closed his
eyes. "Wake me when we get to Shaw," he said. "I need
all the sleep I can get."

Deputy Mayleen Richards glanced again at the clipboard
on the dash to confirm the address. One of the self-storage
facilities on her list was right there in Dobbs, but it
wouldn't open till ten, so she'd decided to start with the
one farthest away on the edge of Fuquay-Varina over in
Wake County. The way the numbers seemed to be running, Six Pines Self-Storage should be—ah, yes, there it
was, a gray cinderblock office with long rows of units out
back, each looking like a single-car garage with a pull-
down door. A high chain-link fence surrounded them all.

She pulled into a parking slot, adjusted the tilt of her
hat, and made sure the blouse of her uniform was prop-
erly tucked in as she got out of the car.

A tall, sturdily built young woman with cinnamon
brown hair and freckles across her prominent nose,
Mayleen Richards had tried sitting at a desk after finish-
ing a two-year computer course out at Colleton Community College, but she was farm bred, used to hard physical
work outdoors. Another two years of trying to fit her
awkward square personality into a comfortable round
hole was all she could take before she quit her job in the
Research Triangle and asked Sheriff Bo Poole for a job.

He knew her parents, knew her, and was always glad to have another officer in the department who wasn't afraid of computers. He'd been disappointed that she preferred patrol duty over an indoor job, but agreed to let her pull a normal rotation. Lately, Major Bryant had been giving her more detective chores, and with the county growing in population, she was hoping to get switched over permanently.

As she entered the office building, a gray-haired woman smiled at her from behind the counter.

"Good morning, Officer. How can I help you?"

Richards introduced herself and explained that she was there in connection with a Brazos Hartley, who had bought the contents of a storage locker from Six Pines. "A couple of racks of negligees."

"How do you spell that name?"

As Richards spelled it out, the clerk swiveled around and began tapping computer keys to bring up the record. "Oh, yes. The Lee Hamden account. Negligees? Is that all it was?"

"Nightgowns and robes. And rather expensive looking. Didn't you know?"

"Honey, all I know's what's on this contract. They don't have to get specific about what they're storing, and we can't go through their things."

"Even when you're auctioning it off?" asked Richards.

"Nope. Even the buyers don't know what they're getting till they've paid over their money. Talk about a pig in a poke. All they can do is look. They can shine a flashlight in, but they can't touch anything and they can't go inside till they've made the winning bid *and* paid for it. Is Ms. Hamden suing him? Her brother said she'd be fu-

rious, but you know, we did everything by the book—
certified letter, advertisement in the paper, everything the
law requires."

"You remember Hartley, then?"

"Hartley? The man who bought the locker?" She
shook her head. "Wouldn't know him from Adam's house
cat if he walked in behind you," she said cheerfully.
"Doubt if I ever saw him. My boss is the one who helps
with the auctions. I stay in here and do the paperwork. I
meant the owner's brother. *Him* I remember. He was here
last week trying to pay his sister's back rent and her stuff
already auctioned off nine days before. He was awful
upset for her, but what could I do? She only left us an ac-
commodation box number at one of those mailing stores
here in town. We ask folks to leave us the name or telephone number of a friend or relative, somebody we can
get in touch with. The way people move around these
days, though . . ."

She shrugged helplessly. "We wind up auctioning off
three or four of our lockers every month."

"Did he say why his sister didn't respond to the certified letter?"

"She never got it. It went to the mail store and bounced
back here when it couldn't be delivered. He said she's
been called out of state to nurse her husband's mother and
didn't realize she'd be gone so long. Soon as she remembered, she called him and told him to come over and pay
me the back rent, late fees. I had the hardest time making
him understand we really didn't have her clothes.
Clothes. That's what he said it was. Didn't say nothing
about fancy nightgowns. Mostly, he said, she was wor-

ried about some pictures—maybe an album?—stored in her locker, too."

"Oh?" Deputy Richards encouraged.

"I had to tell her brother that most people, when they buy one of these lockers? They just keep the stuff they think they can sell at flea markets and dump all the personal stuff."

"Dump it where? Here?"

"If they want to pay the fee. Soon as the auction's over, they go through the stuff right out there in the driveway and bag up what they don't want. We charge to let 'em use our Dumpsters. Otherwise, they have to truck it to a landfill themselves. I had to tell him that nobody goes to flea markets to buy somebody else's pictures, so stuff like that usually gets dumped right here."

"I don't suppose he went through the Dumpster?"

"Oh, honey, after nine days?"

"You didn't happen to get his name, did you?"

"Wasn't any reason to. Although, now that you mention it, I believe I did call him Mr. Hamden and he didn't say that wasn't his name."

"But you told him who bought the contents of the locker?"

"Oh, yes. It's a public sale. Brazos Hartley. Ames Amusement Corporation, Gibsonton, Florida. Don't know how he found us from way down there. Anyhow, here's his phone number and an e-mail address, and I gave Mr. Hamden the same information and wished him luck."

"But all you have on Ms. Hamden herself is this mailing-service box number?"

"And this phone number. But she must have written it

down wrong because I called it and the lady that answered said she'd had that number for sixteen years and nobody by that name had ever lived there."

The gray-haired clerk looked at Mayleen Richards in sudden interest. "So how come you're trying to find her? Was the stuff stolen?"

"All I can say right now is that it's related to an investigation the sheriff's department is conducting," the deputy said. "Could you describe Ms. Hamden?"

"Sorry. That locker was rented six years ago, before I came. She was on our quarterly plan and payments always arrived by check every three months. Nothing on the checks except her name."

"Do you remember what bank?"

The woman shook her head. "Her brother was real cute, though," she added, trying to be helpful. "Curly black hair and gorgeous brown eyes."

Richards thanked her for her time and checked her watch as she went back out to the car. Only a little past ten. Wouldn't take but a few minutes to check out E-Z-Quik Mail.

The lone clerk there was cooperative but he'd only worked there a few months and could add nothing. "I've never seen her to know who I was looking at. Most people using the boxes out there in the vestibule don't come on inside unless they're mailing a package or buying stamps. According to our records, she pays cash for the box a year at the time and it's due to expire the end of the month."

"Is there anything in her box right now?"

"I'm not supposed to let anybody see a client's mail without a court order," the clerk said virtuously, but he went into the sorting room behind the bank of rental boxes and came back a minute later. "Nope. Empty as my girlfriend's head."

The phone number on the form was similar to the one on the Six Pines Self-Storage form. Same prefix, but she'd scrambled the same last four numbers. There was no North Carolina street address for Lee Hamden. The space had been left blank except for the notation "In transit—no permanent address."

"'Course now, there's a lot of that going around," said the clerk.

🦆

Shaw University on the south side of Raleigh had its beginning in an 1865 Bible-study class immediately after the Civil War. Despite integration during the civil rights movement, however, its student body has remained predominately black.

Even though Deputy Jack Jamison passed the school every time he drove into Raleigh, he'd never actually set foot on the campus, and in his sleep-deprived state, he was glad to tag along after McLamb, who seemed to know his way around. They found the dorm where Lamarr Wrenn and Eric Holt shared a room, but neither was in. The kid next door thought Holt might be at his job in the library and that Wrenn was probably in his modern art–appreciation class.

Since classes wouldn't change for another thirty-eight minutes, they headed for the library, homed in on their prey, and were soon crowded together in one of the small soundproof study rooms deep in the stacks.

Of medium height and sturdy build, with light brown skin, closely trimmed hair, and a small gold stud in one ear, Eric Holt was the picture of earnest helpfulness. His eyes met theirs with innocent candor. *Hide something?* those eyes seemed to ask. *Me? Collude with my friends? Cook up a story together? Certainly not.*

"Okay, yeah, it was dumb of Steve and me not to leave our names," he admitted forthrightly, "but hey, Lamarr's our friend. We didn't want to rat him out just because he lost his temper and hit that dude. Besides, the guy was fine when we pulled Lamarr away."

"Fine's not the way we heard it," McLamb growled.

"Well, no," Eric agreed. "He was bleeding pretty bad. I guess Lamarr might even've broken his nose. But he was definitely able to sit there on the top step of that game wagon and cuss us to hell and back. Nothing wrong with his lungs."

"And your friend Lamarr didn't go back later and finish him off?"

"You'll have to ask him that," Eric said earnestly. "He says he went home and I believe him, but the last time Steve Knott and I saw him that night, he was leaving the carnival, heading in the opposite direction from the Dozer."

"Why'd he pop Hartley?" asked Jamison.

"Oh, they got into it about the game. Lamarr said it was rigged. Called the guy running it a thief. One thing led to another. You know how it goes," he said, appealing to them man-to-man.

"Yeah," said McLamb cynically. "We know how it goes."

They came at him with questions from every angle,

but nothing they asked made Eric Holt give up any more information. His whole attitude said that he wanted to help, wished he could help, would certainly help if there were any way in his power to do so, but everything had gone down just as he'd told them.

Lamarr Wrenn was just as helpfully unhelpful. They caught up with him as he was leaving one classroom and heading across campus for another. Dark-skinned with a small chin beard, he was built like a concrete post, tough and solid with big muscular hands that clenched convulsively around his books and looked capable of felling a mule with one blow. He walked with a slight limp that favored his right ankle ("Twisted it playing Hacky Sack yesterday"), but it didn't seem to slow him down.

"Look, man, you make me late and it'll go down as a cut. Steve and Eric already told you what happened, didn't they?"

"You tell us," said McLamb as they strode along with him.

The walks were crowded with students changing classes and they were forced to walk on the grass to keep up as Wrenn plowed his way through.

But it was clear the young men had their stories well in hand. Lamarr Wrenn had thought the Dozer was rigged, he said. He and Hartley got into it. Accusations were made by Wrenn; slurs were spoken by Hartley.

"So when he called me a dumb-ass jigaboo, I smashed his nose in for him. But that's all. Anybody says different, he can talk to me."

McLamb said, "Your friends say you were still steamed when you left them. You sure you didn't go back and have another go at him?"

"Nope, I went home."

"Home being?"

The address he gave was in the old Darkside section of Dobbs. The neighborhood was still mostly black, yet, despite some derelict shanties, it wasn't what you'd call a real ghetto, McLamb thought as he wrote it down. Not when those shanties stood on quarter- to half-acre lots. Not when professional and middle-class African Americans were either remodeling the old clapboard houses of their parents and grandparents or else leveling them to make way for bigger and more modern homes.

"Any witnesses to the time you got there?"

Wrenn shook his head, moving more slowly up the stairs of the building they'd entered, as if it hurt to climb on that ankle.

Nobody lived in the house at the moment, he explained, because it had belonged to his grandfather who died early in the summer. His mother was the old man's only relative and natural heir, but there was some technicality about the deed. Soon as that was straightened out, the house would be sold. In the meantime, Wrenn used it as a crash pad when he wanted to get away from school.

"Wait a minute, though," he said as they pulled up at the doorway of his next class. "There's a nosy old lady lives next door. I think she might've still been out on her porch when I got home."

He gave them her name and address; then the bell rang again and he stepped inside the classroom just as the professor came over to close the door.

The pimply faced teenager minding the desk at the Colleton U-Stor didn't remember Brazos Hartley even though he'd taken the bid on two lockers on the thirty-first of August. He was pretty sure that no one had been around about a locker belonging to a Leonard Angelopolus but Caroline Sholten? He couldn't swear he'd ever met her, but he certainly recalled Mrs. Sholten's angry middle-aged daughter.

"You know how kids used to say 'Your mama wears army boots'?" He giggled. "Well, this lady really did. I mean, she was *huge*. She had on these lace-up boots like a Marine or a paratrooper, and shorts that looked like bib overalls with the pant legs cut off, y'know? And *her* legs were like tree stumps. Man, she was one tough mama! And going on and on about how it was her furniture and her mother meant for her to have it. I told her if her mother wanted to keep the stuff, she shoulda paid the rent before it got auctioned off. I mean, we sent out the letter, advertised in the *Ledger*. Posted a notice at the courthouse. It was a legal sale."

"Did you tell her who'd bought it?" asked Mayleen Richards.

"Yep. Gave her his phone number and e-mail and told her she'd have to find him before he sold it."

"Did she leave her own name or address?"

The kid shook his head.

"What about the owner's address?"

He looked at her as if her deck had a few missing cards. "Well, yeah, but she's dead, remember?"

No point in reminding him that even old ladies have friends and neighbors. "Just give me the address."

It was only a couple of miles away, a fifties-type brick

ranch with empty windows and an air of expectant neglect. The foundation plantings had overgrown their allotted spaces and all the trimwork was in sore need of paint, but help was probably on the way if the real estate agent's sign in the weedy front yard was any indication. It had a new red SOLD! sticker across it. She took down the agent's number just in case no one else could help, then knocked on the door of the house across the road.

"Coming, coming, coming!" called a cheerful, if somewhat trembly, voice and the door was eventually opened by a very old, very frail white woman encumbered by an aluminum walker. She seemed delighted to find a female deputy in full uniform on her front porch. Smiling as Richards introduced herself, she invited the younger woman to come in. "I'm Liz. Liz Collins. Isn't it just wonderful all that we can be and do these days? I'd give anything if I'd been born fifty years later. Not that I didn't have an interesting time of it"—her gnarled hand gestured to a wall of framed photographs beside the door—"but these days I could have maybe made it into space."

Mayleen Richards glanced perfunctorily at the photographs, did a double take, then looked more closely at the young woman in the cockpit of a plane, surrounded by other women in flying gear, getting a medal pinned to her jacket by a general, sitting on the wing of an airplane. "You were a pilot? Which war is this?"

"WW Two," she said proudly. "I was one of the women that ferried planes from the assembly lines over to Europe. They wouldn't let us join the Air Force or fly combat missions, but at least we got to do that much."

From the next room came another cracked and trembly voice. "May I get you some tea?"

"No, thank you," Richards said. She turned, expecting to see another elderly person in the doorway, but no one was there.

"That's only Billy, my cockatiel." The woman laughed and seated herself in a high rocking chair, the seat of which was made even higher by a thick cushion so that she didn't have far to lower herself. "Please make yourself comfortable, Deputy Richards, and are you sure I can't get you some tea?"

"Some tea?" the bird asked again.

Richards smiled. "No, ma'am, thank you."

She explained the reason for her visit and Mrs. Collins nodded immediately.

"Carrie Sholten. Lovely woman. We were neighbors more than thirty years. Her husband died about eighteen months ago and her daughter wanted her to come live near her in Atlanta. Carrie wasn't exactly sure about making it permanent, so she rented the house to his cousin and put her best pieces of furniture in storage while she looked for an apartment. But then, before she could find one, she fell and broke her hip and bless her heart, she never came home from the hospital."

"What about her daughter?"

"Janice? Yes, she came up last month to put the house on the market and get Carrie's things, but that shiftless cousin that was supposed to forward her mail never passed on the letter from the storage place that she was behind on her rent, so they sold everything at auction. Janice was mad as fire over that, but it was all legal.

Nothing she could do about it. She did go find the high bidder and bought back some of the pieces."

"Do you have an address or phone number for her?" Richards asked.

"Oh yes." A telephone and a large businesslike Rolodex stood on the table beside her chair. Mrs. Collins spun the round knob until she found the card she wanted. "Janice Radakovich. She's a civil engineer with the highway department down there in Georgia. Builds roads and bridges. Isn't that wonderful? You young women today!"

&

About the time Deputy Richards was checking out the E-Z-Quik Mail and McLamb and Jamison were winding up their interview with Lamarr Wrenn, Dwight Bryant was ready to walk through the outbuildings at the old Hatcher place with Tally Ames. Not that he'd known the name given to the farm by local residents in this part of the county. All he knew was that Mrs. Ames had said it belonged to her grandparents and now to her.

"They were Hatchers? You any kin to Beth Hatcher over near Clayton?"

When she said no, he gave up trying to find a personal link.

Arnold Ames and their son Val were back in Dobbs, working on the innards of a motor that turned one of the kiddie rides and hoping to get it back in operation by opening time this evening, which is why it was Mrs. Ames who led him out from the carnival. He had offered to bring her in his car, but she had declined.

"Fish's loading the truck with the rest of the stuff Braz

bought so we can store it out there, and then I have to go over to the funeral home, okay? They released his body yesterday."

"You're burying him here?" For some reason, that surprised him. "I was thinking you'd want to take him back to Florida."

"No, we decided to do it here," she said, giving him an odd sidelong glance. She started to say something, then changed her mind.

She had parked the truck over by one of the sheds and the employee they called Fish was already undoing the tarp they'd tied over the load. There was a flash of bright colors inside their plastic covering as he let down the tailgate and rolled off the rack of lingerie Dwight had seen when the van was searched on Saturday. Mayleen Richards had interviewed the guy and reported that he'd spent Friday evening in front of the dunk tank, taking money from the customers who lined up to throw baseballs at the target that would trip a spring and dump their Bozo in the water. Dwight remembered the Bozo, who'd had such an insulting mouth on him that Colleton County youths were elbowing each other aside to pay for the privilege of drowning him, but he didn't remember this Fish.

"Nice enough guy," Mayleen had said. "Borderline retarded, though. Not bright enough to lie."

Mrs. Ames got out of the truck clutching a handful of keys. She wore jeans and work shoes. Her dark hair was pulled back from her face today and tied at the nape with a red scarf.

Since getting the ME's report, Dwight found himself conscious of footwear around the carnival. Not that he really thought Mrs. Ames had stomped her son. All the same, he gave her shoes a close look. These were buff colored with equally light gum soles. They were scuffed and dusty as if they hadn't been cleaned in some time, but no apparent stains. When she walked over to the barn doors, he noticed that the shoes left a crisp ripple pattern on the dirt path.

Fish's shoes were Nikes that had started out white but were now stained and dingy. The stains were either black, as from grease and oil, or were drips of crayon-bright enamels from helping to paint the rides. They, too, left distinct patterns on the dirt.

"Some woman from Georgia caught up with Braz a couple of weeks ago," said Mrs. Ames, unlocking the first shelter. "I didn't see her, but he said she was pretty mad about the locker place selling her mother's furniture."

"Was she mad at him?" asked Dwight.

"Well, she certainly wasn't happy having to buy back the things she particularly wanted. He sold her a table, some chairs, and a framed mirror and he told me he got enough from those four pieces to put him in the black for that particular locker. Braz liked to drive hard bargains."

She threw open the double doors, and Dwight saw a massive oak bedroom suite proportioned for a room with ten-foot ceilings.

"That came out of the same auction," said Tally Ames, "but nobody's called him about it. Over here's the rest of that woman's mother's things."

It looked like ordinary furniture to Dwight.

"Cheap veneers and beat-up postwar era," Mrs. Ames agreed, "but migrant workers will snap it up down in

Florida. Fish, you can slide that rack in behind the dresser here, okay?"

"Okay," he said cheerfully. He was early thirties, about five-nine, and well muscled with a heavy lower jaw and a bullet-shaped head made even more noticeable for being shaved smooth. Around his neck was a gold chain with a cross on it, and the cross banged his chin whenever he stooped to pick up something he'd dropped. Some of the filmy robes kept slipping off their hangers and he bent to retrieve them with a surprising delicacy of touch.

"They're real pretty, Tally. You ought to keep these for yourself."

"I don't think so," she told him with a smile. "Too fancy for me."

They left him to finish unloading the truck, and Mrs. Ames showed Dwight some of the things her husband had bought, including the tools that incited the Lincoln brothers to slash the Pot O'Gold slide.

They were headed for the far side of the compound toward a small shed that stood up on low rock pilings. "Braz's office," Mrs. Ames was saying when she broke off and quickened her step.

"Well, damn!" she exclaimed. "Somebody's pulled the lock off."

She was right. The lock was still closed tightly on the hasp, but the whole thing had been prized right off the door and now lay on the grass near an abandoned hammer. Inside was a shambles. A box of used books had been overturned and more loose papers fluttered off the old battered teacher's desk as a breeze from the open doorway blew in.

"What on earth were they looking for?" Tally Ames wondered aloud.

"Try not to touch anything," Dwight said, "but can you tell me if anything's missing?"

"God, how would I know?" she said tartly. "Braz called this his office, but mostly it was where he kept the books and papers and pictures he and Arnie unload from the lockers. Arnie used to toss them in the nearest Dumpster, okay? But Braz once found a fifty-dollar bill in one of the books. And he was watching a rerun of *Antiques Roadshow* the night they showed how sometimes old tintypes and letters could be worth a few hundred. After that, he got Arnie to give him any papers he was going to toss and he'd go through them. We used to tease him about him and his slow dollar. We thought the only thing he'd found was baby pictures and old income tax returns. Nothing worth even putting in a flea market, much less on eBay."

Dwight heard the "But" in her voice and saw the troubled look on her face.

"There was more?"

She nodded. "He was doing better than any of us ever realized. You gave us his wallet back Friday night, remember? Val was looking through it this morning. There was a little bankbook in the secret compartment. He opened a new account just last winter with a seventy-thousand deposit. We had no idea he had more than two or three thousand, okay? He must have found something really great in the books or papers and he never said a word to us, just sold it and hid the money. Like he was becoming a miser or something."

"You don't know what he found?"

"Whatever it was, he must've got it from Arnie and thought if he told, Arnie would want a cut. Like Arn's ever gone back on his word once he's made a deal."

By now, Fish had finished unloading the back of the truck and had wandered over with a manila envelope. "Here's more pictures Braz had from the new place," he said.

"Mind if I take a look?" Dwight asked as they stepped back outside.

"Keep them," she said. "He'd already looked through them. It's just pictures of the woman in her night things."

Dwight glanced inside and saw what were clearly amateur photos. Most were blurry and taken from such odd angles that her face wasn't clear in any of them. He closed the envelope and tucked it in his jacket pocket to look at later, then went back to his car for latex gloves and an instant camera.

"Why bother?" asked Mrs. Ames as he snapped pictures of the hasp, the hammer, and the condition of the shed. "There was nothing in here worth stealing."

"This your hammer?" asked Dwight as he lifted it by two fingers, being careful not to touch the handle.

"Naw," said Fish before she could answer. "Arnie's got all ours with him in the other truck."

While Dwight was bagging the hammer, Fish stuck his head in the doorway, looked around, and said, "Hey! What happened to all them pictures for the haunted house?"

"What?" said Tally Ames. She took another look. "Didn't Arnie put them in the other barn?"

Fish shook his head. "I stacked 'em right back there. All those skeletons and ghosts and people on fire."

"Now, who would steal junk like that?" Tally wondered.

"You're sure it was junk?" asked Dwight.

"Believe me, I'm sure," she said. "We're not talking old masters or even old primitives on oil and canvas, okay? This looked like some kids had been given a lot of left-over house paint and some old pieces of plywood to paint Halloween decorations on. That's it. There were about thirty-five of them, and Arnie and the boys were going to use them to decorate the outside of our haunted house. Braz thought it was all scrap lumber and old half-empty cans of paint when they opened up the locker and he put his flashlight on it. I think he got it for like thirty dollars and Arn gave him thirty-five for the lot since they'd be useful."

The main part of the compound had been neatly mowed, but weeds were high around the side and Dwight soon saw where two vehicles of some sort had recently driven in there and turned around. Ragweed and golden-rods had been snapped off or crushed down and were barely wilted.

"Any of your people park there?" he asked.

Both Mrs. Ames and Fish shook their heads.

"Who knows you have this place?"

"All our own people have been out here moving equipment in and out," she answered. "And some of the independents know about it. Braz told Skee, the guy runs the duck pond? His wife was like a grandmother to Braz. And Skee probably told the world if it sat still long enough."

Dwight laid a ruler across the tire tracks and took care-ful pictures, but he knew he was just going through the motions. The tracks appeared to be the width of standard tires, the weeds hadn't held any tread marks, and if there had been shoe prints in the dirt immediately in front of the wooden steps, their own shoes had obliterated them.

🦆

Bostrom's Bigfoot U-Store was out on the bypass at the edge of Dobbs, and Bob Bostrom himself was standing in the doorway when Deputy Mayleen Richards got out of her patrol car. He was about her height, of slender build, with brown hair and brown eyes that were wary at first.

"Your feet don't look very big to me," she said in greeting.

The wary look disappeared and he laughed. "That was my dad. Size thirteen triple E. I got my momma's feet, thank goodness. What can I do for you, Officer?"

When she explained and showed him the receipt he'd given Braz Hartley a couple of weeks ago, he led her into his small office and pulled out a file drawer. No computers here.

"Oh, yeah," he said. "Now I remember. Young black guy showed up here wanting his granddaddy's stuff back."

He described the man's outrage in a vivid, almost word-for-word reenactment for her.

"He said, 'Gibsonton, Florida? This white bastard trucked my granddaddy's pictures to Florida? How you got the right to let him do that?'

"I told him, 'The state of North Carolina gave me that right when your granddaddy let the rent run out on his locker and the certified letter I sent him came back.'

" 'But he *died*!'

"I told him even dead people got debts, debts him and his family ought to've paid, and you shoulda seen him puff up at that," Bostrom told Richards. "He was a lot bigger'n me, but I just started cleaning my nails with my pocketknife here"—as if by magic, a wicked-looking switchblade appeared in his hands—"and he climbed back down. I told him to chill. He didn't have to go all the way to Florida. The buyer was with a carnival right here in North Carolina. Ames Amusement."

"So was his grandfather an artist or something?" asked Richards.

"You'd think he was Rembrandt to hear that guy run on about it, but the old man used to come over here and paint right out there in his locker. All the stuff I ever saw looked like the pictures my wife Jane puts on our refrigerator from our grandbabies."

Bostrom showed her the deceased artist's address. It was just over in Darkside, less than a quarter mile away.

CHAPTER
14

DEBORAH KNOTT
MIDDAY MONDAY

When I got back after lunch, I found April waiting impatiently by the rear door of my courtroom. She looked like a teacher again. Her brown curls were tidy, makeup tamed her freckles, and she wore a crisply pressed beige cotton jumper over a short-sleeved white shirt.

"Dwight's taken her out to her place in the country," she said as soon as I got close enough to hear her above passing clerks and several attorneys with their clients, "and her husband didn't know when they'd be back. I called home and Andrew's sober for the moment, so I'm going to go on now and talk to him before I pick up the children when they get out of school." Her voice dropped. "I don't want Ruth and A.K. hearing about this from their cousins. What I need for you to do is go out there when you're through with court this evening and tell her that we'll all be there for the service tomorrow. Minnie and Isabel and Doris and Mae are going to fix lunch and you know them. There'll be enough to feed anybody she wants to come. I expect she'll want her own friends to be there, so you be sure and tell her that, all right?"

"Okay," I said, but I was talking to the air. She was already halfway down the hall and nearly collided with my cousin Reid, who held the door open for her.

He gave me a half-embarrassed grin as our eyes met and he saw my eyebrow arch.

"I see you heard," he said as he came up to me.

Despite what had happened with Dwight and me last night, his behavior Friday night wasn't very commendable.

"Pretty shabby, Reid," I told him. "Even for you."

"What do you mean, even for me?"

"You know perfectly well what I mean. Dwight's your friend."

"Well, hell, Deborah, he's had since June to take it up the next level."

"Take it up, or take Sylvia Clayton down?" I asked snidely.

"That relationship was going nowhere," he assured me.

I gave him a jaundiced look. "And this one is?"

"Aren't you late for court?" he countered, holding open the door so that I automatically entered the courtroom without thinking.

Equally automatically, the bailiff jumped to his feet and said, "All rise!" and there was nothing I could do except take my seat on the bench.

Smirking, Reid sat down as everyone else sat, too, and the clerk handed me a sheet with three add-ons. Janice

Needham was clerking for me today, but her chair was far enough away from mine that I was out of reach of her compulsive fingers. Once I forgot, though, and handed her a form that put the sleeve of my robe within range. She immediately picked off a piece of lint.

"Wasn't it awful about what happened at the carnival Friday night?" she whispered to me while we waited for the DA to confer with one of the defendants and her lawyer. "He seemed like such a nice young man. For a carnival worker, I mean."

"Nice" wasn't the description I'd heard used by any-one except perhaps his mother.

"You met him?"

"Well, not really. But Bradley started talking to him when he got change and then while I was playing, they talked back and forth about what it was like to travel with a carnival and what he did during the winter months. From what he told Bradley, I think he was planning to leave the carnival soon and go into the antique business. I won back three of my quarters and a real cute little bracelet, see?"

She held out her wrist. It was encircled by a tennis bracelet set with pink glass stones. Probably retailed for a dollar ninety-eight at one of those teenybopper stores at the mall. I didn't ask her how many quarters it'd cost her. Besides, it did match her pink blouse and pink headband.

"Pretty," I said, and turned my attention to the grand-mother who took the stand to explain to me woman-to-woman why it was cruel to keep a tired child belted in a car seat when all that precious little thing wanted to do was stretch out across the backseat and go to sleep in comfort.

I asked her if she'd ever seen what a precious little thing looked like after being thrown from a car when it flipped off the road doing sixty miles an hour, then gave her the stiffest fine I could and told the DA to call his next case.

At the afternoon break, I went down to the sheriff's department in the courthouse basement. When I tapped on the open door of Dwight's office, he was half sitting, half leaning on the front of his desk talking to three of his deputies. His face lit up. "Well, speak of the devil! McLamb here was just about to go find a judge to get a signature on this search warrant."

"What do you want to search?" I asked, skimming through the form McLamb handed me.

"Lamarr Wrenn's grandfather's house," McLamb said. "Based on our investigations today, we think it probably contains property belonging to the Hartley guy that was killed Friday night, property that was stolen from a locked storage shed Mrs. Ames owns."

"Really? What sort of property?"

"Some boards that his grandfather painted pictures on."

"Pictures?"

"Halloween things. Skeletons and ghosts and—"

I looked up at Dwight suspiciously. "You serious? Didn't you say they only paid about twenty-five or thirty dollars for those boards? And that they were only going to use them to decorate the exterior of their haunted house?"

"Theft is theft," he said virtuously. "Breaking and entering."

I finished looking over the document. Everything

seemed in order so I signed and dated it, even though it looked like a lot of trouble for a bunch of worthless wood.

Jamison and McLamb left with the search warrant and Richards said she was going to get on the phone and call Atlanta. "See if I can verify the whereabouts of that Radakovich woman on Friday night."

As she left, I closed Dwight's door. "Talk to you a minute?"

"Sure." His jacket hung on the back of his chair and the collar of his blue shirt was unbuttoned with the red tie loosely knotted. He folded his arms across his chest and remained where he was, leaning against the edge of the desk, motionless, as if bracing himself for something bad. "What's up?"

I checked my watch. "I need to be back upstairs in four minutes, so just listen, will you? We can talk about this more after I adjourn this evening."

"You've changed your mind," he said flatly.

"About us? No, why? You having second thoughts?"

He shook his head. I hadn't realized how tense he was till I saw his jaw unclench and his arms relax, but I didn't have time to ask him what was wrong. Dwight's always saying I don't tell him things, and I didn't want him to hear about Tally first from one of my brothers or their wives.

"Look, I couldn't say anything to you about this till I'd talked to Daddy and Andrew and Andrew'd talked to April, only he pulled a drunk this weekend and didn't, so I had to tell her myself this morning."

"Hey, whoa, slow down, shug. Tell her what?"

"Just listen!" I said impatiently. "Remember how Andrew got a Hatcher girl pregnant when he was seventeen and her father made them get married and then she ran off after the baby was born?"

"Oh, yeah, I do sort of remember hearing about that somewhere along the way, but I was still a little kid and it—"

"Dwight!"

"Sorry. So?"

"So Tallahassee Ames is that baby. She's Andrew's daughter. My niece. They're going to bury Braz Hartley out at the homeplace tomorrow morning, and I've got to run."

As I hurried down the hall to the elevator, Dwight called after me, "Come on back when you finish court, hear?"

I'd hoped to adjourn early, but it was after five-thirty before I signed the very last order of the very last case on my calendar and called it a day. I'd already told Roger Longmire, our chief district court judge, that I was taking a half day of personal leave tomorrow, and I didn't want anything on today's docket to have to be carried over because of me.

When I got back down to Dwight's office, the door was closed, but I could hear belligerent voices from inside. A woman's shrill voice floated above angry male tones and both were followed by Dwight's calm bass rumble.

Sheriff Bo Poole's door was open down the hall, so I poked my head in. "What's going on, Bo?"

"You signed the search warrant," he said. "You tell me."

"You mean they really found those stolen boards?"

Before he could answer, Dwight's door opened and I glanced back over my shoulder to see a hugely smiling Lamarr Wrenn step out into the hallway. He wore a Shaw sweatshirt with the sleeves cut out, shorts, and sandals. His right ankle was taped with an elastic bandage. One big arm was around a middle-aged woman in a blue suit who scowled up at him, the other hand carried one of those crudely painted scraps of plywood. The woman was clearly his mother. She was giving him a come-to-Jesus lecture about the evils of theft, and what'd he want with those weird old pictures anyhow, and don't think for one minute she wasn't going to take every penny out of his hide, but he just kept smiling and hugging her as they went on down the hall.

The white man who followed them more slowly was also smiling as he put a slip of paper in his wallet. It was Arnold Ames.

"Thanks for your understanding," Dwight said. "I really appreciate it."

"No problem," said Ames. "A quick dime's better than a slow dollar any day of the week, far as I'm concerned, and this way everybody gets what they want, right?" He shook Dwight's hand. "Good doing business with you, Major Bryant."

"What was all that about?" Bo asked when Ames was gone.

"I'll try to have the full report for you tomorrow," Dwight said from his doorway, "but basically, it's about why Lamarr Wrenn really punched out Friday night's homicide."

"He's not the perp?" asked Bo.

"I don't see how he could be," said Dwight. "The next-door neighbor confirms the time he says he got there. She also says he was wearing sneakers, and whoever stomped Hartley was wearing hard-soled shoes."

"But the Halloween pictures?" I asked.

"Not Halloween," he told us. "Bascom Wrenn, Ms. Wrenn's daddy, got religion big time about five or six years ago and started painting these strange pictures of the Last Judgment—the eye of God, the dead rising from their graves, souls in hell. Lamarr thought they were great, which was news to Ms. Wrenn. She was under the impression that they embarrassed the hell out of both of them. In fact, she was so sure the pictures were evidence that Mr. Wrenn was getting cracked and senile that he used his little pension to stick them in a self-storage unit out on the bypass to keep her from seeing them and he'd go over there to paint."

I laughed. "The storage locker was his studio?"

"Yep. So when he died, nobody knew about the locker and the rent lapsed. Bostrom, the guy who owns the facility, jumped through all the legal hoops—sent a certified letter to his home, posted it here in the courthouse, notice in the *Ledger*, the whole works. Ms. Wrenn says if a letter was forwarded, she doesn't remember signing for one. The sale went forward and Braz Hartley bought the contents of the locker for thirty bucks. Old cans of paint and those hellfire and damnation pictures. His stepfather saw a use for the pictures and gave him thirty-five for the lot."

"Where does Lamarr come in?" I asked.

"After the funeral, when he realized his granddad's

pictures weren't in the house, he went looking them, learned about the locker, then found out that he was too late. Hartley had bought them. That's what the fight was about. Lamarr Wrenn accused him of stealing the pictures and asked for them back."

"I'm guessing he didn't say 'pretty please,' either," I murmured.

"Right. So on Sunday afternoon, he and some friends drove out to the property Mrs. Ames owns over near Widdington, broke into the storage shed where the pictures were, and brought them back to Dobbs, where Jamison and McLamb found them when they searched the house this afternoon."

I didn't like the sound of that "he and some friends." Stevie and Eric? "But what was all that in your office just now?" I asked, hastily moving on from that topic.

"We got Ms. Wrenn and her son over from Raleigh and asked Mr. Ames to come in, too, to see if we couldn't work something out. Like you said, Deb'rah, the theft would probably have been treated like a misdemeanor, even with the breaking and entering, if that's what they actually did. Ms. Wrenn offered him a check for three hundred and fifty if he'd return the pictures and not press charges, and you saw how happy he was to do it."

"Three-fifty on a thirty-five-dollar investment?" Bo laughed. "Wish my retirement fund earned returns like that."

Still chuckling, he switched off his office light, told us to have a good evening, and left.

I looked up at Dwight. "Stevie and Eric were the friends who helped Lamarr steal back the pictures, weren't they?"

"Well, now, shug, I never got around to asking him who his accomplices were, and he didn't volunteer to tell me."

"Thanks," I said softly.

He brushed it off. "Anyhow, if he's telling the truth, the DA would have given him a break because the door was already open. He says that someone else drove up while they were trying to decide whether to pop the lock. They stayed hidden behind the shed till they heard whoever it was rip the lock off the door and realized it was another thief. Wrenn says they were going to rush the guy, but then he twisted his ankle and the guy got away before they could even see who it was."

"The idiots!" I fumed. "What if he'd had a gun?"

"What if he was a she?"

"A woman?"

"All they saw was from the legs down. Jeans and dirty sneakers."

He didn't have to spell it out. I see too many women charged with the whole range of crimes to think that men have a monopoly.

"You're thinking Polly Viscardi? She wears work shoes, though. Work shoes with bright pink laces."

"Now don't you reckon whoever did it has ditched whatever shoes they had on at the time? They'd be pretty bloody."

I thought about it and agreed he had a point.

"So tell me about Miz Ames being Andrew's daughter," Dwight said. "And what's with Andrew?"

"You off duty now?" I asked.

He nodded, leaned across his desk, and hooked his jacket off the back of the chair with one finger.

"Then come ride over to the carnival with me and we'll talk on the way."

By the time we got out to the festival grounds, I'd told him all I knew about Tally and how Andrew and April had reacted to the news. In return, he told me about the unexpectedly big bank account that Braz had secretly squirreled away and how hurt Tally had seemed over the discovery. He also shared what Mayleen Richards had learned while backtracking on Braz's storage-locker buys. There was a Georgia woman who'd bought back some of her mother's furniture, which would seem to do away with any motive. Besides, Mayleen had talked to a couple of people down there in the transportation department who had gone out to dinner with the woman in Atlanta Friday evening.

The owner of the other furniture buy, a massive set of oak bedroom furniture, had been located as well.

"It was part of his ex-wife's divorce settlement, but after they sold the house, she didn't have any place to put it, so he stored it for her, paid the first three months' rent and after that, forwarded all the notices on to her. Mayleen said he sounded sorta happy it'd been forfeited. Said he never had a good night's sleep on that bed from the minute she bought it."

That left the negligees as the only other buy in North Carolina.

"And it looks like your guess that she was keeping it secret from her husband might be on the money," Dwight told me as I pulled into the parking lot beside the Agricultural Hall. "She sent a brother to try to save the stuff, not her husband. And she seems to have let it drop rather than making an issue out of it that might get back to him."

"She had the locker six years? That's some affair," I said. "Sounds like a divorce would've been easier."

"What would be easier is if you'd get a bigger car," he said in exasperation, untangling himself from the seat belt.

Even with the seat pushed back as far as it would go, Dwight has trouble getting his long legs in and out of my Firebird and he mouths off about it every time he rides with me. (There's a reason so many law officers favor Crown Victorias and pickup trucks. Most of those men are as big as Dwight.)

Although the sun had set, it wasn't completely dark yet, but the carnival was in full swing. Toe-tapping country-western music poured from the loudspeakers. The Ferris wheel was turning and the Tilt-A-Whirl held shrieking teenagers, but there seemed fewer people on the midway than on Friday night. It was still early, though.

I didn't recognize the young woman working the Guesser, at the front of the midway. We watched while she guessed a little girl's weight and was off by four pounds. "You must have hollow bones, honey. Pick yourself a bear."

The child happily chose a green one, which her dad clipped to the belt loop on her jeans; then she scampered away toward the Ferris wheel.

"Guess your age, guess your weight," the woman began when I approached her.

"Sorry," I said. "I'm looking for Tally Ames. Do you know if she's working this evening?"

"At the Dozer," she answered, already losing interest in me and gazing past my shoulder to catch the eyes of the people entering behind us.

Almost immediately, we ran into the carnival's patch, Dennis Koffer. He didn't recognize me from Friday night, but he had a smile for Dwight. "How's it going, Major? You here tonight on business or pleasure?"

"Some of both." He shook hands and turned to me. "Have you met Judge Knott?"

"Judge, it's a pleasure," Koffer said, offering his hand.

Nothing changed in his manner that I could pinpoint, yet when he heard my name, I sensed that he recognized it and knew my relationship with Tally.

"Anything you can tell me about your investigation?" he asked Dwight, relighting the cigar that seemed permanently attached to the corner of his mouth. "I mean, anything besides what Arnie told me about the kid that punched Braz out?"

"Nothing yet," Dwight said. "I may need your help tomorrow. We're going to come back and interview everybody again. See if anyone's remembered something useful."

"Sure. You've got my pager number. Just give me a buzz." At that moment, almost on cue, the pager went off. After glancing at the number displayed, he said, "Y'all enjoy yourselves tonight," and hurried back the way he'd come, trailing a cloud of fragrant cigar smoke.

I noticed Dwight noticing Koffer's sturdy leather shoes as the man walked away and I punched his arm hard. "I thought you were off duty."

"I am." All the same, he looked closely at the place where Koffer had stood. The ground had been trampled into dust and we saw that his shoes had left little triangles across the instep and heel.

We walked on down the busy midway, occasionally bumping into people we knew, though most were strangers. Invitations came thick and fast from the colorfully lit game stands to come on over and try our luck, test our skills, step right up and have a little fun.

"You gonna win me a stuffed animal to guard my bedroom door?" I teased.

He shot me a sidelong glance and his lips twitched. "Never noticed that you needed one," he said dryly.

That was so like the old Dwight that I laughed in relief and linked my arm through his.

"What?" he said.

"I really was afraid things might change between us," I confessed. "But you were right. They haven't, have they?"

"Well, one thing's changed," he drawled. "Or weren't you paying attention last night?"

"Oh, I was paying attention."

The tingle was suddenly back and I could have jumped his bones right there. (It really had been a long dry summer.)

"I even took notes," I added demurely.

As if reading my mind, he said, "How about we deliver April's message and get out of here?"

We drew near Tally's Dozer, and remembering the errand I was on made my thoughts take a more serious turn.

At first, I thought the game was unattended because I couldn't see anyone looking out over the top. We went around to the door flap and I opened it to peer inside. "Tally?"

She was seated on a low stool at the rear of the space, leafing through a magazine. "Oh, hey, Deborah! When did you get here?"

She rose and came out to join us.

"You know Major Bryant, of course."

"Oh yes." Her smile was so like Andrew's, I wanted to go right over to his house and throw him back under that cold shower. Anything to bring him to his senses.

"Arnie told me how it all came out this evening. The kid that stole back his grandfather's pictures? And the mother paid three-fifty to get them back? She must've really loved her father."

"More like she loved her son and was glad you and your husband weren't pressing charges," I told her.

She gave a sad shrug. "Kids do crazy things sometimes."

I put out my hand to her. "Tally, April came to see you this morning while you were out at your place with Dwight here."

"Oh?"

"She wanted to meet you and tell you to be sure to invite as many of your friends tomorrow as you like. She and some of my sisters-in-law—your aunts—will be serving lunch after the service, and they don't know how to fix for less than an army."

That got a small smile. She started to speak when the booth on the far side of the Dozer suddenly exploded with flashing strobe lights and ear-piercing sirens that seemed to go on for a full ninety seconds. Everyone stopped in their tracks and turned to watch as the winner of the Bowler Roller stepped up to claim his prize.

"Thank God that only happens about two or three

times a night," said Tally when the lights and siren finally cut off. "Flash is one thing, but that damn siren's a killer."

"Pulls them in, though, doesn't it?" I said, watching young men line up to try their luck at setting the bells and whistles off again.

"That's the whole point," Tally said with a resigned shrug.

One of her customers called for change, another was ready to cash in her prize chips. While we waited for her to come back, I glanced around the end of the tent where little children were splashing their hands in the water, trying for prizes at the duck pond. Across the way, a teenager was demonstrating to potential customers how easy it was to climb the rope ladder to reach the prizes at the top.

From the other side of the Dozer tent came the entrancing odor of fried dough sprinkled with sugar and cinnamon. I was ready to follow my nose when Tally returned. Someone else immediately claimed her attention, though.

"Hey, Tal?"

A rough-looking man, late forties probably, with bloodshot eyes, full tattoos on both arms, and a day's growth of whiskers leaned wearily against the end of the Dozer.

"Sam? When did you get in?" Tally said. "Did you get them?"

"Yeah, Arnie's there. You seen Polly? How come she didn't open up tonight?"

Dwight and I followed their eyes across the crowd to where Polly's Plate Pitch was still dark and shuttered.

"She ain't in the trailer and the girls say they ain't seen her all day, neither."

Tally shook her head. "I don't know, Sam. It's been so crazy here. You want to go ahead and open it up for me?"

"I'll open it, but I can't work it. I missed some of the road markers coming in and got turned around, wasted an hour. I gotta go get some sleep, Tal. I nearly run off the road just before I got here."

"That's okay, I'll find somebody. Here, Deborah," she said, untying her money apron and handing it to me. "Mind the Dozer for me a minute? Make change? If anybody wants to cash in for a prize, ask them to wait or come back later, okay?"

"Hey, wait!" I called. "I don't think—"

Too late. She had disappeared into the crowd, leaving me holding the bag in the shape of a money apron.

"I don't think this is something appropriate for a judge to be doing," I told Dwight, who just shook his head in amusement.

"Don't look at me, shug. If it's bad for a judge, think about a deputy sheriff."

"Oh, well. She'll probably be back before anybody wants anything."

We stood there by the Dozer and watched as the man went over, pulled some keys from his pocket, and began unlocking the flaps. One part folded down to reveal the words POLLY'S PLATE PITCH in bright red letters. The other part folded up and locked into place. It was lined with small multicolored lights that began chasing themselves as soon as he flipped a switch. Stacks of shiny plates in all colors and sizes gleamed beneath the lights. The game is a simple one: You just toss a quarter onto any plate. If it stays in the plate, then you could win one of the large stuffed animals dangling from a rod in the back. After surfing some of the carnival sites on the web yesterday morning, I had learned that the harder it is to win, the bigger and nicer the prizes.

Skee Matusik's Lucky Ducky next door was a play-till-you-win with every player a winner. His prizes probably cost him a dime at the most. Same with the balloon race across from him. But the Bowler Roller, Polly's Plate Pitch, and the rope climb next to it all had big prizes, so I knew they had to be a lot harder than they looked.

"Change, please!" someone called from the Dozer, and I stepped up into the well of the wagon, took the woman's two dollar bills, and handed back eight quarters from Tally's money apron.

It was fascinating to stand back here and watch quarters tumble over the side spills into the baskets beneath each station. I had a vague idea that the Harvest Festival Committee was supposed to get a percentage of the carnival's take, but how was it decided? The honor system? I found myself thinking about cash-only businesses and the IRS. No paper trails here. How would the government go about guessing how much money the games on this lot took in? 'Course that line of logic's what got my daddy into trouble with the IRS all those years ago. He was never convicted for making or distributing white lightning. No, his conviction was for income tax evasion.

"I'm ready to cash in," said a man's pompous voice from the other side, a voice I recognized at once.

Reluctantly, I looked over the countertop and saw a

startled Paul Archdale, the attorney who'd probably be running for my seat in the next election.

"*Judge?* Judge Knott?" Disbelief and disapproval were in his eyes. "What on earth are you doing in there?"

"Research," I said blandly. "I thought I ought to see what goes on behind the scenes at a carnival so I can better understand why some of our rowdier citizens flip out. What about you?"

"Supporting the festival," he said with returning righteousness.

He tried to hand me the poker chips he'd collected. I knew there was a system for equating chips with prizes, but I didn't have a clue what it was.

"My goodness," I told Paul. "You *have* supported the festival here tonight if you've played long enough to get that many chips."

He flushed and muttered something about getting lucky.

"I'm afraid you'll have to come back in about ten minutes when the owner's here," I said. "I have no idea how the prizes work."

Archdale huffed away impatiently.

Dwight was leaning against the end of the Dozer with a broad grin on his face. "Research?"

I shrugged. "All I could think of."

Across the way, the man Tally called Sam finished opening the booth just as Tally reappeared with a young woman who didn't look much older than sixteen or seventeen.

We saw her giving the girl last-minute instructions, then the man left them with a weary wave of his hand and headed toward the trailer area. The girl stepped into the booth and smiled at the people who had immediately paused to play the simple-looking game.

Tally started back through the throng to join us. Before she'd gotten halfway to us, though, screams pierced the air. Even the music pulsing through the loudspeakers was no match for the girl's terror. Plates went crashing as she stumbled from the booth, wide-eyed and gibbering and pointing to the huge stuffed pandas and Sesame Street characters hanging at the back.

Dwight rushed over and I followed.

There among the prizes hung the body of a woman with bright red hair.

Polly Viscardi.

CHAPTER
15

It was a repeat of Friday night, only this time it was me, not Sylvia Clayton, that Dwight was telling he'd see the next day. Unlike Sylvia, though, I didn't split right away.

The carnival was immediately closed down, of course, much to Paul Archdale's dismay. As soon as the announcement came over the loudspeakers asking people to please clear the lot, he marched straight up to me and demanded his prize.

"Prize?" I was outraged. "Paul, someone's just been killed here."

"Yeah, and I'm real sorry about that," he said stubbornly, "but I dropped thirty-seven dollars on this game and I'm not leaving without my prize."

"How many chips you got, Mister?" Tally said from inside the Dozer. "Four? Okay, here you go."

From the prize rack over her head, she unclipped a bubble pack that held a bright yellow-and-black submersible flashlight that looked like a knockoff of a name brand.

As he walked away somewhat mollified, I muttered, "And may he use it to illuminate a place where the sun don't shine."

Tally shot me a startled glance and gave an involuntary giggle. "And here I thought you were from the high-class side of the family."

"Don't make any snap calls till you meet the rest of them," I said, and went around to the front to start folding down the sides for her.

All around us, the other game stands were being closed down, too, as uniforms took over the lot again, canvassing all the operators, asking if anyone had seen anything before Polly's body was discovered. Patrol cars with flashing red and blue lights had converged on the midway till the EMS truck could barely squeeze past. Instead of loudspeakers with music and handheld mikes with pitches, the night air crackled with radioed dispatches.

Down at the gate, a news van with a mobile transmitter had appeared and I saw someone from the Dobbs *Ledger.* I suspected that the media would be taking a second carnival death more seriously than the first time around.

The man from the Bowler Roller had finished shutting up quickly, and when he came over to help tie down the tent flaps, Tally introduced us. "Deborah, this is Windy Raines. Believe it or not, Windy, she's my aunt."

"Really? Now, how come I don't have any aunts like you?" he said, leering rakishly, a leer spoiled by the fact that he was missing a couple of teeth and was probably nearing sixty.

"Behave yourself," Tally warned. "Her boyfriend's that deputy sheriff over there."

I started to say Dwight wasn't my boyfriend, then remembered that well, yes, he was. It was going to take some getting used to.

Across the way, the crime-scene van was back. Yellow tape looped around the Plate Pitch and floodlights lit up the interior till the stacks of glassware blazed in the glare. Beyond the hood of a patrol car, I saw Dwight in the center of a knot of men, both uniforms and civilians. I recognized Arnold Ames, Dennis Koffer, Skee Matusik, and a couple of prominent men who were on the county's festival committee. A moment later, they were joined by an unfamiliar heavyset man who listened silently as Ames and Koffer appeared to be bringing him up to speed.

"Ralph Ferlanski," Tally told me. "The other owner. He owns the Ferris wheel and Tilt-A-Whirl and the swings."

"And the generators," Windy reminded her with a hint of bitterness in his tone.

"And the generators," she agreed equably, not letting herself get drawn into whatever problem he had with the other owner.

"God, this is bad as a hurricane," said Skee Matusik, who had evidently been invited to take himself away from the Plate Pitch area. "They're saying tomorrow may be dark, too."

"The hell you say!" Windy Raines exclaimed. "How they expect us to make our nut?"

"The teenagers'll be back for you guys," Matusik said

bitterly, "but I might as well go on and make the jump now. Nobody's gonna bring the kiddies out to a place where somebody's getting killed every time you turn around."

Tally's jaw tightened, and I looked down at the scrawny little man coldly. "In case you've forgotten, Tally's son is one of those people who got killed, and I'm sure he didn't lie down and die just so you could have a bad day. Any more than that poor woman over there."

"Oh, hey, Tal! I'm sorry. You know I didn't mean it like that. Polly and me, we might not've got along, but you know how much Irene and me loved Braz."

"It's okay," she said wearily.

"Lord, lordy," said Raines. "Polly gone, too. Midway's not gonna be the same without that redheaded spitfire keeping the ashes stirred."

We finished securing the Dozer and tying the tent flaps closed.

Thanks to Dwight, I found myself sneaking close looks at their footgear. Tonight all three wore those unisex leather work shoes with thick soles. Raines's were calf-high lumberjacks, laced with leather strings, while Tally's were regular low-tops laced with round cords. Matusik's were ankle-high with regular brown laces that stopped two holes short of the top pair. His and Tally's shoes left ridge patterns in the dirt, but Raines's were so old that if they'd ever had a tread, they were now too worn to show. On the other hand, they didn't seem to have been cleaned lately and the discolorations looked like normal dirt and grease to me. Certainly no huge blotches of dried blood on the dark brown leather to say they'd stomped a young man to death three nights ago.

Having finished with the Dozer, Tally moved on to the ears-and-floss wagon next door, but the two young women working there—Candy and Tasha—had everything under control, they said, and were almost finished. Both were teary over Polly's death.

"They bunked in together," Tally told me as I followed her down to their other grab wagon, the one that sold corn dogs and cold drinks. "Candy, Tasha, Eve, and Kay. Kay's the one found her. They bunk at one end of the trailer next to us, and Polly and Sam bunked at the other end. Polly's been like their den mother this time out."

We found the other grab wagon empty and abandoned. Tally wasn't surprised.

"Towners!" she muttered, swinging up into the wagon. "Eve and Kay were working this one alone because our regular cook's been stoned since Friday afternoon, but I had to pull Eve off yesterday to work the Guesser, so we hired someone local to help Kay. Then tonight when I pulled Kay off to cover for Polly, the new girl said she could handle it. Everything was all made. She would've had to keep moving, but really, there's nothing to it. Looks like she took off the minute we left, though."

She checked the money box beneath the counter. Empty. "Another no surprise," Tally said grimly.

The window counters and grill were a mess.

There was a bucket of clean soapy water under one of the counters. I hung my jacket on the outside knob, stepped up into the wagon, squeezed out the dishcloth, and got busy.

"What are you doing?" Tally asked. "You'll wreck your clothes."

"They're washable," I said, glad that I'd chosen to wear a cotton pantsuit and low shoes this morning.

"But you're a judge."

"So? I'm also a pair of hands, and you can use some help."

While she turned off the grease vat, stowed the food in a refrigerated chest under the counter, and moved stuff out of my way, I washed off everything that felt greasy or sticky. We made a good team. There's something about working together that lets down the roadblocks and fosters trust. Soon she was telling me about Polly Viscardi.

"We've known her for years, Arnie and me. She and Irene were good friends, too, but this is the first time she'd traveled with us. She was a player, all right."

"How do you mean?"

"You met her, didn't you?"

"Not really. We tossed a few quarters at her plates, but I can never get anything to stick, and then I saw her with you Friday night." I remembered bright red hair, the pink laces on her shoes, and that off-the-shoulder ruffled blouse as she flirted with the men in our party to encourage them to keep tossing quarters. "She seemed . . ." I tried to find the right words. "I don't know. She looked very feminine, but I felt she might be sort of hard underneath?"

"That was Polly, all right. She had an eye for anything in pants, but they didn't get in *her* pants unless she saw a use for them. Like poor old Sam. He was just a roughie at the beginning of the season and she was shacking with Mike, our cook. Then one day, boom! Mike was back in the bunkhouse and Sam was in her bed, okay? I don't think either of them knew what hit 'em."

"How did Mike take it?"

"You mean was he the one killed Polly?"

"Scorned lover? Jealousy?"

"Scorned and jealous, yeah. Do anything about it? Nah. Just kept getting stoned. Eve took it worse."

"Eve?"

"She's Mike's daughter. I don't think she was pissed at Polly so much for dumping her dad as because he quit pulling his full weight here and that made more work for her and Kay." She put the mustard jars in the ice chest. "And of course, Tasha was with Sam before Polly moved in on him."

"Really?" That fresh-faced kid I'd just met at the floss wagon and the road-worn Sam?

"Sam's got a great sense of humor," Tally said. "And he's dependable. You get to appreciate things like that when you're out here on the road."

"Who else didn't like Polly?"

"Well, you heard Skee. No love lost there. She didn't think he did all he could for Irene before she died and she got mad because Irene was barely in the ground good before he moved another woman into their doublewide, somebody who took him for almost everything he and Irene'd built up together. By the time that little possum belly queen did a rake 'em and scrape 'em on him, all he had left was his camper truck and his Lucky Ducky. And Polly wasn't above rubbing it in about what a jackass he'd been. Like some juicy young thing was going to love him for himself alone."

My nose wrinkled as I thought of the woman who could crawl in beside Skee Matusik's scrawny body or kiss that nearly toothless mouth. "Some men don't ever take a good look in the mirror. Don't you reckon she earned whatever she got from him?"

Tally sighed. "Maybe she did. But when I think how hard it was for Irene out here on the road with her bad heart and all, and then to have some little whore walk away with everything she'd worked for? I tell you, if it hadn't been for Braz, we wouldn't have let Skee book in with us this season. But Irene was good to him and he knew she'd feel bad if Skee went down the slop chutes, so he talked me into it."

"Anybody else have problems with Polly?" I asked.

She was silent for a moment and I didn't push it. Just kept scrubbing.

"Oh, well, hell, doesn't matter anymore, does it? Your deputy's probably snapped to it already. It was Braz, okay? They didn't get along worth a damn. And don't ask me why. I don't think it was over Skee, though, 'cause he used to razz Skee about that little bitch, too. Braz was another that thought women couldn't resist him. Maybe he came on to her and she slapped him down too hard? I didn't ask and they didn't bring it to Arn or me. Sometimes it's better not to know stuff when you're going to be living this close with somebody for the season."

She sighed. "Val and me, we went over and picked out his casket this afternoon. The last thing we'll ever do for him. Poor Braz. I should have made more time for him. Been a better mother."

All I could do was make consoling noises. There are never any easy words.

By now, the wagon was almost spotless. I rinsed out the dishcloth I'd been using, then went and dumped the bucket in the weeds behind a shuttered balloon-bust stand while Tally turned off the lights and closed down the flaps.

"Thanks," she said. "I really appreciate it."

"Hey, what's family for?" I said, draping my jacket around my shoulders.

She turned and looked at me steadily. "You're not just shitting me, are you? You really mean it."

"I mean it." I looked straight back into those blue eyes. "I made a promise almost twenty years ago that you would be part of our family if you ever wanted to be."

"To your mother?"

I nodded.

"Do you know, I only saw her that one time, but I still remember her as if it was last week. She was the nicest woman I'd ever met." She finished locking the wagon. "You don't know what it meant to me when she put that bracelet on my wrist and it was just like yours. I mean, you were her daughter, so sure, you'd have a pretty one. But mine was just as pretty and shiny. And that candy! No chocolates I've ever had since tasted as good as what she gave me that day."

"Till the day she died, she was sorry she didn't just put you in the car and bring you home with us," I said. "She went back a week later with Andrew, but you were gone."

Tally's face lit up. "Did she really? Because she promised she'd come back to see me, and when my mom came to take me away, I told her I couldn't go till Mama Sue came—that's what she told me to call her, okay? Soon as I said that, Mom slapped me and said I'd been played for a fool. That your mother never had any intention of coming back." She shrugged. "I always wondered."

"Oh, Tally," I said helplessly, my eyes misting over.

If Mother had followed her first instinct, Tally would still be Olivia and we would have grown up together like sisters. Life would have been so different for her. No baby at fifteen. College. A settled life instead of gypsying from town to town. Different for me, too, maybe. She would have been there for both of us when Mother was dying. And she was just enough older that she might have kept me between the ditches instead of taking it off road, straight through the underbrush.

We faced each other across that wide, wide river of might-have-beens and she gave me a wry smile.

"If wishes were horses," I sighed.

"Yeah," she said. "C'mon. I'll buy you a beer, okay?"

At her trailer, she pulled a couple of long necks from the refrigerator. "Want a glass?"

I shook my head and we went back outside. Her trailer and Polly's were at right angles with only a few feet between the back ends. Several lawn chairs were there between the two doors, which were about fifteen feet apart, and a charcoal grill stood off to the side. We could hear the murmur of girlish voices inside the other trailer, and Tally went over, stuck her head inside, and called, "You guys all right?"

I gathered that Kay was tearful still, but no longer hysterical.

"Where's Sam?" Tally asked.

The girl who'd been working the Guesser earlier in the evening—Eve, daughter of the spurned cook—came to the doorway. "He was so zonked that we thought maybe it was better not to wake him up. Just let him sleep. He doesn't need to see Polly like that anyhow."

She stepped out onto the grass and gave me a neutral nod as Tally introduced us. She had long dark hair that reached below her waist. At the Guesser earlier, she'd had it tied back. Now it fell like a dark lustrous veil across her shoulders and down her back.

"Candy and Tasha and Kay are in there really freaking," she told Tally. "First Braz and now Polly. What's happening here, Tal? Somebody picking us off one by one?"

"Of course not," Tally said briskly, pulling keys from her pocket. "Look, why don't you take the girls and go find a grocery store? Get some fresh fruits and salad greens?"

Eve frowned.

"They were saying earlier that they wanted to do laundry. Maybe you can find them a Laundromat?"

"Okay," said Eve. "I've got laundry, too. Might as well be doing that as sitting in there scaring ourselves to death."

She reached for the keys just as Deputy Mayleen Richards rounded the front of the trailer.

"Mrs. Ames? Can you tell me which trailer was Polly Viscardi's?"

"This one," Eve told her, pointing to the other trailer.

"And you're one of her roommates?"

"Yes, but we already told those other officers we didn't see anything."

The other three young women had come to the door by now. They ranged in age from late teens to very early twenties. All four of them wore sneakers, shorts, and T-shirts. With six people sharing one trailer, there couldn't be much space for extra clothes.

Richards took down their names, but when she asked to see Ms. Viscardi's quarters, they tried to talk her out of it.

"Her boyfriend's in there asleep," said Tasha protectively. She was a tall coltish girl, all arms and legs with a long face and small dark eyes. "He was driving all day and half of last night. He doesn't even know Polly's dead yet. Do you have to wake him right now?"

"It'll have to be done sooner or later," the deputy told her, "but I can start with you-all. Which of you saw Ms. Viscardi last?"

It turned out that they couldn't be sure. Certainly not today.

"She was already up and out by the time I woke up around nine-thirty," said Candy, who was probably the oldest, but also the smallest, maybe five-two with blond braids pinned up across the top of her head. "We thought she was still asleep, didn't we?"

The other girls nodded.

"Her door was closed," said Kay, the baby of the group, "but when I peeked in around noon, the room was empty."

"Had the bed been slept in?" Richards asked.

"We couldn't tell," said Candy. "Polly never made the bed except when she put fresh sheets on. But she didn't make coffee, either. Usually the first person up starts it. The pot was still sitting on the drain board when I got up."

"I didn't see her on the lot today," Tally said.

"What about last night, then?" said Richards.

"She was here." Tally gestured to a nearby lawn chair. "Sam had gone to pick up some plush and—"

"Plush?"

"Stuffed toys for prizes. We drew a bigger crowd this weekend than we expected so Sam drove down to Florida to bring back enough to keep us going through Kinston next week."

"I see."

"After we closed up last night, we sat out here and talked awhile."

"Who's we?"

"Me, the girls, Polly, my son Val, only he went to bed around twelve-thirty. My husband was already in by then, too. Windy Raines, Skee Matusik, and a couple of the independents came by for a beer. Windy and Skee left right before I went in around one. Polly was still here then, right, Eve?"

"We all turned in about then, but Polly said she wasn't sleepy yet. She was going to read awhile at the table."

"Yeah," said Tasha. "That's right. I remember waking up around four to go to the donniker and the light was still on out here and her magazine was turned down on the table. She'd left the door unlocked, too. Her door was closed, so I turned off the light and locked the door before I crawled back in my bunk."

"You were gone a long time," said Candy. "I needed to go, too, and I thought you were never going to come back."

"Sorry," Tasha said tightly. "You should've come and knocked. I took Polly's magazine in with me and I guess I lost track of the time."

"Who didn't like her?" Richards asked.

"Nobody," Eve said flatly, and the others murmured prompt agreement, closing ranks against the law.

"She was like a mother to us," said Kay, beginning to sniffle again.

"What about you, Mrs. Ames?"

"This was the first season she'd worked with us," Tally said. "Far as I know, she got along with everybody."

I took a swallow of my beer and kept my face completely blank. Tally was family now, wasn't she?

"How did she die?" Tally asked, going on the offensive.

"We're not sure yet if it was suicide or murder," the deputy said frankly.

"Suicide?" gasped Kay.

Richards nodded. "Does that seem unlikely to you?"

"Well . . . ," said Eve. "She *had* been a little quieter than usual, didn't you think?"

Candy nodded. "Like she had more on her mind than making her nut."

"I didn't notice," Kay said tearfully.

Tasha was skeptical. "Even if she was worried about something, she wouldn't off herself. She'd either stomp whoever was messing her over or get somebody else to do it."

Stomp was probably not her best choice of words given the work shoes that sturdy woman had worn, and I about strangled on my beer.

"You okay?" Richards asked when Tally had stopped slapping my back and I was able to quit coughing.

"Yeah, sorry," I said. "I must have swallowed wrong."

She turned back to her agenda. "Mrs. Ames, how did Ms. Viscardi and your son get along?"

"Val? Fine."

"No, I meant your other son. Brazos Hartley."

"The same, so far as I know. I don't think they had much to do with each other, okay?"

"She didn't have any reason to want him dead?"

"No, of course not! What are you saying?"

"Nothing. Just trying to see if there's a connection between your son's death and hers."

"If there is," Tally said stiffly, "I don't know what it could be."

The other four professed to have noticed no tension between Polly and Braz.

With that, Mayleen Richards said she was sorry, but she was going to have to take a look inside if that was all right with them. She and I both knew that she'd need a search warrant if they refused. But the trailer belonged to Tally and she offered no objections.

As it turned out, the girls' worries about bothering Sam weren't necessary. He slept right through Mayleen's search, even when the deputy lifted the mattress beneath him.

"Didn't even turn over," Kay marveled.

"Yeah, he could sleep through a tornado," said Tasha without thinking.

The others went silent for an instant, then started chattering like finches, but Richards didn't pick up on that slip of Tasha's tongue. She asked again if anyone had anything to add, and when they all shook their heads, she headed back to the Plate Pitch.

The girls took the keys to the truck and went off mournfully with duffel bags of dirty laundry and a shopping list from Tally.

"If I can just keep them from running off on me for three more weeks, we'll have our nut for the winter," Tally said, watching Eve maneuver the truck through the parking lot.

She offered me another beer, but I was still nursing my first one and passed. I hadn't eaten since my early lunch with Portland, which now seemed a million years ago. The moon was rising and another beer would put me right over it. But it was pleasant to sit here in the cool early fall night and listen to Tally talk about life in the carnival: on the road all summer, their winters in Gibsonton, Florida—Gibtown to its citizens—a town founded by a giant and a half woman, where everything was zoned Residential/Show Business instead of Residential/Agricultural as it was in our corner of Colleton County.

"What does that mean exactly?" I asked.

"Means you can have an elephant in your backyard if you want to."

I heard about January trade fairs where the latest thrill rides can sell for close to a million dollars or a pizza trailer with ovens and icemaker for a hundred thousand. I heard about buying goldfish wholesale for seven cents apiece, where to buy the best stuffed toys for the least amount of money, and why iguanas don't make such good prizes. ("Too hard to keep warm on the northern routes.") She told me how to cool the marks and how you can get sucker sore after weeks on the road.

"Like the time we were with this little gilly outfit up in Pennsylvania. I was working a shoot-till-you-win hanky-pank. That's what the sign said: SHOOT TILL YOU WIN. So up steps this big wide farm lady. She looks at my store, she reads the sign, she lays down her money and picks up the gun, then she looks at me and says, 'Hey, lady. Which one of them things is Till?' "

She talked of the friendships and how much she missed Irene Matusik, who really had tried to mother her and grandmother her sons.

"When did she die?"

"Last winter. Her heart had been bad for years and last October, right after we finished the season, it just quit on her. She died in her sleep, all peaceful—the way I hope I go when it's my time, but God, how I miss her!"

She spoke of how Eve and Skee were third-generation carnies and how young Kay was first-of-May. "We picked her up in Georgia and I think she's going to be a keeper."

"You really like the life, don't you?" I asked.

"Yes and no. Every new place is a challenge. But it's rough at times, like being nibbled to death by ducks when equipment breaks down, your help runs off or gets drunk, and the festival committee lies about the draw and then tries to stiff you on the percentages. That's why we're thinking of becoming forty-milers. Sell off some of our stuff and just play small festivals around the Carolinas and Virginia in the summer, do something with the farm for the fall, maybe work the flea markets in the winter."

"That would be great," I said, thinking of the spice they'd add to family reunions. I couldn't wait to see Aunt Sister's reaction to this new grandniece. Especially if I could persuade Tally to contribute fried elephant ears to the picnic table instead of banana pudding or pimento cheese sandwiches.

I told her about Daddy and as much of his first wife as I could, about my brothers and their children, and about

A.K. and Ruth, her half siblings; but that seemed to make her uncomfortable so I remembered something I'd read about on the Internet and I asked, "Did you ever do a hey rube?"

"Me personally? Nope."

"Not even when those guys were ripping up your Pot O'Gold?"

"For three drunks?" Her voice held amused scorn as she shook her head. "You only do one when you need a lot of backup quick, okay? First one I ever saw was at the Brandywine Racetrack, about a month after I was with it. One of the towners had some problem with a guy on one of the rides so he got about thirty of his buds together about eleven o'clock one night and they all climbed up and over the back of the ride to attack the eight guys who were crewing the ride. Well, the guy on the mike at the ride booth saw what was happening and he hey rubed over the mike, which brought about fifty carnies running. It was a real short spat."

She smiled in memory. "If you yell 'Hey Rube,' everyone drops everything to assist. I mean, games are empty, rides stop in midturn, food's left to burn on the grill, so it's a serious thing. I've only seen about five in all my years."

As she spoke, her husband and son rounded the corner of the women's bunkhouse.

The boy gave me a curt nod and went on into their trailer, but Arnold Ames sank down into one of the webbed chairs.

"Judge," he said.

"Please. Call me Deborah."

"She's no judge here, Arnie, okay?" Tally said.

He shrugged.

"Get you a beer, hon?"

"That'd taste good."

"Deborah, you ready yet?"

Again I passed and she stepped inside the trailer.

"I probably ought to be going," I told her husband. "But it's been good getting to know Tally."

"Don't leave on my account," said Ames.

I listened for the sarcasm beneath his words, but there didn't seem to be any. He had a nice face. Not handsome, but pleasant. I guessed him to be midforties. A receding hairline. Shrewd green eyes. The hard wiry build of a man who does physical work outside.

Tally struck me as a complete pragmatist, a woman who'd seen too much crap to put up with anything she didn't like for very long. If she'd stayed married to Arnold Ames for going on twenty years, it had to be because he was good to her. That was enough for me to cut him all the slack he needed tonight.

Tally came back with an opened bottle of beer, and he thirstily chugalugged several swallows.

"TV people were all over the front end," he said. "They get back here?"

Tally shook her head. "What's happening with Polly?"

"They've taken her to Chapel Hill. They think she killed herself."

"Why?"

He reached out to touch her hand. "They're not saying, but from the questions they asked, and the way they were being extra careful to bag up her shoes . . ."

"What?" Tally prodded.

"They may be thinking she's the one killed Braz."

CHAPTER
16

It was a little past nine when I left Tally and Arnie. People were gathering around the two trailers, bringing lawn chairs and coolers, ready to spend the rest of the evening talking about Polly and Braz and offering what comfort they could. Even though Tally seemed to accept me now, I knew my presence would make the others uncomfortable, so I drew a map to show Arnie how to get to the farm, then I hugged Tally goodnight and repeated April's invitation to bring as many of their friends tomorrow as wanted to be there.

Windy Raines, with rough courtesy, offered to walk me to my car, but I told him I'd be fine.

As indeed I was. Officers still milled around the Plate Pitch, but the reporters with their cameras seemed to have moved on and there was no sign of Dwight, either, till I got to my car and found a prowl car parked alongside. The window was down, and he seemed to be catching a cat nap behind the steering wheel.

"Hey," I said softly. "You asleep?"

He opened one eye. "Nope. Just wondering if I ought to come looking for you. See if you're all right."

"I was talking to Tally."

"I figured."

He yawned, got out, and stretched. "She okay?"

"I think so. It'll probably be better after tomorrow's over. Do you want to come to the funeral?"

"Yeah, I probably ought to be there."

"Arnold Ames thinks you think Polly Viscardi killed Braz."

"Does he?"

"Dwight!"

"C'mon, Deb'rah. Be fair. You know it's too soon to say about things like that."

I subsided, knowing he was right.

He looked at his watch. "Still early. Not even nine-thirty yet. You reckon Mr. Kezzie's still up?"

"Yeah," I said reluctantly, knowing where he was going with this and knowing I couldn't put it off any longer. "What about Miss Emily?"

"She's a night owl," he said. "Want to follow me out?"

"Slow as you drive? I could tell my whole family and be home in bed before you get to your mother's."

He smiled down at me. "Don't count on it. I got me a blue light here. You break the speed limit and I'm pulling you over."

Despite his threat, when we drove back through town, he turned off at the courthouse and I knew he was going to pick up his truck rather than drive the prowl car out to Miss Emily's. All the same, I kept it under the speed limit all the way out to the homeplace as I tried to decide how I was going to tell Daddy.

The moon was high in the sky, shinier than a newly minted quarter. I turned in at the rusty old mailbox that bore only a number on the side, crested the ridge, and eased down the long driveway. There was a light on at the back of the house, but the dogs came off the front porch to greet me. As I looked more closely, I saw Daddy sitting there on the swing in the deep shadows cast by the tall magnolia trees that grew along the path.

"Was wondering if I was gonna see you tonight," he said, when I got out of the car.

I turned and looked down the slope to the edge of the yard and our family graveyard. With the moon nearly full, I could see Duck Aldcroft's funeral tent and a dark mound beyond.

Daddy got up and joined me in the yard. I slipped my arm through his and together we walked down to the newly dug grave. That dark mound was the dirt that had been dug up, covered now with carpeting that I knew to be navy blue, though it would have been hard to tell in the moonlight even when it was this bright.

"Never could understand why grave diggers feel they got to hide the dirt," Daddy said. "You reckon they think people don't know that's what's gonna be covering them?"

"Have you talked to Andrew today?" I asked.

"No, but the last I heared, he's sober now. Seen a lot of April and the girls, though," he added dryly. "They and Maidie's got enough to feed the five thousand. Eating table's full of cakes and pies."

The old rosebushes that grew around the graves of both his wives were already starting to drop their leaves, and that reminded me. I looked at Daddy, stricken. "I forgot to order flowers!"

"Don't you worry, shug," he said, patting my hand. "You know April won't gonna forget something like that. And I told Duck to make sure Tallahassee has what she wants for the coffin. They's gonna be plenty of flowers."

The grave had been dug next to the little stone carved in the shape of a kneeling lamb that marked the grave of Daddy and Annie Ruth's first baby boy, a stillbirth. It was as if the gods had required a sacrifice for all the strong, healthy boys to come.

And now another boy was joining him that none of us had ever met, either.

With my arm still linked in Daddy's, we walked over to Mother's grave and I put my hand on her stone: SUSAN STEPHENSON KNOTT. It's not that I think dead spirits inhabit the graves of their bodies, but this was as close as I could physically get to both my parents.

I took a deep breath. "Dwight's asked me to marry him," I said, speaking as much to my mother as to my father.

Suddenly, unexpectedly, I found myself too choked up to continue.

At last, Daddy asked quietly, "How did you answer him, Daughter?"

"I told him yes."

He pulled his arm free of mine, stepped back, and tilted my chin up till the moonlight fell full on my face. His own face was stern and, in this light, looked as if it, too, were carved from marble.

"Except for when you decided to run for judge, I ain't never said a word to you about the way you lived your life, the things you done, the men you been with. Have I?"

"No, sir."

"I figured you won't hurting nobody but yourself and what you done was your own business. But if you marry Dwight and mess up—well, now, that's gonna hurt a lot of people."

"Daddy—"

He held up his hand. "Hear me out, Deb'rah. I'm right partial to Dwight. He's a good man and he deserves a good wife. You gonna forsake all others and cleave only to him so long as you both shall live?"

"Yes, sir." Tears streamed down my face and my hand still lay on Mother's stone as if it were on a Bible.

"All right, then." He opened his arms to me and held me against his chest till I quit crying.

CHAPTER
17

Tuesday continued fair and sunny, but weather forecasters were predicting a change by the weekend. Normally, I like autumn rains that help the trees unleaf and let winter wheat sprout so that newly disked fields turned bright green. Now I was hoping they'd hold off till after the harvest festival ended Saturday night so that Tally and Arnold wouldn't have a financial loss to pull them down further after the loss of their son.

I'd forgotten to set the alarm and didn't wake up till nearly eight. That was so surprising, I reached over and picked up the telephone just to reassure myself I still had a dial tone. I had half expected a call from April or Andrew or Minnie or Dwight. Instead, the phone stayed silent while I showered and then struggled with panty hose. I always forget to check for runs and the first two pairs I tried had them. In the *second* leg, of course.

The dress I put on was a sleeveless navy with a matching long-sleeved jacket that was cropped at the waist. Instead of my usual pumps, I found a pair of Cuban-heeled navy shoes more suitable for walking around a sandy-soil graveyard. For sentiment, I wore my silver charm bracelet again.

Lipstick, a dash of mascara, a touch of blusher, and I was ready to roll by eight forty-five.

Still no phone calls. I wondered if Dwight had chickened out of telling Miss Emily.

I'd left my car parked by the back door, and when I slid in behind the steering wheel and started to fasten my seat belt, I saw an unfamiliar manila envelope that had slipped down between the two seats. Puzzled, I opened it and found a thick stack of color photographs. They all seemed to be of the same woman in different clinging outfits. When I looked closer, they appeared to be nightgowns in colors that ranged from sexy black satin that shimmered in the camera's flash to demure white lace and pink ribbons, with all the rainbow in between. But they were such crazy poses that it took me a minute to realize she must have taken the pictures herself, holding the camera out at arm's length. Nothing could be seen of her face, though, except a chin line here, a brow there, or, in overhead shots, her dark curly hair and dangling earrings above more lace and silk.

I recognized that these must have come from the self-storage locker of negligees that Braz had bought, but how—?

Then I remembered Dwight struggling with my seat belt. The envelope must have slipped out of his jacket pocket. With a mental note to hand it back to him at the funeral, I stuck it up between the sun visor and the roof.

When I got over to the homeplace, most of my sisters-in-law were already there, aprons tied over their Sunday dresses, working as a team as they directed the kids to set up lawn chairs out under the shade trees and on the porch that wrapped around three sides of the house. It was a school day, yet all the children seemed to be here. A long table had been set up on the porch nearest the kitchen door and I found Minnie and Jessica covering it with several snowy white bedsheets that were kept for just that purpose.

Jessie immediately voiced the curiosity the others must be feeling. "Deborah! You've met her. What's she like?"

"Does she have tattoos?" asked Will and Amy's youngest.

"Didn't see any," I said, answering the easiest question first. "She looks like anybody else. Very nice, but very sad right now."

"Does she look like Ruth or A.K.?" asked Zach's Emma, who was filling napkin holders from an enormous package.

"Yes," I said, looking around for Andrew.

Out at the grave site, Duck's people had set up rows of folding chairs under the tent. The closed casket was already in place with a blanket of red roses covering the polished wood. Duck and several of my brothers, somber in dark suits and white shirts, were down there with more of the children. But no Andrew.

"Which?" said Emma.

"Which what, honey?"

"Which one does she look like?"

"Both of them. Same eyes, only black hair."

I slipped past before they could bombard me with more questions. Inside the kitchen, Maidie was sugaring a huge vat of hot tea since everybody knows you might as well not bother with sugar at all if you try to add it after the tea is iced. Never tastes the same.

"Stevie? You and Reese can go ahead and set them ice chests out on the porch, too," she said.

I turned, and there was my nephew back from Chapel Hill in a gray tweed jacket, blue shirt, and tie. As my glance fell on him, he immediately grabbed the ice chest and retreated, which let me know I wasn't the only one hoping to avoid awkward questions.

Amy and Doris were making coffee in the two big party urns Mother had bought thirty years ago when one of the boys got married here at the homeplace, and Haywood and Isabel arrived with Jane Ann and a box full of plastic cups, plates, forks, and spoons.

Since Haywood immediately demanded more information, I tried to tell them as concisely as I could.

"She's not Olivia anymore, I guess y'all heard that?"

"Tallahassee," said Robert's wife Doris, disapprovingly. "Now you got to say that's a real peculiar name to call yourself. Like me changing my name to Raleigh or Fuquay-Varina."

"Actually, wasn't Varina a woman's name?" asked Isabel, going off on her own tangent. "Somebody from Civil War days?"

"If you have a problem with that, Doris," I said, "just call her Tally. That's what everybody else does."

"I didn't say I had a problem with it," Doris said huffily. "I just said it seemed peculiar. I can say that, can't I?"

"Doris, honey, you can say anything you want," said Minnie, who'd stepped inside the kitchen, "but let's let Deborah tell us what we need to know before they get here, all right?"

Doris thought about flouncing off (Doris does that a lot), but she was too curious, so she subsided and listened as I explained that our niece Tally had been married almost twenty years to someone named Arnold Ames, that they lived in Florida, that they were part owners of the carnival playing the harvest festival, that she owned the old Hatcher place over near Widdington, that she had a second son named Valdosta (Doris frowned at that name), who was about sixteen (the girl cousins perked up their ears), and that they'd probably be accompanied by a lot of their carnival friends.

"I hope you'll all remember that Sunday's a workday for them when they're on the road and they live in trailers too crowded for a lot of clothes they wouldn't normally need, so some of them might not be dressed up. But Braz was their friend and I'm sure they'll be mourning for him just as sincerely as if they were in suits and ties and Sunday dresses."

Several started to scold me for even suggesting that they'd judge a person's worth by their clothes, but I knew it would undercut the ones like Doris and also help the kids keep an open mind.

Another car arrived with A.K. driving April and Ruth. No Andrew.

"He just flat refuses to come," April said despairingly. "And there's nothing I can say that Seth and Mr. Kezzie haven't already said. We'll just have to make the best of it."

Duck Aldcroft had sent a funeral car for Tally and her family, but they weren't due for another half hour.

I slipped out of the house while the others were exclaiming and tsk-tsking, and a few minutes later I was easing my car's low-slung chassis across a couple of erosion barriers in the lanes between the homeplace and Andrew's house.

As I expected, he was out back at the pens with some of his rabbit dogs.

"Don't you start on me!" he said as soon as he saw me. "I'm not going and that's that. You can just turn around and march yourself right back over to Daddy's. You hear?"

"I hear," I said, and kept coming till I reached the step of the little viewing house he and the boys had built in front of the quarter-acre training pen so that they could watch the dogs in comfort when the weather was rainy or cold.

I didn't say anything, just sat on the step and waited while he raked the dog dirt out of the gravel yard of each pen, filled their pans with fresh water, and checked their ears for mites and ticks. His hands were gentle with them, if a bit unsteady, and his face still had a pasty look from all the liquor he'd drunk this weekend.

"You had no call to tell April," he said angrily.

"I didn't go looking for her, Andrew. She came to me. To find out why you'd crawled in a bottle to hide."

He glared at me. "I won't hiding!"

I just sat there and looked back at him.

"I won't hiding," he muttered.

"No? What do you call this?"

He turned back to the dogs without answering, but

when next he looked at me, he said, "You don't go on, you're gonna be late for the burying."

I shrugged. "She'll have lots of other aunts and uncles there." I let a moment go by. "No father, though."

"I ain't—" He broke off with a disgusted wave of his hand. "Oh, hell, Deb'rah. She don't want me there."

"You won't know that for sure unless you go."

I stood up and walked over to the dog pens. "Show me your hands."

"Huh?"

"Your hands," I said.

Puzzled, he held them up. I reached across the fence, took his right hand in mine, turned it over, and traced the scar there with my finger. "How'd you get that?"

"Aw, you know how. Guy in a bar had a knife."

"And you took it away from him."

"I was liquored up," he said dryly. "You telling me to go have a couple of stiff ones?"

He started to pull his hand away, but I held on to it and pointed to another ragged scar at the base of his thumb.

"You weren't liquored up when Jap Stancil's bulldog went after Jack."

He did pull his hand away then.

"You're not a coward, Andrew, so how come you're so scared of meeting her?"

"I wouldn't know what to say after all this time," he said plaintively. "Besides, she'd probably just spit in my face."

"Yes," I conceded. "There is that possibility. So let me see if I've got this straight. You're not afraid of switch-blades or bulldogs, but you *are* afraid of a little spit, right?"

"Shit, Deb'rah." Against his will, the barest hint of a smile crossed his lips.

"Daddy's got soap and water," I told him. "And if she really does want to spit in your face, well, don't you think you owe her that much?"

His eyes were anguished. "But what'll I say to her?"

"How about 'I'm sorry'? How about 'I was a stupid kid who didn't have the brains God gave a monkey'? How about 'I was wrong. You *are* my daughter and I'm glad to meet you'?"

"Yeah," he said with a shaky smile. "I guess any of those would do."

One nice thing about men — they don't take forever to get dressed.

While Andrew splashed around in the bathroom, I laid out his suit, shirt, and tie, found fresh underwear, dark socks, and his dress shoes, then got out of his way. He was a little damp around the edges but ready to go exactly twelve minutes after he caved.

Even so, Duck Aldcroft's funeral car had already arrived with Tally, Arnold, and Val, and Daddy must have been out front to welcome her. Tall and dignified, his hair bright silver in the sunlight, he was escorting her to the front row of chairs as we came down the slope. Arnold and Val both wore sports jackets, shirts, and ties as did the other owner, Ralph Ferlanski, and Dennis Koffer, the show's patch. Tally looked beautiful in a dark green pantsuit and man-tailored white silk shirt. Some twenty-five or thirty other carnival people arrived in a collection of motley cars and trucks. All were neatly, if more casually, dressed, and they followed the Ameses awkwardly, uncertain of the protocol of a family graveyard. There was a little glitch as Duck's people tried to get them to take seats under the canopy and they held back. They clearly thought they should be the ones standing and that our family should sit.

While Duck was sorting them out, I took Andrew's hand and led him to the front row where Tally sat between Daddy and Arnold. She looked up as though in relief at seeing my familiar face, and I gave her a quick hug.

"This is Andrew," I whispered in her ear, "and he's scared out of his mind that you're going to spit in his face."

Her blue eyes were huge in her drawn face as she looked up at him somberly.

Standing there between the coffin of his grandson and the daughter he'd denied for so long, Andrew suddenly looked as if he'd been hit with a poleax. His face crumpled.

"They didn't tell me you were so pretty," he said brokenly. "Oh, Livvie, baby, I'm so sorry. About your boy, about you—I was so dumb back then."

I don't know what she'd planned to do or say when she finally met him. What she actually did do was look deep in his eyes, then put out her hand to him and say, "You were seventeen back then."

Daddy got up and gave Andrew his chair. Duck found him another a few rows back, and I went and stood between Seth and Dwight.

Tally had said they didn't want a religious ceremony and Duck did the best he could, but it's hard when you're so used to Bible Belt rituals. He read Housman's "To an Athlete Dying Young" and talked about youth's bright promise cut short. He started to call for prayer, caught himself, and instead suggested that everyone close their eyes for a moment of silence in tribute to Brazos Hartley.

I knew from experience that when Duck says a moment of silence, he means the full sixty seconds. Sixty seconds seems forever when you're trying to think reverential thoughts about someone you've never known.

Eventually, he murmured a soft "Amen," and there was a general rustling and throat-clearing.

"I'll ask everyone but his immediate family to rise now and join in while Annie Sue Knott leads us in 'Amazing Grace.'"

We're all more or less musical, but Herman and Nadine's Annie Sue has the best voice in the family and it rang out pure and sweet as she set the pitch and timing for the rest of us. The boys and their wives and children were right there with her by the third note—bass, alto, tenor, and soprano, our voices blended in the old familiar harmonies:

> *'Tis grace hath brought me safe thus far,*
> *And grace will lead me home.*

CHAPTER
18

🦆 Most funerals are not totally somber and Braz's was no exception.

After Duck Aldcroft escorted Tally, Arnold, and Val up to the house, his people quickly lowered the casket into the ground, filled all the dirt back in, mounded the excess, and covered the grave with the blanket of roses. They took away the chairs and the navy blue carpeting, and they left the matching navy blue tent discreetly lettered ALDCROFT FUNERAL HOME to shelter the grave and the flowers heaped there from sun and rain. As Daddy had promised, there were plenty of wreaths and sprays from the rest of the family and one as big as a tractor wheel that Ralph Ferlanski, the other carnival owner, must have sent. It was composed of large white spider mums, yellow daisies, and the biggest bronze mums I'd ever seen. Gold lettering on the burnt orange ribbons read FROM YOUR CARNIVAL FAMILY.

Family's where you find it, isn't it? And I was proud of mine today. They were everywhere, talking, making folks welcome, urging people to fix themselves a plate of fried chicken, sliced ham, meatloaf, chicken pastry, and vegetables of every kind. And what about another serving of cake, pie, or peach cobbler? They fetched ice and slices of lemon for tea, cream and sugar for coffee, fresh cups of water. They showed people where the bathroom was and made sure there were plenty of paper towels.

Kay, the girl who'd found Polly Viscardi's body, was about the same age as Jane Ann and Jessica, and Candy and Eve weren't much older. All five of them sat along the edge of the old board porch, swinging their legs while they ate, and my nieces were peppering them with questions about carnival life and listening to the answers with such uncritical interest that I could feel a definite easing of tension.

April swooped by and gave me a hug on her way to the front parlor where Andrew, A.K., and Ruth were trying to bridge the years with Tally. The rest of the family were tactfully giving them space so as not to overwhelm her with so many of us at once.

Arnold and their son Val had gone out to eat on the front porch with Daddy, Dwight, Stevie, Reese, and those of my brothers who live close enough to come. The rocking chairs and swings were as full as the plates the men were balancing on their knees, but several offered to get up and give me their seats. I told them to stay as they were and perched on the steps with a red plastic cup of iced tea to listen with the others as Arnold described their tentative plans for the farm.

"You going to become a farmer?" Haywood asked dubiously, making short work of a drumstick.

"Not like you people." Arnold took a sip of tea and set

the cup down on the floor beside his chair. "We were thinking about turning the place into a Halloween attraction. If it all works out, we could come in off the road next year or year after next at the latest. Become forty-milers. We've already got the haunted house and if we weren't hauling it up and down the eastern seaboard, losing bits and pieces every time we jump, I think we could make it something really special. I've got a good mechanic working for me right now, and Val has some great ideas for pop-ups and illusions if we can only figure out all the wiring and lighting."

We'd all been sneaking glances at Val, trying not to stare as we cataloged every feature of this new twig that had popped out on the family tree, and Arnold's words gave us permission to look our fill. I knew that after he left with his parents this afternoon, my kin would be saying how he was built just like Reese at that age, how his hair was like the little twins', his hands and feet as big as theirs, and *Did you see the way he cocks his head when he's listening? Just like you do, Daddy.*

From his wheelchair on the other side of Haywood, Herman said, "I'm just a plain ol' everyday electrician, but that sounds like the kind of thing Annie Sue'd love to mess with. You need to talk with her."

"Yeah? The one who was singing down there? She knows electrical gimmicks?"

"When she was twelve," I laughed, "she wired her mother's electric stove so that every time Nadine turned on one of the back burners, the doorbell rang."

"And remember the time she wired the toilet seat in y'all's bathroom, Herman?" Haywood chuckled as he related another family legend for the newcomers' amusement. "It played 'Remember Me' every time he lifted the seat so's to remind him to put it back down when he was finished."

Val laughed out loud and Arnold nodded. "Sounds like someone we could use, all right."

For his parents' sake, the teenager seemed to be making an effort to be friendly today, and he said, "Tell them about the corn maze, Dad."

"Oh, yeah." Tally's husband borrowed a match from Daddy and lit a cigarette. "We thought we could put four or five acres into a really elaborate corn maze."

"You mean that fancy-colored corn?" asked Robert, who was working on a ham biscuit. "They's a pretty good market for Indian maize over in Cary and Apex."

"That's another possibility," said Arnold, "but I was talking m-a-z-e, not m-a-i-z-e. I want to grow tall field corn and have paths all through it for people to get lost in. Pumpkins, too. Charge five bucks apiece to go through the maze, two bucks for the haunted house, and maybe sell the pumpkins for a couple of bucks each."

"How much land you got over there?" Seth asked, interested.

"Eighty-three acres."

"Woods? Creek?"

"Yeah, why?"

"Well, if you had you a tractor and a flatbed, you could give hayrides, too. Little kids love them."

"Yeah, you're definitely gonna need to buy a tractor, but we could lend you plows and disks to get you started," Zach said.

When they started talking the merits of one tractor over another and just how much horsepower Arnold would need and where he might find a good used one, I gathered up the plates of those who'd finished eating.

Dwight stood up, too, and said, "Here, let me get that door for you."

He held the screen door wide, then followed me on down the hallway. As we passed the parlor, I glanced inside. Tally was leaning back against the faded couch cushions and looking a little more herself while April and Ruth made light conversation. A.K. still looked uneasy and Andrew looked dazed, but I had a feeling it was going to work out. It was probably way too late for any true father/daughter relationship, but just connecting ought to help the healing on both sides.

Dwight and I went straight through the house to the back porch to dump the empty plates in the trash barrel and fix a couple for ourselves now that the line had thinned out. We passed Minnie, Isabel, and Zach's wife Barbara in the hallway, on their way out to the porch with their own plates. Nadine, Doris, and Maidie were at the kitchen table in deep conversation with a couple of carnival women I recognized by sight though not by name.

Outside, the rest of the crowd were in groups spread out around the yard. Some were seated in lawn chairs under the shade trees, others were braving the sun on a knee-high wall next to a border of gardenias, hydrangeas, spireas, and forsythias, bushes whose flowering time was finished for the year. We paused to watch Windy Raines and Skee Matusik, who were giving some of the younger kids a demonstration of two-man juggling. They were surprisingly good. Windy was talking trash a mile a minute and Skee kept adding in more lemons from a basket little Bert held out to him till one of them suddenly lost the rhythm and lemons went flying all over the grass.

As the children scrambled to pick them up and asked to be shown the first moves, Zach's Emma came out with a box of Band-Aids for Skee, who had raw blisters on both his heels. Bert was still of an age that Band-Aids are wonderful. He immediately found a half-healed hurt on his hand and demanded one, too. With his sun-wrinkled skin and old, discolored tattoos, Skee Matusik was an unlikely grandfather figure, but I guess his years of working the Lucky Ducky had made him wise to the ways of children. Before tending his own hurt, he very seriously and very carefully unwrapped a Band-Aid, smoothed it across Bert's small hand, and said, "There you go, Bo."

At that moment, Tasha came around the corner with Sam, who had cleaned up better than I expected. A good night's sleep, a shower, and a shave made a world of difference. He wore clean khakis, a long-sleeved dark purple knit shirt, and brown loafers with no socks. By now, he must have been told that Polly Viscardi was dead, but from the proprietary way Tasha was filling a plate for him, he wasn't in heavy mourning.

I saw Skee and Windy exchange lifted eyebrows and heard Windy mutter, "Guess he gets to keep on sleeping in the cathouse."

Almost against my will, my eyes went to Tasha's feet. Blue leather sandals with thin soles.

Adding a slice of tomato to my plate of field peas and butter beans, I followed Dwight out to a bench under a pecan tree. He looked very nice today in his tan slacks and shirt and a tweedy brown jacket that matched his brown eyes. I resisted the impulse to smooth down the unruly cowlick that always stood up.

"At least Andrew and Tally are talking," I said. "That's a good sign, isn't it?"

"How'd you get him over here?" Dwight asked. "Seth said he wasn't coming."

"Seth just didn't use the right argument."

He bit into a chicken thigh. "I see you told Mr. Kezzie."

"Daddy spoke to you?"

"No, but when I got up to open the door for you just now, he gave me a wink."

"He's really pleased about it," I said. "Probably feels I'm getting the best end of the bargain. What about Miss Emily? Did you tell her last night?"

"Yep."

"How did she take it?"

He laughed. "You mean you didn't see the skyrockets going off?"

"Seriously?"

"Yeah. Oh, and she gave me this."

He hooked a ring from his pocket, a lovely, old-fashioned square-cut diamond in an antique setting. A stray spot of sunlight through the thinning leaves caught the stone and it flashed blue fire. "She gave her own ring to Rob when he and Kate got engaged. This was her mother's."

He held it out to me, but I couldn't take it. Agitated butterflies were tumbling around in my stomach so wildly that for an instant I thought I was either going to pass out or throw up.

"What's wrong?" Dwight said as I took long deliberate breaths in and out to steady myself.

"You okay?" he asked, starting to look worried.

I nodded. "Stupid of me. Bad reaction. It's just that telling your mother, my father, and now your grandmother's ring—it's really going to happen, isn't it?"

He closed his hand around it. "Not if you hate the whole idea so much that you're gonna keep turning green every time you think about it," he said grimly.

"I don't, I'm not," I protested. I took his hand, uncurled his fist, and slipped the ring on my finger. It was a perfect fit.

"I can't wait to start wearing it," I lied, handing it back for safekeeping till he had told his son and I would have to put it on for all the world—and my family—to see. "When are you going up to tell Cal?"

"I would've already gone if Polly Viscardi hadn't been killed last night."

"It wasn't suicide? She didn't kill herself because she'd killed Braz?"

"Nope. It's murder with a sloppy attempt to look like suicide."

"You can tell that quick? Before the autopsy?"

"All Percy had to do was look at the rope with a magnifying glass," said Dwight, speaking of Percy Denning, the deputy who'd had extra training as their crime-scene specialist. "Whoever killed her used a rough jute rope. Looped it over the pipes that supported the canvas roof of the stand, then hoisted her up. Percy could tell by the direction the fibers had been rubbed that the line had been pulled across the pole and tied off while it supported her whole weight. If she'd tied it off first, then jumped off the edge of the platform like we were supposed to think, the fibers would have been rubbed in the opposite direction."

"Then she wasn't the one who stomped Braz?"

"Oh, we've still got her tagged for that."

I looked at him questioningly.

"Her shoes. We've sent them to the SBI lab for confirmation. She'd cleaned them up pretty good, but Percy's pretty sure from the heel print in the Dozer and the sample he scraped out of the crack between the heel and the shoe itself that she's the one stomped Hartley to death. The blood type's consistent with his."

"Wait a minute! Does that mean *her* death was revenge for his?" I didn't like this scenario one little bit. Not when the three people most likely to want Braz's death avenged were Tally, Arnold, and Val.

"Too soon to know," he answered.

"What about time of death?"

"Sometime between one A.M. and daybreak. The night guard was supposed to make the rounds at twelve, two, and four, but there's just his word for it that he did. Even then, there was lots of time in between. He says he would have noticed if there was anybody unauthorized on the lot."

"What about authorized?"

"He said the patch—Koffer—was still roaming around at midnight, so we talked to him, too. Something about measuring one of the game stands to see if it was longer than the independent agent claimed. I gather they pay by the running foot for the privilege of booking in with the carnival and some of the agents try to fudge the figures. He says it cuts down on the hassles just to measure when no one else is around. He also says he was asleep in his own trailer by one o'clock."

"Polly's bunkmates say the last time they saw her was around one. That they went to bed and she stayed up to read."

"Yeah, Richards told me. They say anything else she might not've heard?"

Feeling like a total snitch, I repeated the gossip Tally had told me about Polly's love life, about her current lover whom she'd taken from Tasha, and her former lover—the corn dog cook who was also Eve's father. Probably none of it was relevant, but I'd have felt even worse if I didn't tell him and it turned out to be important.

"Tally didn't ask me not to repeat it," I said, "and she's clicked on the possibility that we're more than friends. All the same—"

"Don't worry, shug. It's probably common knowledge on the lot. They won't know it came from you."

I glanced at my watch. A quarter past twelve and I was due in court at one.

"I need to get rolling, too," Dwight said. "Want to ride into Dobbs with me?"

"And you'll bring me back this evening?"

He nodded.

"Okay. Just let me go say goodbye to Tally and Arnold."

As we walked back through the house, I almost bumped into Stevie, who did an abrupt about-turn and ducked into the bathroom.

I leaned close to the door. "You can run but you can't hide forever, Stevie Knott. You and I are due for a little prayer meeting."

I tiptoed away. Let him think I was waiting outside the door to snag him.

Out on the porch, we found that several of the carnival people had already left and the Ameses were getting ready to leave themselves. Tally wanted to walk down to the grave site alone with her son and husband, so I hugged her goodbye and said that I'd get over to see her again before the carnival closed.

Then I hugged Andrew, who gave me a bear hug back. Lastly, I told Daddy I was going to leave my car there for the time being and ride over to the courthouse with Dwight. He's played too much poker to give us away, and as for the others, they take Dwight so much for granted that no one seemed to think it odd that he'd make the round-trip out from Dobbs twice in the same day. Indeed, April was still so clueless that she even smiled up at him and said, "We're going to have to get you and Sylvia out for supper one night before too much longer."

Dwight turned a becoming shade of red, which made my brothers laugh and rag him about wedding bells in his future.

We were halfway to Dobbs before I remembered the pictures I'd found.

"Doesn't matter," Dwight said. "Doesn't look like those lockers have anything to do with Hartley's death after all."

"But what about the person who tried to break in the shed out at the farm when the gang of three were liberating Lamarr's grandfather's pictures?" I asked. "How do you explain that?"

"I don't. Sure would've helped if they'd gotten a good enough look to say if the person was male or female. It might be sheer coincidence, you know. A burglar totally unconnected with the carnival, just looking to take what he could."

"So instead of ransacking the house or unlocked sheds, he—or she—headed straight for the most securely locked outbuilding on the place?"

"Okay," he conceded, "but if it *was* Viscardi, we still don't know why she would want Hartley dead. That story she told us about his blackmail attempt? Maybe he had something on her more serious than who she was sleeping with. Something she couldn't get out of just by having him beat up."

"She really did have him beat up?"

"Oh, yes. Jamison interviewed that Sam Warrick and he admitted it. Didn't want the Ameses to know, but from what we gather, everybody knew it but Mrs. Ames, including her husband and her son."

So we were back to the Ameses again, with yet another reason to dislike Polly Viscardi.

Even with Dwight driving, we had plenty of time to get to Dobbs and he kept the truck on back roads that were more direct as the crow flies but meandered through the country. Summer was definitely winding down. Wild asters made patches of blue along the ditch banks, and wasteland was yellow with coreopsis, sneezeweeds, and goldenrod. Pokeberries hung in clusters from dark purple stalks and sassafras leaves were bright red and orange against the pines.

"We still don't have a viable theory as to how Viscardi killed Hartley without being seen," he said.

I'd been thinking about that myself ever since last night when Arnold told us about Polly's shoes being bagged.

"Her game is one that's pretty hard to win," I said. "That's something I picked up on the Internet. Unless the coins have a lot of backspin or land just right, they simply won't stay on the plates. And remember, you don't have to buy chances to play. People just step up and start tossing. In fact, her main reason to be there was to keep them back behind the foul line."

Dwight looked dubious. "Okay, so maybe she could leave it for the two or three minutes it'd take her to get across to the Dozer, do Braz, and get back. But why didn't anybody see her enter or leave?"

"Windy Raines's Bowler Roller," I said. "Remember last night when we were talking to Tally? Those strobe lights and the siren? How we all stopped and stared over there and it seemed to go on forever? Even people playing the Dozer went around to that side to watch till the siren stopped. That must have been when she did it. The Bowler Roller's another one that's hard to win, but it does happen three or four times an evening. All she'd have to do is wait till it went off, then take advantage of all the lights and noise and people looking there instead of at the Dozer."

"Makes about as much sense as anything we've been able to come up with," Dwight said, pulling around a tractor and flatbed loaded with irrigation pipes. "The ME couldn't tell if the injury to the back of his head was before or during the actual stomping. Mayleen thinks she either hit him over the head or got him to lie down by telling him it would stop his nosebleed. She says her grandmother used to put a cold spoon on the roof of her mouth or cold metal across the bridge of her nose to stop the bleeding."

"Cold quarters?" I wondered.

CHAPTER
19

I convened court at precisely one o'clock. Janice Needham was clerking for me again. The courthouse grapevine had learned of my relationship to Tally Ames and her murdered son, and Janice leaned in to me solicitously to say, "Bradley and I are so sorry, Judge. We had no idea he was kin to y'all."

"Thank you, Janice," I said. "I do appreciate you and Brad thinking of us."

She looked expectant, hoping for some direct-from-the-horse's-mouth tidbit that she could pass around at the next break, but I glanced over to Tracy Johnson, who was prosecuting this afternoon, and nodded for her to call her first case.

"People versus Martin Samuelson, Your Honor."

To my surprise, it was the same elderly black man who'd recently stood before me charged with DWI. I'd suspended his license. Now here he was back with heavier charges.

"Mr. Samuelson," I said, "didn't I suspend your license just two weeks ago?"

The old man nodded.

"And didn't you promise me that you wouldn't ever drive again when you'd been drinking."

"Yes, ma'am."

"But you did. *And* you drove with a suspended license."

"Yes, ma'am."

"Why, Mr. Samuelson?"

"See now, I didn't want to drive," he said, "but I couldn't just leave my car on the side of the road. I had to get it home, didn't I?"

"But your car should have been at home," I told him. "A suspended license means you can't drive even if you're completely sober."

"Yes, ma'am, I know that, and that's why I got my nephew to drive me to the ABC store. But on the way home, there was this roadblock up ahead, and Leon, he didn't want to go through it. I don't know why, so he just drove in the tobacco field and left me setting there. Well, it was only a half mile from my house and I had to get my car home, didn't I? And I won't going to drive on the highway. I was figuring to go through the fields once I got turned around."

The trooper who'd pulled him, Ollie Harrold, testified that he was assisting in a license-check roadblock when he saw Mr. Samuelson's Ford drive into a tobacco field about a hundred yards away. "The driver jumped out and ran through the field and disappeared. After maybe ten minutes, the person in the passenger seat got out and went around to the driver's seat. It was almost stuck in the sand, but he kept rocking it till he got it backed out of the field and onto the road, and that's when I went down and asked him for his license."

Harrold also testified that he'd administered the Breathalyzer test and Mr. Samuelson had blown a point-oh-eight. Not so long ago, that would have been well under the legal limit. Not anymore, though. And under the required sentencing a Level One DWI meant a mandatory minimum of thirty days' jail time.

"Your Honor?" said Harrold, who knew what sentence the old man was facing. "I know Mr. Samuelson, and I know he's telling the truth about not intending to drive."

A case like this one is precisely why I hate mandatory sentencing. Nothing left to the discretion of the judge except to decree guilt or innocence. My hands were tied.

The intent of mandatory sentencing is noble. It's supposed to ensure that everybody will be treated roughly equally under the law. Black, white, brown, red, or yellow. Rich or poor. A Daughter of the American Revolution or a just-off-the-plane Nigerian immigrant. Christian, Jew, Muslim, or atheist. Almost no wiggle room for bigoted judges (think there aren't any left?) to come down hard on some groups and easy on people just like themselves. As with most noble intentions, however, the law of unintended consequences always comes into play and here I was with Mr. Samuelson, who hadn't meant to drive. If his superior hadn't been out there on that roadblock that day, the patrolman would probably have found a way to get Mr. Samuelson and his car back home without anything official going down in the books.

Once he'd written the ticket, though, all the legalities were set inexorably into motion.

I could see the pleading in Harrold's eyes for me not to do what the law required, and I leaned back in my chair to think of my options. I wasn't helped by the throbbing that had begun on my right foot.

Even though they're pretty and had cost more than I usually pay, the low-heeled navy shoes I'd chosen for the funeral were reminding me why I seldom wore them, funeral or no funeral. I've never had corns but I do have a rather prominent bony knob at the base of my big toe and some shoes rub me raw there if I wear them more than a couple of hours. I slipped my foot out to ease the pain and concentrated on Mr. Samuelson's dilemma. Mine, too. Nothing would be served by sending an eighty-three-year-old man to jail for thirty days. He hadn't deliberately gone out to break the law. If his nephew hadn't left him with his ox in a ditch, so to speak—

A glimmer of possibility gleamed through the legal underbrush. A legal out no doubt inspired by the Book of Luke: "And which of you shall have an ass or an ox fallen into a pit, and will not straightway pull him out on the Sabbath day?"

I looked at Mr. Samuelson. "Sir, did you feel this was a real emergency?" I asked. "And that you had no other choices?"

"Oh, yes, ma'am. I won't going to leave my car there. Time I might could get somebody to fetch it, it'd be stripped down to the axles. They's some bad people out there, Your Honor."

"There is a legal term called the Doctrine of Emergency," I said, "and it protects those who perform technically illegal acts during an emergency from the legal consequences of those acts. I hereby declare that Mr.

Samuelson's actions were covered by that doctrine. Case dismissed."

"Thank you, ma'am," Harrold murmured quietly as he stepped down from the witness-box.

Tracy just shook her head and called her next case.

Hey, if it was good enough for Jesus, it should be good enough for the state of North Carolina.

I slipped my foot back into my shoe and that place at the base of my big toe protested. I decided then and there that these shoes weren't going back into my closet. As soon as I got home, I was going to put them in the Goodwill box. Let somebody else wear them.

Somebody else?

One train of thought immediately coupled itself to another, and then another, till I had a whole line of freight cars pulling out of the station loaded with possibilities.

Well, damn!

Tracy moved into routine cases of excessive speed and seat belt violations, but I gave her only half my attention. The other half was chugging around the carnival lot as I remembered all I'd seen and heard these past few days. The things Tally and Dwight had told me, the things I'd gleaned from the Internet, the things I'd wondered about. All came together in such dovetailing clarity that it was all I could do to sit there and rule on these misdemeanors. I might not know why Braz was killed, but I had a pretty good idea why Polly Viscardi was.

While the ADA sorted through her shucks before calling the next case, I scribbled a note to Dwight and called the bailiff over. "Give this to Major Bryant, please, Mr. Overby. And if he's not there, see if they can locate him?"

He nodded and went out, and for the next hour and

forty-five minutes, I did my best to pay attention and dispense justice.

When I recessed at three for the afternoon break, Dwight was waiting outside in the hallway talking with Reid and my other former law partner, John Claude Lee. I'd've paid a nickel to have heard what Reid had to say to Dwight the first time they met after that Saturday morning sunrise surprise, but now was not the time to ask.

"You wanted to see me, Your Honor?" Dwight said formally.

"Yes, please." I held the door of my temporary chambers open.

When we were inside with the door closed, and before I could speak, Dwight put his arms around me. "Sorry," he said, "but I've been wanting to do this all day."

God, he kisses good! As slow and deliberate as his driving. And with the same attention to all the road signs.

"Much as I'd like to pursue this line of thought to its logical conclusion," I said, stepping back a little breathlessly, "I have to get back in there in fifteen minutes and you've got a lot of ground to cover, too."

"I do?"

"Those shoes that Polly Viscardi was wearing when she died. Are you sure they're hers?"

"Huh? Yeah . . . well, pretty sure. Pink laces, little bells on the lace tips. Why?"

"Look at my poor foot," I said, and slipped off my shoe so he could see the red where a blister was trying to form beneath the sheer nylon.

"I've got six people out there doing a canvass of the carnival and you call me back to show me your blister?" He gave a sudden grin. "Am I supposed to kiss it and make it all better?"

"Only if you have a foot fetish," I said, smiling back. "No, you're supposed to think about Skee Matusik's blisters. I've had these shoes three years and they still look like new because they hurt my feet so much I can't wear them for very long at a time. Skee's on his feet all day. Those are not new-looking shoes he's been wearing the last two days, but they were certainly brand-new blisters.

"I don't know what he was wearing Friday night," I said. "I didn't notice. But on Saturday, it was dirty white sneakers. Yesterday it was the leather shoes he had on at the funeral, but the laces are way too short. Even leaving the top holes untied, he could barely make a bow. And you saw those blisters on his heels today at lunch when Jessica brought him Band-Aids. Those can't be his own shoes that he's wearing."

"Matusik killed Hartley?" Dwight asked. "Why?"

"Sorry," I said, and I really was. For better or worse, Tally's first son had been part of our family, lost to us before we knew he existed, as forever unknowable as my father's first son. "I don't know enough about either of them to even begin to guess. He and his late wife were supposed to be like grandparents to Tally's boys. Tally said the only reason they let Skee come out with them this trip was because Braz begged them to on account of their close relationship. But if the shoes Polly was wearing turn out to be Skee's, then he has to have been the one that killed Braz, not Polly. And after he finished killing her late Sunday night or early yesterday morning, he must have switched shoes. Put her pink laces in his low-top shoes, and his short laces in her ankle-high ones. He's a small man, and she was a sturdy woman, so their feet would have been roughly the same size. Only his laces weren't long enough to go through all the holes."

Dwight frowned. "Maybe his first laces broke and those were the only length he could find."

"Look at your own shoes," I said, pointing to his black regulation lace-ups. "It has to be like Percy Denning's rope fibers. If you took your laces out, I bet you could see exactly how much space is between the holes. They'd be worn where they go through the metal eyelets. Can't you call the SBI lab and at least ask them if those pink laces have always been on those particular shoes?"

"I can do better," Dwight said decisively. "I can send them the shoes Matusik's wearing now and have them check both pairs for fingerprints while they're at it."

"Once word got around about how Braz died," I said, "he couldn't get away with wearing the sneakers. He had to know that sooner or later someone would be around asking about hard-soled shoes and he'd be jammed up if he couldn't produce his."

"I was having a little trouble with the idea of Polly Viscardi crossing the midway to kill Hartley," said Dwight, "but Matusik only needed to step around the corner of the tent when that Bowler Roller siren went off."

"Did he kill Polly for her shoes," I wondered aloud, "or because she saw him go into the Dozer?"

"Why don't I just go ask him?"

He tousled my hair the way he used to when I was ten, then he was off, too.

Court ran late again, but Tracy, Janice, and I made an efficient team. We finished the traffic calendar and were actually back on schedule when I adjourned at five-forty.

Downstairs, Dwight had Matusik in custody. Bo Poole let me join him behind their new one-way glass while Dwight and Raeford McLamb questioned him. When I got there, he was still stubbornly denying everything. Eventually though, the questions got to him as they hammered away on the two pairs of shoes. With the ones he'd been wearing the last couple of days on their way to the SBI lab in Garner, and confronted by his own blistered heels, he sullenly gave it up about thirty-five minutes after I arrived.

"Yeah, all right," he snarled. "I stomped the little bastard. World would've been a lot better off if somebody'd done it when he was a baby."

"Why?" Dwight asked patiently.

"He saw me put a pillow over Irene's face."

"Who's Irene?" asked McLamb.

"My wife. Last fall. She had a bad heart. Wasn't much use for me anymore. Yeah, yeah, I know what you'll say. Just like Polly and Tal. Yeah, she was the one good with money, good with kids, kept us going with the duck pond and balloon bust, but she didn't want to do what a wife's supposed to do for her man anymore and there was Bubbles with hooters out to here and she wanted me as much as I wanted her. Or I thought she did. Only she wouldn't do it with me long as I was married to Irene and everything was in Irene's name. I mean, Irene was old and sick.

She won't gonna live long anyhow, y'know? Doctor said so. Told me I was lucky to've had her long as I did when he signed the death certificate. So I got drunk one night and came home and did it. Only I didn't know Tal had kicked Braz out that night and he'd crashed on our couch. Can I have something to drink?"

They brought him a can of Pepsi.

"You say Braz was there," Dwight reminded him as the scrawny little man lifted the can to his mouth and drank deeply.

"Yeah. Bastard was gonna run right over to Tal and Arnold to tell them. Everybody thinks Bubbles took me for everything I had, right? Wasn't her. It was Braz. He made me sign it all over to him that night. He sold my doublewide and my balloon bust right out from under me. Left me with nothing but my camper truck. Let me say the duck pond was still mine, but he took a percentage of it, too. That's why Bubbles left me. I couldn't give her nothing. Didn't have nothing to give her if I'd wanted to. Everybody laughing at me, and then he was going to sell my Lucky Ducky. Said he was going to cash out end of the season, the little money-sucker. Leave me to starve, would he? Huh! I cashed him out. Gave him a mouthful of money to pay his way to hell."

So this was really how Braz had accumulated so much money so fast. Not a lucky self-storage buy or a shrewd eBay sell, just plain old ordinary blackmail.

Instead of Polly as I'd first thought, it was indeed Skee who'd taken advantage of the Bowler Roller's flasher and siren to kill Braz. And it was he who'd ransacked Braz's trailer and tried to search the shed, looking for the paper records that might let the Ameses figure out where the money came from.

"Polly saw me come out of the Dozer Friday night and she was going to try the same trick."

"More blackmail?" asked McLamb.

"Like I had anything left to pay her off with, y'know? I told her to come over to my truck after everybody else had gone to bed and I'd sign over the title to her. Stupid cow."

The rest was as we'd deduced: the faked suicide and the switching of the shoes and their laces.

Bo and I went back to his office and he was shaking his head. "You'd think after he screwed up the murder of his wife, he'd have thought twice about trying his luck a second time."

"Yeah," I said, wondering what Tally would say when she realized where Braz's money had come from and how he'd profited from the death of a woman who was supposed to have loved him like a grandmother. I was glad I wasn't going to be the one to tell her.

Dwight left the mopping up to his deputies, but it was still full dark when we finally headed back to the farm. He had popped a Willie Nelson tape in the player and ol' Willie's wonderfully craggy voice was crooning the words of that sweet, sweet song "Let It Be Me" as the moon rose behind us. We had the windows rolled down, cool autumn air washed over us, and I thought how good it was to be with someone who was as easy with my silences as I was with his. Any other man, I'd have to be doing the charm thing—making small talk, buttering his ego, flirting. But Dwight was just Dwight, so I didn't need to bother with any games.

The porch light had been left on for us when we got to the homeplace, but I didn't see Daddy's truck.

Maidie had heard us, though, and came to the door to peer out past the light and make sure it was us. "Mr. Kezzie's gone over to Cotton Grove. Y'all eat yet?" she called.

I looked at Dwight and he shook his head.

"Thanks, Maidie," I said, walking up on the porch, "but I've got something at the house and—"

"I'm not inviting you to eat here. I saved something from lunch and I made some fresh cheese biscuits just in case y'all get hungry later—for *food,* that is," she added with such a sly smile that I knew she'd guessed.

I could never slip anything past her.

Plastic boxes stood neatly stacked on the kitchen table and Dwight carried them out to the truck. Maidie had been my rock Mother's last summer, and as I kissed her warm brown cheek goodnight, I said, "What do you think Mother would say?"

"Well, honey, I reckon she'd say it's way past time you quit messing around and did something sensible for a change. And then I expect she'd say for you to go on along now and fix your man his supper."

🦆

We drove in tandem through the lanes over to my house and when we got there, we discovered that we were hungrier than we realized. I kicked off those shoes and dumped them in the Goodwill box I keep by the garage door and slid out of my dress and into a light robe while Dwight hung his jacket and tie over one of the chairs and started opening the boxes. I brought plates and utensils. We had our choice of practically everything that had been on the table at lunchtime, and Maidie's hot cheese biscuits were just the right accompaniment to supper.

While we ate, I pulled out scissors and the stack of photos Dwight had dropped in my car.

"What are you doing?" he asked curiously.

"You did say these aren't needed anymore, didn't you?"

"Yeah."

"There's a glue stick in that drawer behind you," I said. "Can you reach it without getting up?"

He could.

In none of the pictures was there enough of the woman's face to form an image. I snipped the chin and mouth from one, the cheek and ear from another, hair and brow from still others. As I cut, I glued each piece to a sheet of paper as if putting together a jigsaw puzzle. In the end, one eye was still missing and the image looked like an abstract Picasso portrait. Nevertheless, it was enough.

"I'll be damned!" said Dwight, reaching for a third biscuit. "Brad Needham's a cross-dresser?" Then he laughed. "Bradley Needham, Lee Hamden. Of course."

"Different strokes for different folks," I said, staring at what I'd created and suddenly wishing I hadn't.

"Suppose his wife knows?"

"If she did, he wouldn't have had a storage locker since they married. He probably stopped by it and took out a few things or deposited new stuff whenever he was on his way in or out of town. The rooms look like your standard Holiday Inn."

I gathered up all the pictures and my collage and dumped them in the garbage pail.

"Hey!" said Dwight.

"Why not?" I asked. "What would be the point of letting Brad know we know? Of telling Janice? Or anybody, for that matter? There's nobody else in these pictures. Who's he hurt?"

I thought how terrified he must have been, but how brave, too, to come out to the carnival and strike up a conversation with Braz just to see if Braz would recognize him. I wished there were some way to let him know the pictures had been destroyed and his secret was safe, but I didn't see how that could be managed without alerting him that someone had connected him to the pictures after all.

As if I'd spoken all this, Dwight said, "Yeah, you're right. Dump 'em."

I smiled at him. "Where's my ring?"

He fished the old-fashioned circle of gold from his pocket and slid it on my finger. The square-cut diamond flashed and sparkled in the kitchen lights.

"Want to stay over tonight?" I asked.

(Ping!)

CHAPTER
20

MID-OCTOBER

The carnival left town in the small hours of Sunday morning to make the jump to Kinston for four days the following week before working their way back to Florida for the winter.

I got to see Tally a couple of times more before they left. The day after Skee Matusik's arrest, she was numb with disbelief. "He killed Irene? And Braz knew? But he loved Irene. How could he keep quiet about something like that?"

She and Val were still wary with the rest of our family when they left. Too soon to tell whether they'll actually move to the Hatcher place and become more familiar to us. She says that's what she wants, but I've heard the ambivalence in her voice. There are reasons she's with the carnival that have nothing to do with Carol or Andrew. I've listened to her talk about great dates they've played, the crowds, the excitement, the fun of keeping someone peeling off the dollar bills like that first evening when she had Reese going.

Arn? I think he could sublimate with his lockers and eBay, but I remember my own brief years of wandering in the wilderness, free as a leaf torn from the tethering tree and blown by a capricious wind, and I have a feeling Tally will always want to load up the trailers every spring with plush and slum and hit the road for Anywhere, USA.

We'll see.

About three weeks after the carnival left the county, Dwight turned on the little television in my bedroom to catch the late-night news.

At the commercial, I went in to brush my teeth and was rinsing when I heard Dwight call, "Deb'rah! Quick! Come here, you gotta see this!"

I dashed back just in time to hear the news anchor say, "—Bascom Wrenn, who died in Colleton County this past spring. Outsider, or Visionary, Art has won growing recognition among serious collectors worldwide, and Joseph Buckner of the Buntrock Gallery just off Fifth Avenue in New York is here to tell us about this significant new find. Mr. Buckner?"

Mouths agape, Dwight and I watched while the camera panned over crudely painted boards and Mr. Buckner explained the significance of the stick skeletons and roaring flames, and rhapsodized over the Eye of God, the Tree of Knowledge, and the Biblical exhortations in ungrammatical white printing that covered every square inch of the scraps of plywood now hanging on the gallery walls.

He was aided by a large young black man chicly

dressed in a dark suit and one of those black silk shirts with the banded collar and no tie that I've only seen on movie stars when they broadcast the Oscar ceremonies. It was Lamarr Wrenn, that erstwhile economics major, looking like a seasoned New Yorker as he fingered his small chin beard and spoke of his grandfather's naive but utterly sincere attempt to paint the Rapture.

The camera caressed the ecstatic, semi-hysterical paintings, paintings Arnold Ames had planned to nail onto the outside of his haunted house. Validated by the cool ivory walls of a Fifth Avenue gallery, they had suddenly acquired an oddly compelling aura.

Back on the screen, the gallery curator was answering our local anchor's question.

"It's always difficult to put a dollar price on pictures that haven't had their value tested in the marketplace," he said. "But conservatively speaking, we'll be surprised if this important body of work doesn't bring at least two hundred thousand."

"Conservatively?" I croaked.

Laughing, Dwight clicked off the television and pulled me down on the bed beside him. "Wonder how Arnold Ames feels about his quick dime now?"

GLOSSARY

The following were used in the text of this book and were gleaned from personal conversations or from postings on Internet chat boards. They are but a fraction of the colorful terms used by the carnies themselves.

Agent—The concessionaire who works a store (as opposed to a clerk, who just takes the money).

Bozo—The clown who works the dunk tank and entices players with insults and a clever pitch. The clown makeup is for his own protection so he won't be recognized when he's off duty since some of his customers take his insults personally.

Cake eaters/Rubes/Clems—The paying customers, particularly those at rural or small-town venues.

Carnival—The loose affiliation of independent ride owners and concessionaires that provides traveling outdoor amusements for the public to enjoy.

Cool the mark—Send a tapped-out patron away happy . . . or if not happy, at least resigned to his losses so that he does not complain to the police that the game is rigged.

Cutting up jackpots—Swapping stories with fellow carnies and bragging about the money taken off the hairy mooches (loaded marks).

Dark night—An evening when the carnival is closed unexpectedly. Usually due to rain.

Donniker—Rest room or toilet.

First-of-May—Someone newly with the carnival.

Floss—Cotton candy.

Forty-miler—Concessionaire who doesn't travel far from his home base.

Gaffed game—One that is rigged so that the agent can control how much stock is thrown.

Gilly outfit, Gillies—Small carnivals that only work rural areas.

Hey Rube!—The call for help when a carny is in serious bodily danger from outsiders.

Jump—The move from one location to the next town.

Mark—The paying customer. Dates back to when agents would let someone with a full wallet win and give him a congratulatory slap on the back with a chalked hand so that other agents would see the chalk mark and know that here was someone loaded with money and ripe for plucking.

Nut—The show's operating expenses. According to carny lore, the term originated on a circus lot. An owner owed a lot of money and to prevent him from leaving town without paying, his creditor took the nuts off the wheels of his wagons and kept them till the debt was paid. To make your nut is to break even. If you're showing a profit, you're "off the nut."

Outsiders—People who are neither associated with the carnival nor part of carnival life.

Patch—The go-between for a carnival and local authorities. If bribes need to be paid, whether in cash, passes, or plush, he pays them. He also fixes the problem ("patches the beef") and smooths things over with any unhappy customer.

Plush—Stuffed toys given as prizes.

Pop-ups—Hidden props, usually triggered by a pressure mat or electric eye, that pop up at eye level to startle the customers in a "dark house" (a horror/haunted house attraction).

Possum belly—An auxiliary storage space beneath an equipment truck. It's usually empty when the rides are set up and therefore often doubles as a sleeping place for green roughies. (Women who use it for casual sex are scornfully called "Possum belly queens.")

Rake 'em and scrape 'em—Take the marks for every penny by every means both foul and fair.

Razzle-dazzles—Add-up games with virtually impossible odds of winning and the distinct probability of losing serious money.

Roughie—Unskilled laborer who helps set up or tear down the rides and equipment.

Route markers—Small red arrows posted on the roadside by the advance agent or carnival owner to show drivers the route. Arrows point straight up, left or right, and down. Down means to slow down. More than one means a turn coming up. Route markers are essential for drivers who can't read.

Sharpies—Carnivalgoers who have practiced a game till they can win almost every time (which is why some games post the warning ONE PRIZE PER DAY PER PERSON).

Stores/Joints — What an outsider calls a game or concession. Run by agents or clerks. There are three kinds:

(1) Hanky-panks — You win every time. Maybe not a great prize, but still a prize.

(2) Alibi stores — You could win, but if you do, the agent will try to avoid giving you a big prize by saying you violated some rule of the game. If he's really good, you'll continue to play.

(3) Flat stores/Flatties — You flat-out won't win. Most of these games are gaffed. What you'll get for your money is the fun of trying, plus an entertaining spiel from a smooth-talking agent. (Keep your wallet in your pocket!)

Sucker sore — A carny's state of mind after being on the road so long that he's fed up with the public. He's tired of their questions, tired of their stupidity, tired of their corrupt elected officials or police force.

Sunday schooler — A clean show with no alcoholic beverages on the lot, no erotic suggestiveness, no razzle-dazzles, no overly gaffed games.

Throwing stock — The percentage of a store's gross revenue (usually 25 to 30 percent) that is given back to the players as prizes.

ABOUT THE AUTHOR

MARGARET MARON grew up near Raleigh, North Carolina, but for many years lived in Brooklyn, New York, where she drew her inspiration for her series about Lieutenant Sigrid Harald of the NYPD. When she returned to her North Carolina roots with her artist husband, she created the award-winning Deborah Knott series, a series based on her own background. Knott's first appearance, in 1992's *Bootlegger's Daughter,* earned four top awards of the mystery world—the Edgar, the Anthony, the Agatha, and the Macavity—an unprecedented feat.

Slow Dollar is her ninth Deborah Knott novel.

More
Margaret Maron!

Please turn this page
for a preview of

*LAST LESSONS
OF SUMMER*

available
wherever books are sold.

She awoke in darkness, groggy and disoriented. Voices floated up the stairwell as from a radio someone had forgotten to switch off. A heavy thump shook the old house and she heard a woman's impatient voice. "Would you be careful? You're going to dent it."

Amy crept across the landing and cautiously peered through a front window. Light streamed from the open front door and she watched two men hoist a chest into the back of a large white van. A pair of chairs, part of her grandmother's dining room furniture, stood on the paved drive, and when the men moved aside she saw at least two more chairs already aboard. She tiptoed back to her room, found her cell phone, and dialed 911.

The dispatcher answered immediately. Amy whispered her name and explained that her grandmother's house was being robbed.

"Address?" asked the dispatcher.

Amy told him, he repeated it back, then said, "Now

if you'll just keep the line open, we'll make sure you stay safe until a deputy gets there."

With the dispatcher's soothing voice in her ear, Amy stopped shaking. "I could see the van from the landing. Should I try to get the license number?"

"Ma'am, if they don't know you're in the house, I think it'd be better for you to stay put."

"They're making an awful lot of noise down there. I don't think they'll notice."

"Ma'am—"

"Shhh!" Amy hissed and opened the door.

The smell of cigarette smoke was so strong on the landing that she instantly froze until she heard the woman say from some distance, "Put out that cigarette. Right now! She never allowed smoking in the house."

"So what's she gonna do?" asked a boisterous male voice from even farther away. "Call the sheriff on us? She's dead. Remember?

"I mean it!" the woman said imperiously.

"Okay, okay."

Amy tiptoed down to the railing, but this side staircase was for utilitarian service and from directly above she could only see a spill of light from the main entry hall where a grander staircase rose to this floor at the center of the house. Shadows flickered across the lower walls as the thieves moved back and forth. From their voices, there seemed to be three of them, a woman and two men.

Emboldened, she went back to the front window, but the light was too dim to make out the numbers on the license plate. Nor could she read the printing on the side of the van from this angle, though there seemed to be a picture of a child holding something.

As she turned from the window, someone flicked on the lights directly below and she heard him start up the stairs.

"You wanted a dresser out of her bedroom, right?" he asked.

There was no way to get back to her own room and nowhere to hide on this uncluttered landing, no convenient drapes, no broom closet or empty cupboard, only the tall case clock. She cowered next to it, knowing she would be seen the instant anyone drew even with it.

She heard his footsteps mounting higher on the bare treads, felt the vibration as he reached the landing, heard his breath coming hard from the climb. She herself stopped breathing when he fumbled along the wall and bumped into the clock so that it swayed against her shoulder.

She heard him mutter, "Where's the damn switch?" Then the hall light overhead came on so abruptly that she was momentarily blinded.

"Will you get your butt back down here?" the woman called from below "There's no room for nothing else on this load but the table. You and Jimmy'll have to take it apart to get in on, though. You got a screwdriver?"

"I thought them things was pegged," said the man, but to Amy's infinite relief, she heard him turn toward the stairwell.

"And shut off that light," snapped the woman.

The landing immediately went dark.

Amy's legs turned to water and she sank to the floor,

unable to make herself leave the safety of the clock's bulk and cross the landing to her room.

Her cell phone glowed in the darkness. She held it tightly to her ear and whispered, "You still there?"

"Listen, ma'am," said the dispatcher. "Don't you do that anymore. We've got a patrol car—"

Static buzzed along the ether.

"You're breaking up," Amy said softly. "I can't hear you."

More static. Amy stared at the face of the cell phone and watched while the battery icon registered empty and the little screen faded to black. Too late to realize that she had not charged the phone in three days nor thought to plug it into the car's charger on the drive down.

The dispatcher had said a patrol car was on its way. On its way from where, though?

She huddled on the floor beside the clock and leaned her head against it until her pulse slowed to the clock's steady tick.

"Hey, Paulie!"

It was the voice of the same man and it sounded as if he were at the foot of the stairs again.

"What?" answered the woman.

"There's a car parked out here."

"What?"

Amy heard the outer door open, then mingled exclamations from the three below.

They knew she was here.

Terrified, she leaped to her feet and raced silently down the wide hallway, stubbing her bare toe on the corner of the old blanket chest that stood outside her grandmother's bedroom. Blanket chest? She lifted the lid and felt inside.

Empty!

The hall light blazed on and running footsteps pounded along the staircase.

(Think, Pink! Do, Blue!)

She slid into the chest and lowered the lid. It smelled of mildew and dust motes prickled her nose.

"Who's here?" the woman called from the end of the hall. "Anybody here?"

They must have opened the door to her room and switched on the light. She heard disjointed phrases: "—suitcase—shoes—should've checked, dammit!"

"—not in the bedroom."

Closet doors banged in the distance, then the woman's artificially friendly voice advanced along the hallway. "Come on out, honey. You don't need to be afraid. Nobody's gonna hurt you."

"Let's just go," said a lighter male voice.

The one they called Jimmy?

"Yeah," said the other man.

"No!" The woman sounded out of breath and was puffing loudly. The chest creaked when she sat down on it. "She's somewhere in this house and we need to find her before she—"

"What's going on here?" demanded a voice of authority.

"Oh, shit!" said one of the men.

"Don't shoot!" cried the other.

"Now, now. You don't need to be waving that gun around, honey." The chest creaked again as the woman stood up. "I believe I know your brother. Aren't you Steve Richards's little sister?"

"I'm Deputy Mayleen Richards. Sheriff's department. And you are?"

"Pauline Phillips. This is my son Jimmy and my—"

Amy was listening so intently that she forgot to keep pinching her nose against the dust prickles. It was not a very loud sneeze but it sufficed.

Someone instantly lifted the lid and she squinted at the sudden light.

Two men, an older heavyset woman, and a sturdy young woman in uniform with a gun in her hand stared down at her.

One of the men said, "Well, hey there, Cousin Amy. Welcome back."